A THREAT IN THE SHADOWS

HIS HEART LEAPED. The pistol was steady, it was deadly, it was held against his forehead by a black-gloved hand. Behind it a shadow in the darkness said softly, "Make no sound, Jake Wilde. Not even the very slightest murmur. Or I promise you I will blow your handsome little head right off."

He wanted it to be another dream, but he knew it wasn't. He was tinglingly awake, every nerve alert, every pore of his skin prickling with the exhilaration of danger.

How many of them were there? One?

A movement to the left, in the corner of his eye, flickered across the stripe of moonlight.

Two.

Had they come in through the window? Climbed the ivy-smothered wall? His mind flicked through the options. Had Janus sent them? Were they Shee? Hardly— not with a gun.

Mortal, then.

Thieves.

To steal what?

The mirror.

He opened his mouth to yell. A great slab of sticky adhesive was slapped across it. His arms were grabbed and yanked behind him. He felt the tight cords scorch his wrists.

He moaned a savage curse into the pillow.

Too late.

Other Books You May Enjoy

CATHERINE FISHER

THE DOOR IN THE MOON

OBSIDIAN MIRROR BOOK 3

speak

SPEAK

An imprint of Penguin Random House LLC

375 Hudson Street

New York, New York 10014

First published in the United States of America by Dial Books,
an imprint of Penguin Group (USA) LLC, 2015
Published in Great Britain by Hodder Books, 2015
Published by Speak, an imprint of Penguin Random House LLC, 2016

THE LIBRARY OF CONGRESS HAS CATALOGED THE DIAL BOOKS EDITION AS FOLLOWS:
Fisher, Catherine, date.
The door in the moon / Catherine Fisher.
pages cm.—(Obsidian mirror ; 3)
Summary: "While Jake and Sarah are pulled through the Obsidian Mirror, landing in the
violent, unpredictable time of the French Revolution, Oberon Venn must decide between
staying mortal or losing his soul in the faerie realm"—Provided by publisher.
ISBN 978-0-8037-3971-0 (hardback)
[1. Time travel—Fiction. 2. Fairies—Fiction. 3. Fantasy.] I. Title.
PZ7.F4995Do 2015 [Fic]—dc23 2014028161

Speak ISBN 978-0-14-242679-1

Printed in the United States of America

1 3 5 7 9 10 8 6 4 2

Didst thou not lead him through
the glimmering night?

1

On summer nights? On sweet summer nights
Wintercombe is a house of shadows!

Nothing moves in its hundred rooms but a drift of
curtain at a window, and halfway along the Gallery,
the gilt hand of the grandfather clock.

The cloister gate, always hung with a row of
rusting iron implements, creaks very softly in the
sultry stirring of the air.

And, oh my dear, the night smells wonderfully
of roses!

Letter of Lady Mary Venn to her sister

WAS IT THE moon that woke him?

Because as he opened his eyes, a low slant of light lay
across them like a silver blindfold, making him turn
his head aside in annoyance on the hot pillow.

Jake lay sprawled among the sticky web of his dream.

He had dreamed of a hot, dirty room.

*His father had been standing in it, struggling to take off
a mask—the sinister crow-beaked mask of the plague doctor.
"For God's sake, Jake, help me with this, will you? I can't
breathe."*

*Jake had reached out. But the mask would not come away
from his father's face. It was stuck. And then its eyes came*

alight, yellow as gold. Strange garbled words emerged from its opening beak, and his father was gone; the bird-faced creature had become someone else, and the language it spoke was a garble of clicks and warbles, some Shee-tongue of the Wood, a speech of trees and grubs and scurrying insects.

Jake snatched his hand away, cried out "Dad!"

And that one word had wiped everything away.

He was awake and the dream was lost.

It left only moonlight, and the dusty canopy of the bed above his head; he lay still, staring upward, empty and crooked, the single bedsheet all tangled around his knees and chest. He was breathing fast and listening hard, sheened with sweat, because his father was still lost, still out there, somewhere in some other time, suffering.

Worry became anger; he slipped into the familiar tormenting whirlwind of rage. It was taking them so long to control the mirror! And Venn's neglect infuriated him.

He made himself breathe out, trying to let the fear go, pushing his hair from his eyes. Then he rolled over, edged a book aside and saw the small green figures of the bedside clock.

Three fifty a.m.

A curtain drifted in the open window.

A floorboard creaked.

He whispered, "Horatio? Is that you?"

No answering chatter. That wasn't unusual. The marmoset had taken to sleeping wherever it felt like in the vast dim house; sometimes curled up cozily in the kitchen with the seven cats, sometimes swinging on the dusty chandeliers of the empty bed chambers. After all, it had plenty of choice.

From the next room came the deep growl of Wharton's snoring. Jake grinned, lay back, turned over.

Into an ice-cold circle of metal.

His heart leaped. The pistol was steady, it was deadly, it was held against his forehead by a black-gloved hand. Behind it a shadow in the darkness said softly, "Make no sound, Jake Wilde. Not even the very slightest murmur. Or I promise you I will blow your handsome little head right off."

He wanted it to be another dream, but he knew it wasn't. He was tinglingly awake, every nerve alert, every pore of his skin prickling with the exhilaration of danger.

How many of them were there? One?

A movement to the left, in the corner of his eye, flickered across the stripe of moonlight.

Two.

Had they come in through the window? Climbed the ivy-smothered wall? His mind flicked through the options. Had Janus sent them? Were they Shee? Hardly—not with a gun.

Mortal, then.

Thieves.

To steal what?

The mirror.

He opened his mouth to yell. A great slab of sticky adhesive was slapped across it. His arms were grabbed and yanked behind him. He felt the tight cords scorch his wrists.

He moaned a savage curse into the pillow.

Too late.

→·←

Sarah was lying suspended in the green depths of some crystalline ocean, a dark dreamless place of infinite silence, when a voice spoke in her ear.

It was a tiny piping voice and it sounded worried. It said, "Mortal, listen, I really think you ought to wake up."

"Why?" she muttered.

"Because something very strange is happening."

Fish swam in and out of the words. She wondered why she dreamed of underwater, because she had never dared set foot near the sea. In her future world at the end of time, it was a poisoned, venomous place. Nothing lived there. The coral reefs were dull with dead plankton. Janus's dark tyranny had killed the world.

Her thought turned into a silver-and-blue jellyfish and pulsed rhythmically away through her brain.

She said, *"Strange?"*

The word woke her; she sat up.

The attic room was dark and hot. Through the window, wide-open, drifted the eternal whisper of the trees of Wintercombe Wood, and the distant hoot of an owl somewhere far down the valley.

"What sort of strange?" she whispered. "The baby?"

Lorenzo's wails erupted at all hours of the night.

"No. Not quite sure who." The wooden bird sounded apologetic. For a moment she couldn't even see it; then the moon came out and the silver light showed her its tiny form, stuck with false feathers. It was perched on the wardrobe, its single beady eye turned to her. "Only that whoever they are, they don't seem to be properly mortal and they're already inside the house."

Alarmed, she said, "The Shee?"

"Oh no. I'd certainly know if they were Shee."

Sarah was already out of bed. She grabbed jeans and a top and flung them on. "Where in the house? Why haven't the alarms gone off?"

"Don't ask me." The faery bird tipped its head to one side.

"The coin!" Fear flickered through Sarah like lightning on the dark moor. "Do you think they could be after the coin?" But then, no, no, they couldn't be, could they, because no one else here even knew she had it, the half of the broken Zeus stater, the only object in

the universe that could destroy the mirror. She forced herself to be calm, pulled on her shoes, stood up.

Don't panic.

The coin was safe. Hidden in a very secret place. Hidden until she could find the other half and bring them both together, and cancel the future—Janus's terrible future—before it ever even happened.

"I'm going out to take a look," she said. "Stay here. Don't let anyone see you."

"Don't worry." The bird shuddered delicately. "I won't. Even the spiders on the cobwebs won't see me. They're usually Summer's spies, did you know that?"

Sarah had already moved to the door. Before she opened it, she took a breath and pushed her cropped blond hair behind an ear.

Then she stepped out into the corridor.

It was mid-June and the weather had been hot for weeks. The ancient house smelled of wax-polish and lavender and roses—of sweet mingled midsummer scents, phlox and honeysuckle. All its windows were wide, as if it struggled to breathe, as if down here in its deep combe beside the rushing river it was slowly being suffocated by the heat and pollen and the leaf-heavy branches of the trees.

The attic corridor stretched, white-painted, into the dark. She didn't put a light on, but walked softly along it to the top of the servants' stairs and stood listening, straining to pin down every tiny sound in the sleeping house.

A creak.

A murmur that might have been a voice.

She frowned. The mirror was down in the medieval part of the building, the Monk's Walk, safe behind Piers's defenses of alarms and lasers. Surely no one could get at it there. And there had been no alarm from the gates, so no vehicle could have even tried to come up the drive.

She listened again.

Tiredness came out of the night and washed over her. Briefly the green ocean slid back into her memory, beckoning and cool. The Shee bird was surely wrong— or playing some mischief.

She'd strangle the manky little thing.

Then, as she turned away, a sound came from up the spiral stairwell, the ghost of an echo. Immediately Sarah was flitting down, silent and quick, avoiding the boards that creaked, slipping through the arch at the bottom, ducking behind a great vase on its pedestal.

She peered around it.

Before her the Long Gallery, a corridor wider than a room, stretched the whole length of the house, its white ceiling frosted like a cake with patterns of pargeting, its walls lined with ancient bookcases, great vases, statues of Greek philosophers and Roman senators.

The main bedrooms were along here, Jake's, Wharton's . . . and Piers's, though she wondered if that odd creature ever had to sleep. Right down the far end was Venn's room, but she knew all too well that it would be empty, because he was rarely in the house these nights.

As she frowned with anger about that, she saw Jake's door slowly open. A sliver of light widened.

She was relieved, went to step out and say "Did something wake you too?"

Until she saw him shoved into the hallway, the shadow behind him. And the gun.

→→·←←

They had let him dress and pull his boots on, and Jake was glad of that because behind his fear his fury was intense, and when it came to kicking someone, he could do a lot more damage this way. He wasn't blindfolded, but the two men—he was sure now there were two of them—kept behind him, and they each had smeared their faces with dark camouflage. They wore hoods and black coats. One was bigger than the other—the tall one did the talking. They smelled oddly of oil and some vaguely familiar sweet scent.

When he was a kid, just after his mother left, he'd had a phase of sleeping fully dressed with all sorts of daft kids' weapons stuffed under his pillow. Maybe it had been from films or stuff he'd been reading then, or because of all the disturbance in his life. He'd had a constant fear that something would happen in the night and that he had to be ready for it. It never had.

Until now.

As the tall man shoved him forward, his eye caught a flicker of movement in the darkness at the end of the gallery. For a moment he was sure someone was there, but as he stared he saw nothing but shadow.

"Remember, Jake. Not a sound." The muzzle of the gun caressed his cheek, the gentlest of reminders. "Now walk."

They followed him along the corridor. He tried to step on as many creaky boards as he could, but Wintercombe Abbey had its own secret vocabulary of creaks and squeaks, and they rarely woke anyone used to the breathing and stirring of the ancient house.

But as he passed a windowsill a dark mass uncoiled and sat up.

The tall stranger hissed; the gun swiveled.

Jake made a squirm of alarm through his taped mouth. For a second he thought it was Horatio; then a pair of green eyes opened and stared at him intently.

"Leave it." The smaller shadow spoke sharply. "Can't you see it's just a cat?"

"Bloody thing."

"Hold your nerve. Look. That's the door."

They had stopped at the door to the Monk's Walk.

They obviously knew their way around the house. Jake slid a look back; the cat was watching, its fur bristling.

The taller man crouched, his long coat sweeping the dusty floor. He drew out a small tool, made a few deft arrangements to the ancient lock. It clicked, and the door swung open.

Jake swore silently. He was sure now they were after the mirror, the black obsidian glass that was the precious doorway to time. They must have a way to deal with all of Piers's security.

But the cat had seen them, and the cats—all seven—talked to Piers. With any luck, this one might be slinking along the skirting board to wake him right now. Anxiety tingled in Jake. He had to play for time. Not let this happen.

"You first." The tall man caught his arm and thrust him through the door. Deliberately Jake stumbled into the dim interior, fell on the cold stones, and rolled away fast into the darkest corner, tugging the bonds on his wrists with furious energy.

The man swore. "Where are you? Get up! Or I'll blow you to bloody smithereens."

And wake the whole house? Jake thought. I don't think so. One thumb was almost free. Ignoring the scorch of rope on skin, he fought to separate his hands.

Then a cold blade point was touched lightly to his cheek.

"Naughty, Jake." A whisper at his ear, clear and quiet. He looked up, straight into the smaller thief's eyes. They were bright and mischievous, and he knew all at once that this was the more dangerous of the two.

"Seems to me you're getting some silly ideas, Jake. About bolting. About raising the hue and cry on us. Do you think we don't carry a few silent weapons too, Jake?"

The blade of the knife, sharp as a pin, pierced the skin under his right eye. Jake kept utterly still.

"That's better. Because, believe me, your throat would be cut, and we'd be through that mirror, before your friends got their dainty little toes in their furry little slippers. No point in being dead, eh Jake? Not with your father still to find."

Astonishment shot through him. What the hell did they know about his father? Before he could breathe, he was hauled up between them and dragged along the stone arcade of the Monk's Walk, stumbling through the gothic fingers of moonlight that stabbed down through the broken tracery.

Far below in its deep ravine, the Wintercombe rushed over its rocks, but the sound was no longer the dreadful thunder of the spring floods. It was a murmur, a song, a pleasant liquid ripple and splash.

It hummed under his feet.

Sarah had made herself invisible with the terrible ease Janus's gift had given her. It was an ability she loathed, but as soon as she had seen the two dark figures behind Jake, and the moonlight glinting on the pistol muzzle, she'd used it without hesitation.

They passed within touching distance of her. Flattened against the paneling, head sideways, she dared not breathe. They opened the door and shoved Jake through.

A creak followed, on the hessian matting.

The cat.

Those Replicant creatures could see her, she knew, so she whispered, "Get Piers! Hurry! Tell him I'm going after them," and slid into the Monk's Walk, breathing more easily because there were no creaky boards down here, just cold stone.

Far ahead, shadows flitted through moonlight.

She slipped after them, thinking fast. Surely the lasers around the mirror would stop them. And Maskelyne would hear—the scarred man slept down here now, in some monkish cell piled with books and circuitry, close to the mirror that infatuated him. She raced through slots of moonlight, through the terror of not being able to see her own arms and legs, of being nothing but a wisp of spirit and snatched breath. Into the labyrinth.

It was a funnel of malachite mesh, a tangle of wir-ing and computer monitors, and in its heart, dark as a great venomous spider, lurked the obsidian mirror.

She stopped dead.

Seeing it here in this darkness, tied down in its tan-gle of cables, it seemed a sinister vacancy, a moonlit door to nowhere, to non-places outside the very uni-verse itself.

It had always made her afraid. Now as she crept on, breath held, it seemed to reflect the terror inside her.

→⁊·⁊←

Keep calm, Jake told himself. They couldn't have sto-len the bracelet because Venn kept it on his wrist and never took it off, and without a bracelet, they wouldn't dare use the mirror.

The thought was a relief, but he was trying not to panic. They had hauled him, struggling hard, through the green mesh and he had seen with disbelief that no lasers had triggered and no alarms howled.

Whoever they were, they were experts.

He tried to yell, fought so hard a flask toppled from a bench and smashed, a star of glass shards.

"Hold him! Hold him still!" The small man walked up to the mirror and pushed back one dark sleeve of his coat.

Around his wrist curled a silver snake bracelet with a stone of amber.

Jake swore, kicked free, turned to flee, but the tall man gripped him with wrathful ease. Already the mirror had opened into a throbbing emptiness, the wide black doorway into time. Jake yelled, *"No. No! You can't do this!"*

"Just watch us, Jake."

They grabbed him, one on each arm, and before them was nothing but darkness, and they forced him forward and leaped into it. But just as Jake felt the throbbing terror of the mirror envelop him, his eyes widened in astonishment.

A small hand, cold and invisible as a glass glove, had slipped into his.

And *journeyed* with him.

❖

The cat waited until the black vacancy had collapsed, until the room had stopped shaking, until the mirror stood silent and solid. Its own fur and whiskers were flattened with the terror of the implosion, its green eyes wide.

Then it padded to a secret infra-red beam that crossed the floor, and very deliberately, put a paw on it.

Every alarm in the house exploded into noise.

2

I have long forgotten where I was born. Maybe
I had no birth. Maybe memory cannot last the
centuries I have endured. In truth I have journeyed
among beings that were hardly men, even unto the
courts of kings and wizards. Always I sought wisdom,
from chained dragon, from forbidden tract, from
demon and angel.

I have read the great stones. I have stolen the
apple from the Tree.

And out of all my sorcery I have made that which
will destroy the world.

From The Scrutiny of Secrets *by Mortimer Dee*

WHARTON'S DREAM WAS definitely a nightmare.

He was back in the stark white classrooms of Compton's School, standing, in some ridiculous pajamas, before a class of bored and belligerent boys. Lounging at the front desk, wearing a shirt, tie, and slim gray trousers, was Summer.

The faery creature propped her small bare feet on a chair and looked around curiously. "Hello, George! So this is where you used to work. It's a bit grim."

He ignored her, and cleared his throat. "Gentlemen, please! This term we'll be studying Shakespeare's greatest comedy, *A Midsummer*—"

"My play!" Summer blew him a graceful kiss. "George, you're doing my play. How very sweet of you!"

The boys sniggered. Wharton glared. He knew this dream. He loathed this dream. Because, any minute now, all hell would break loose.

"You know"—Summer swung her legs down and stood—"it's so lovely being in your dream. Venn only dreams about Leah, and Gideon isn't allowed dreams anymore. But yours are so easy, George."

She reached out a red-nailed finger and touched his pajama lapel. A white rose sprouted from the buttonhole. "Let's do my play. Shall we?"

Before he could answer, he felt his ears grow, his nose thicken. His hands clenched up into hooves, he sprouted a coat of velvety gray hair. He opened his mouth and all that came out was a startled bray.

Summer giggled helplessly. "I always knew you could act, George."

He was nothing but a donkey-headed man in pajamas, and the boys roared with delight as he shook his head and stamped and hee-hawed his wrath, until suddenly the school fire bell erupted into sound, and he sat up so fast in bed that he almost cricked his neck.

For a moment hot humiliation was a sweat all over him. He put both hands to his ears, bemused.

The bedroom door crashed open. "Alarms!" Piers gasped. "Intruders! *Go!*"

Army training kicked in. Wharton was out of bed in an instant, trousers dragged on, dressing gown grabbed. He opened the wardrobe, pulled out the shotgun, loaded both barrels. "Who? How did they get in?"

"No idea." The little man was hopping with anxiety, his white lab coat inside out.

"Shee?"

"Doubt it."

"Where's Venn?"

"*Away.*"

Wharton scowled. He knew what *away* meant. "You mean in the Wood?"

"Where else!" Piers looked sour.

"And Jake? Gideon?"

"No sign."

"Okay. Move. *Move!*"

They raced down the corridor. The door to the Monk's Walk was wide; Wharton swore, backed, swung in, and held the shotgun steady.

The corridor was empty.

Piers whispered, "Oh hellfire. If the mirror is gone I am *dead*. Worse than dead. *Eviscerated.*"

Wharton shook his head. "Not just you. How the hell could anyone get in here?"

He moved from cover to cover, dodging down the stone cloister, through pale slots of light. The short summer night was black; the moon had risen; he could smell the warm stirring leaves of the Wood.

At the arch, he waited, listening. Nothing. He yelled, "You in there! Put your hands up and stand still! Or I'll blast you to kingdom come!"

Still nothing.

He exchanged a glance with Piers. The small man, or genie, or whatever he was, crouched behind a pillar and shrugged.

So Wharton took a breath, breathed a prayer.

And went in.

→·←

High in the highest attic of the Abbey, Gideon had no dreams. He lay in the hammock Piers had set up for him, one long leg dangling over the side. His eyes were closed but there was no sleep for him anymore, because Summer had stolen his sleep, and now he had nowhere he could go to escape from the terrible fear of his endless life. The Shee, those faery creatures of the Wood, had stolen more than his dreams. They had stolen *him* once, long ago, made him their changeling, taken him into that place they called the Summerland, the unplace where time didn't exist.

He was mortal, but ageless.

Young, but old.

He loathed them. And even here, in this house, they still had him trapped.

Even though he kept all the windows of the room firmly locked and barred, even though he didn't want to, he could hear the moon anoint the leaves with silver. The faintest stir of branches came to his Shee-sharpened senses. Out there green buds unfurled, insect wings of finest gossamer unfolded. And then, slowly at first but growing in the dark like a wave of sound, just as they did every night, the nightjars began to sing, an eerie rasp, like a choir of sinister voices.

He opened his eyes.

They were singing for him. The Shee were calling him, taunting him, mocking him through beak and bill, tormenting him with their songs of the wood, of the sweetness of the Summerland, the long unchanging days of music and hunting and cold laughter.

He hissed with despair.

Then the alarms exploded. He leaped out of the hammock; at once, swift and light as a shadow he was out and running, down and down the stairs, along the corridors, skidding into the labyrinth just as Wharton was threatening the last cobwebbed corner of the room with the shotgun.

"What is it! What's happened? Is it the mirror?"

"Don't ask me." Wharton seemed reluctant to put the weapon down. He prowled around in bewilderment; almost, Gideon thought, disappointment. "Don't understand it all. No one here. Nothing missing. No damage—just this flask smashed on the floor. Piers, if one of those blasted cats of yours has set off that alarm, I will personally . . ."

He stopped.

The black cat had leaped up onto the workbench and was sitting right in front of Piers. It made a few urgent mews.

Piers stared. *"What!"*

The cat mewed again, at length. Then it began licking its tail with furious concentration.

Piers's face was as white as his coat. "Forget eviscerated," he breathed. "I'll be hanged, drawn, and quartered."

"Tell me," Wharton said. "Tell me!"

Piers absently made his hand into a fist and blew into it. When he opened it, he held a handkerchief, which he used to mop his face. "I used to be trapped in a bottle. I hated it, but looking back, it was a quiet, comfortable life." He looked up. "Someone's kidnapped Jake."

"Jake?" Wharton was stunned, but Gideon said quietly, "Who?"

"Don't know. Tertius couldn't get a good look at

them. Two men, with weapons. Not Shee, human, but with something strange about them. *Journeymen,* for sure, because they had a bracelet and they forced him at gunpoint into the mirror. They may have come in that way too."

Wharton had to sit down. He dumped the shotgun on the bench. "Jake . . . dear God! But . . . the alarm . . ."

"The cat did that. These people were like shadows. Nothing registered them. As if . . . they didn't exist. Experts."

"Or Replicants," Gideon said at once. "Replicants don't really exist." He turned to look at the mirror and saw his green coat glimmer in its dark depths. "But why Jake? Do they think they can get some kind of ransom for him? And it means they must have access to the mirror, in some other time."

His quicksilver reasoning left Wharton feeling befuddled. "Jake. Kidnapped! It's unbelievable!"

He couldn't seem to get it into his head. "And where's Sarah? Surely she must have heard . . ."

"Ah," Piers said. "Yes. Well. You haven't heard the worst of it. Sarah's gone too."

"Gone?"

"Not kidnapped. Oh no. Seems she followed them in, invisible. The cat says they had no idea she was there."

"But . . ." Wharton struggled with it. "Sarah has no

bracelet. You need physical contact with whoever is."

"She'd have held on to Jake." Gideon allowed himself a rare smile. "She's crazy, that girl. But *when* have they gone? Can you track them?"

Piers leaped up and ran to the mirror. A whole new console had sprouted from its side in the last month; now he tapped the controls nervously. After a minute he said, "Far enough, it seems. Between two and three centuries, but I'm not really able to pinpoint accurately . . . We need Maskelyne on this. Quickly."

As he said it, each of them wondered why the scarred man had not been first here. His care of the mirror was obsessional, as if it was part of his soul.

"I'll go and find him." Gideon left them to it, slipped out, and ran down the stone steps at the end of the Monk's Walk. He had been this way once before—since the spring he had explored every crack and corner of the building, every room and garret and cellar, because he had nowhere else to go and nothing else to do. If he put one foot outside the safety of the Abbey, the Shee would be on him like flies. He had betrayed Summer, helped Sarah steal the coin from her. If Summer got her claws on him he would certainly pay. But, he thought acidly, these days she didn't seem to care. She had Venn to distract her.

At the dimmest turning of the stone stair was an ancient Gothic porch doorway and through that another tiny stone stairwell led down into the cellars. Why did the scarred man have to lurk in the very depths of the earth? Gideon wondered. Mortals seemed to have this urge to dig themselves in—to find dark corners and caves, to build houses, to hide from the sun and the sky. He couldn't understand it. Living locked up in the Abbey, not even able to climb the trees or stand under the blue sky, was becoming unbearable for him. Day by day he was getting more irritable, more tense. He wondered how much more of it he could stand.

The door at the bottom was small and heavily ornate with great black wrought-iron hinges—the metal made him shiver, but he knocked urgently. "Maskelyne? Are you there?"

No reply.

He turned the handle and went in, ducking under the low lintel.

The room was as bare as if no one lived there. A neatly made bed, a table with a pile of papers and a pen, a photograph of Rebecca—which she had surely placed there herself. Gideon looked at her face smiling out at him, her plait of red hair. Did she know she was the girlfriend of a ghost? Because whatever Maskelyne was, he was not Shee and maybe no longer even mortal.

Then he paused, curious.

Next to the photo lay a large leather-bound book.

There was something strange about the book. As

Gideon looked with his Shee-sight, it seemed to glimmer, to be faintly doubled or trebled in outline, as if it existed in several dimensions at once, superimposed over and over on itself. It was a phenomenon he had seen before, in his wanderings through the crazy slanted worlds of the Summerland, and it always intrigued him.

He walked cautiously over to it.

The thick volume was bound in calfskin. Once it had been dyed a lustrous purple, but now it was faded and powdery at the corners.

On its cover, a diagram of occult letters was inscribed. Around it a delicate silver chain lay open and unlocked.

He shuddered. He had heard the Shee whisper about books like this—grimoires, spell-books, the possessions of the greatest sorcerers. The faery creatures feared them, because in them were spells that could command obedience, and the Shee loathed to be under mortal beck and call. In fact, if they saw this, they would certainly try to tear it to shreds.

Reluctant but fascinated, Gideon reached out and opened the pages.

They were of crisp yellow parchment, slightly greasy to touch, and their margins were an intertwined tangle of knots and branches, as if some great tree grew all the way through the book. Drawn by some long-dead scribe, demons and monkeys and men and monsters lurked among the leaves. Gideon leaned closer. Small silver birds sang in there, and a dog with three heads that barked faintly, and a snake of gold and turquoise scales that slithered in and out of the dark unreadable letters.

He turned another page.

This time the margins showed two dragons fighting, their open jaws breathing out flames, so red and yellow that he felt their heat.

And lying in the fold, paper thin and faded to the palest of purples, was a flower.

His fingers picked it up, carefully, felt the strangeness of it. It was a flower from no mortal plant and from nowhere in the Summerland either. It lay in his palm like a fragile proof of worlds beyond even all those he had known.

"Come away from that book."

The voice from nowhere made him jump; he turned fast.

Maskelyne stood in the darkness of the embrasured wall, though Gideon knew for a fact he had not been there seconds ago. A dark man in a dark coat; his scarred face made him half demon and half angel. He came forward swiftly and slammed the book closed, keeping his hand on it. "Are you a fool to look on things you know are dangerous!"

Gideon had jerked his fingers back with the speed of a snake. Now he thrust his hands in his pockets and shrugged. "Don't fear me reading your secrets, master. I never learned letters."

"Some books don't need to be read." Maskelyne fastened the chain tight and locked it with a tiny key, which he put in his pocket. "Some books will infect you like leprosy."

"So why keep it, then?"

Maskelyne glanced at him sidelong, the scar on his face jagged and deep. "That's my business. What's going on? Who's taken Jake?"

He turned and walked out quickly; Gideon ran after him. "You know?"

"The mirror told me. Just now, as I slept, the mirror whispered to me. It murmured its displeasure. It's angry, Gideon, and I fear that."

He ran and the changeling ran after him, up through the stairs and dim rooms to the labyrinth. Piers had cleared the workbench; he and Wharton sat waiting, gloomily.

When he saw Maskelyne, Wharton jumped up and said, "Find out how far."

Maskelyne went to the panel. His slim fingers touched the controls. It wasn't as if he operated the thing, Wharton thought suddenly, but rather as if he communicated with it, in some bizarre way.

"Well? Can you tell? Where have they taken him?"

"Before 1800. Or within a few years of that date. But they came from another period. More like 1900."

"Could it be Symmes?" Piers said hopefully.

Wharton shook his head. "No. John Harcourt Symmes had had his accident and gone into the future by then. The mirror was locked up in his empty house in London for ten years, just moldering under a dust-sheet, until his daughter, Alicia, came."

"Well, it seems someone else used it during those years. Someone who moves from period to period with practiced ease. A real *journeyman*." Maskelyne turned away and sat down. He looked deeply troubled. "I'll do the best I can to find out who. Meanwhile, someone has to go and tell Venn. Jake is his godson, after all."

Piers and Wharton looked at each other in dismay.

"Not me," Piers said. "Gideon."

"Are you mad?" Gideon shook his head. "I can't go back to the Shee."

"And I must stay with the mirror." Maskelyne stood and stared into its darkness thoughtfully. "This incursion has changed something. Since the spring we've spent weeks working without much result, but these intruders have done what we could not. They have woken the mirror again." He turned his handsome side to them. "I need Venn's bracelet and he needs to know what's happened. You'll have to go and get him, George."

Wharton said, "To the Summerland? God forbid! I went there once down a well and—"

"Not there. He's with Summer, in the Wood," Gideon muttered.

"Great. And how do I find them?"

"Don't worry about that. They'll find you."

The big man sighed. "Right," he said. "If no one else has the guts . . ." He took a breath, turned, and marched firmly from the room.

Into the silence, Piers said, "Crumbs. I don't envy him."

Gideon was silent. Part of him wanted to flee after the man into the green freedom of the Wood. But he managed to stay still. Only, deep in the pocket of his coat, his fingers played with the strange, paper-thin, stolen flower.

3

My gift, she said, is the cowslip,
The silver of the moon.
The bees' kiss to the flower's lips
on the hottest afternoon.

My pain, she said, is the wasp sting,
the scorch of the fiery sun;
the scream of the dying fledgling
as the weasel's work is done.

Ballad of Lord Winter and Lady Summer

JAKE FINALLY WORKED the tape free. He spat it off, took a breath, then whispered, "Are you in here? Sarah?"

There was no answer. He was disappointed, and then glad because there would have been no point in her getting locked up too. She needed to be free.

They had brought him through the mirror into a place of total darkness. He had had a glimpse of a candle, a single tiny flame somewhere in the distance, a sense of space, an echoing dimness, and—

Sarah's hand had slipped from his just as the tall man

had untied his wrists, hustled him through a door, and bolted it firmly behind him.

He looked around cautiously.

"Is anyone in here?"

His own voice came back at him, resonating as if from a high ceiling.

He threw the tape on the floor in disgust. He could be anywhere . . . For a moment a wave of despair and sheer anger crashed over him, made him clutch his hands into fists and want to yell aloud. How could they do this! Snatching him from the search for his father, the long fruitless work on the mirror . . .

Yet . . . the mirror had worked for them. Allowed them to *journey.*

That had to be a small wan hope.

Breathing deep, controlling his fury, he groped, hands out. Almost at once he stumbled against the edge of a table and fumbled his way along it. On the surface he felt a few small cold objects, and among them, a square box. Shaking it, he smelled oil, knew it for a tinderbox, and struck it. The tiny blue flame spurted in the dark, steadied and grew. He saw a candelabra with six candles.

He lit them quickly, then picked the whole thing up and looked around.

His heart leaped with terror.

Men and women stood around him in crowds. Silent

and unmoving, they stared at him out of the gloom; their eyes glassy in the flame light. No one spoke. Each of them was rigid, their clothes a crazy motley of ages and times, Elizabethan players, a Roman centurion, medieval women. For a moment he thought he had interrupted some fancy dress party, but the silence was too unreal, the stillness too complete, and he understood with another shiver of fear that they were not even alive.

Then, piled in a corner, he saw a heap of legs and hands and feet, of severed limbs and spare torsos, of severed heads all gazing blankly up and out, and he knew these were waxworks.

He allowed himself a shaky laugh.

They looked so real!

He made himself move toward them, but as soon as he did, the candle flames cast huge wavering shadows; everything seemed to shift slightly, the figures to move, the light glittering in their eyes.

It gave him the creeps.

In front of the ranks of waxworks were three booths containing more complex figures. Still as statues, frozen in attitudes of waiting, a Scribe sat with pen poised, a Dancer balanced on tiptoe. The nearest was an Indian Conjurer in a striped coat sitting before a table with three balls upon it.

Jake looked at it closely, bringing the candles up. And perhaps he touched some handle, because to his shock the figure suddenly came alive, and he stepped back with a gasp as it turned its head and fixed him with glassy eyes.

Music squeaked from its rusty interior.

The automaton picked up a cup and showed nothing beneath it. Then it replaced the cup and with a jerky, impatient action, picked up another. A small red ball lay there.

Jake watched. The figure covered the ball, then revealed that it had vanished. Lifting the third cup, it showed that the ball now lay there, and the dark painted face smiled a brief smile, nodded, bowed, and was still.

Machines. Very old ones. Wind-up. Clockwork.

Jake raised the candles high, wax splatting on the floor. He was in a low, raftered room, maybe an attic. It was crammed with the waxworks, and though he knew what they were, he didn't want to stay here, among these lifeless eyes that watched him.

"Jake!"

It was a whisper; it made him run to the door.

"Sarah? Is that you?"

"Who else would be mad enough to come?"

It made him grin. "I'm glad you did. Where the hell are we?"

"Not sure." Her voice was close to the outside of the door, as if she had her lips to the keyhole. "The two men have gone. Down a wooden stairway and out into a street, I think. They've locked the door behind them. It's dark out here—there are corridors, wooden, all rotting, stairs, plenty of locked rooms. Maybe we're in some sort of storehouse or warehouse. It's hard to tell. What's in there?"

"Waxworks. Automatons."

"What?"

"Mechanized puppets. Used for entertainment. We can't have *journeyed* too far back. Look, Sarah, they can't be leaving me here alone for long. They'll be back soon. Can you get me out . . ."

"No chance. There's a huge lock." He heard her rattle it. "And the door itself is solid."

"Right. Then listen. Get a weapon—"

"Jake, this is not a game. I'm not smashing someone over the head."

"For the lock! To break the lock."

She breathed out, tense. "Oh. All right. I'll look around." She seemed to move away, then her voice come back. "Don't go anywhere."

He was about to be sarcastic until he realized she was probably as scared as he was, so he forced a laugh. "I won't. Thanks for coming along, Sarah."

"Venn won't thank me," she whispered.

Jake pulled a face. That was only too true.

➤·◄

Sarah moved away from the door, reluctant. Judging from the glow coming under it, Jake had found light of some sort, but she had nothing. Groping the walls was useless; there were no electric light switches.

She made her way along the corridor.

It was low roofed, but some dim illumination filtered from somewhere, so gradually she realized she was walking on trampled earth, and that the walls were painted a dingy green. Here and there they were stained as if by past water leaks, and scuffed as if many people had rubbed and run their hands along them.

Was this a school?

Some sort of theater? A slum?

At the end was a door that creaked open at her touch, revealing a stairwell. She leaned over and looked up. The stairs turned in a wide square into the dark. Sarah waited, listening. The building was utterly silent around her. Then, on some higher floor, something made a small popping sound.

"Hello?" she murmured.

The stairwell took the word and sent it back to her, fading into nothing.

Her hand on the greasy banister, she started up.

It was a bare, bleak stair. She could smell damp, and a sweetness, and a faint but reassuring hint of onions. Twice more the popping noise came; she paused to listen to it, and it was distant, as if outside.

By the time she reached the top landing she was breathless, and her calf muscles were tight with strain.

Facing her was a dilapidated door, with one phrase on it, scrawled in red paint, vivid as blood. It said *VIVE LA RÉVOLUTION!*

"Oh no," she said, very softly.

She forced down the handle; the wind snatched the door from her and flung it open.

She stared in delight and dismay.

She was standing on a narrow balcony and before her spread the massed rooftops of a great city. Gray stone and red tile glittered under a cloudless blue sky. Sunshine blinded her; she had to shade her eyes to look, and she saw balustrades and gables, a crammed tangle of alleyways and streets and lanes pierced by the high spires of countless churches, the twin towers of a mighty Gothic cathedral, the silver flash of a river under its bridges.

Where was this?

Not London, she knew. The sun was too bright, the design of the buildings all wrong.

Was this Paris?

The cathedral must be Notre Dame.

She looked for the Eiffel Tower but obviously it didn't exist yet—she had only seen pictures of it and the TV transmission of its ruined end, when Janus's troops had entered the city at the start of his career. If it was Paris, it was old and dirty and its streets narrow.

Directly below her was a mean boulevard, lined with trees. Carts and carriages rumbled along it, noisy on the cobbles. The popping noise made Sarah grip the rail and look down carefully; there was a market of some sort going on. Voices and vendors' cries, the bleat of ewes and crowing of a caged cockerel rose up to her, the stench of a city without drains or sewers. But beyond that a gang of drunken men were firing muskets wildly into the air, and a barricade of tattered furniture and broken timbers had been heaped haphazardly across the street. She stepped back quickly.

The clothes of the women told her this was the eighteenth century. She knew little about that period in France, except that there had been a great revolution, and rich people had been guillotined, hundreds of them.

That was all she needed.

She turned, ducked back inside, and ran down the stairs. Jake would know more. Passing a broken banister, she went back and pulled it out; the black wood cracked loudly and she froze, listening, and thought she caught some other noise, a rumble deep in the bowels of the building.

Suddenly scared, she made her way down, telling herself not to be stupid, that all anyone would see was a broken stick moving by itself in thin air.

Then, halfway along a landing she heard a bang

somewhere below, a loud shout that might have been her name.

Abandoning caution she turned into the corridor and raced along it.

But the door to the waxwork room was wide open.

And Jake was gone.

→·←

He had meant to be ready for them, to hide among the waxwork figures, but they had obviously expected that and been almost silent; they'd come in fast, at least five big men all with flaring torches, and grabbed him before he could even scramble up. A black cloak was flung around him, the hood pulled firmly up and over his face.

He squirmed, took a breath, and yelled, "Get your hands off me!"

One of the men snorted a laugh.

Jake was bundled out. It was hard to see anything; he smelled the outside before the warm air hit him. The stench of the cities of the past was something he was becoming used to, but this was more pungent even than plague ridden Florence—rotting vegetables, dung, the sour acrid sting of some leather or tanning works that started his eyes watering. And the brilliant unmistakeable heat of the sun.

They pushed him up into something that swayed like a carriage; he felt a grimy velvet bench, then men squeezed in beside him on each side. The door was slammed, horses were whipped up.

As the vehicle moved, he was flung against the man to his left, who swore at him.

Jake went very still.

He thought fast. First, Sarah must have been left behind. She could hardly have climbed on the coach, and though it was traveling slowly, she could never have followed it through the crowded streets.

Because he could hear a crowd out there now, a babble of voices, the coachmen yelling at people to get out of the way, the slap of hands against the paintwork, angry cries in French—*French?*—against the window.

He managed to throw the hood back from his eyes.

There were five men in the coach with him, all huge, all armed. Three sat opposite, cudgels on their knees. One held a pistol, cocked, near the window.

For a moment Jake was flattered; then he realized the weapons were not for dealing with him.

There was a riot going on out there.

The streets were alive with a raging mob. He saw snatches of faces, stalls turned over, shops being stripped of food. Women struggled away with trailing armfuls of cloth, an old man staggered under a cask of wine. There were barricades of heaped furniture; twice the coach had to back up in front of them. And he could smell the tension, the wild unleashed anger out there in the city, smell it in the billows of smoke from burning houses, in the crackle of flames, the spilled fruit and cabbages squashed under the wheels of the carriage.

"*Liberté!*" he heard. And then, clearly, "*Vive la Révolution!*"

"Bloody French lunatics," one of the men beside him muttered. Another, the one with the pistol, said, "Shut up," and rapped the ceiling hard with one fist. The carriage speeded up, turned a corner, throwing Jake back in his seat. The window blinds were yanked firmly down and fastened.

But he had seen enough.

This was Paris, surely, sometime during the Revolution, a time of riot and anarchy. They'd called it the Terror. And he had managed to lose Sarah in it.

He spoke up. "Where are we going?"

Silence.

"Why have you brought me here? Who sent you? Is it money? For a ransom?"

No one answered, so he said, "Venn will never pay it. He wouldn't care . . ."

One of them snorted. "No one wants your money, boy."

A thought struck Jake like a joyful blow. "Is my father behind this? Dr. David Wilde? Did he—"

A huge hand took hold of his jaw. Strong fingers pushed into his cheeks, squeezing them together.

"Shut your mouth, cocky little *monsieur,* or I'll see to it you'll be missing a few teeth to talk through. Deliver you whole, she said, but a bit of damage in transit wouldn't be my fault. Get that?"

He nodded.

When the hand withdrew he sucked his cheeks in, still feeling the bruising grip. As the carriage rattled on, he thought about that single word.

She.

Who was she? Summer? Was this the Summerland after all?

Conserve energy, he told himself. Watch, listen, stay alert. He was suddenly so hungry his stomach churned, but no one spoke to him again, and as the coach turned corners and rumbled under archways, he sensed that they were crawling deeper and deeper into the dense mass of the city, into its packed and stinking heartland, the filthiest slums and alleys.

Jake swayed beside the morose men.

He was in a lot of trouble here.

And this might just be the start of it.

→⋗⋖←

Sarah sat wearily against the wall among the wax-works. She felt sick, a little giddy. A point of pain was beginning behind one eyebrow. She had been invisible too long.

Back in the Lab, there had always been stories and

rumors about the children who died, about the early failed experiments, when Janus's scientists had been inexperienced and the powers he had designed untested. She remembered too the terror of the white blankness creeping over her whole mind, as if her whole personality would somehow vanish away if she let it.

Two hours—two and a half at the most—was the safe limit. She might be over that already. With a sudden panic she raised her head, terrified even as she made it that the *switch* might not work anymore, that she might have to stay like this forever.

But her arms and legs and feet and hands were there. She gazed at them in relief.

She felt better at once.

There was no way out. The building was a locked tenement, empty and derelict. The main door was firmly bolted. So she just had to . . .

Something clanged.

She leaped up and darted into the crowd of waxworks.

With a rattle of keys, two men hurried in. Ragged, dirty, roughly dressed in soiled aprons and breeches, one big and one stooped, they walked between the waxworks, talking loudly and laughing boldly, as if to keep away the silent stares of the still figures.

Sarah's eyes watched them. These men were nervous, in a hurry to get out.

They hurried to the three automata, dragged out a

wooden packing case lid and fitted it over the Conjuror, carefully, then lifted it on two poles and staggered out with it, locking the door behind them.

After a few minutes they came back for the Dancer, the case wobbling as they lifted it.

One of the men glanced around, clearly scared.

"Hear that?"

"What?"

"Thought I heard something. Like breathing."

Standing among the crowd of waxworks, Sarah let her eyes go still and vacant. She stared ahead, fixed.

→⋅←

When the men came back for the third time, the big one gazed at the waxwork crowd uneasily. "Bloody glad to be out of this lot," he muttered.

The stooped man cackled. "Tell that to the contessa."

Over the third figure, the Scribe, they placed the wooden lid, carefully, wary of its waxen face, its poised fingers holding the plumed pen. A corner of the purple velvet cloak got snagged in the packing case; the men shoved it in, impatiently.

Then they lifted the heavy wooden box.

"Lot heavier, this one," the smaller man complained.

Awkward, they staggered out with it.

4

On the final, terrible night of the Kebron
expedition, halfway down the glacier, when the
men were in the last stages of exhaustion, one of
them looked up and thought he saw a woman,
small and slender, walking beside Venn on the top
of the ice, and talking to him. She wore summer
clothes and was barefoot.

He knew he was hallucinating. The temperature
was 30 below zero.

Later, at base camp, he mentioned it.

Venn managed a wintry smile. "We can never
get away from our nightmares" was all he said.

Jean Lamartine, The Strange Life of Oberon Venn

WHARTON STRODE THROUGH the silence of
the midnight Wood.

It had never looked more beautiful.

Above the leafy canopy of the trees, the sky was
darkest blue and scattered with stars. An owl hooted;
below, to his left, almost hidden in its deep bed, the
Wintercombe rippled over rocks and lichened boul-
ders, its surface glinting with bubbles.

The path he walked was ridged with tree roots, the
undergrowth on each side sweet with night-scented

flowers and ghostly foxgloves. Moonlight slanted in brilliant diagonals through the dark masses of the trees, and once, when he stumbled and put his hand against a trunk, the moss was so deep and wet that his fingers sank into it.

Of course, the Shee knew he was here.

At first it had been the lightest of touches, on his hair, his face, as if he had snagged invisible cobwebs. Then a moth landed on his shoulder. A gnat bit him gently on the cheek.

Grim-faced, he walked on. Moonlight lit the depths of the forest, showing him green, treacherous, enticing places off the path, secret clearings, the glimmer of dark crags.

On midsummer night the Wood scared him, maybe more than any place he'd ever been. Its stillness, its watchfulness, its complete Otherness, crept into him. Nothing here was human. It was ancient and unconquered and he knew it would watch him live or die without the slightest vestige of emotion. Just like the creatures that lived in it.

He stopped.

Quite suddenly the path divided before him into three, each track twisting away between the trees.

He cleared his throat.

"Is anyone here? I need to speak to Venn. Oberon Venn."

Stupid. They knew who Venn was.

Only a high rustle answered him. Looking up, he glimpsed a scatter of dark bats, circling the branches.

He caught hold of a tree branch to duck under it.

It became a long, slender hand.

Wharton yelled, leaped back. A shock of sweat broke out all over him. His heart slammed in his chest.

"I'm so sorry, sir," the tree said. "It's just that I heard you call."

It was an ancient, crooked specimen, maybe a rowan. Now he looked carefully, it seemed a bit like a wizened old man, all bent up, the bark crumbling like leprous gray skin. A few sparse leaves clung to it.

"You can speak?" he said.

"Indeed. My voice is all that is left to me."

Wharton glanced around. The Wood fluttered with moths. "Left of what?"

"My mortality, good sir. Of my human life."

Fascinated, Wharton edged closer. The voice was a faint breeze in the branches. One gnarled knob of trunk watched him like a blinded eye.

"Summer did this to you?"

The tree rustled with anxiety. "My Lady Summer was good enough to be angry with me, yes. But I deserved it." A leaf drifted sadly down. "It happened just a few days ago. I am a monk of the Abbey here. They warned me, the Abbot and my brothers, but I still love to leave the precincts and wander in the Wood. And so I began to encounter the fiends."

Wharton nodded, grim. "You poor devil."

"Not that They are, in fact, true demons. Some of the holy Fathers say these beings are angels that fell between Heaven and Hell. Neither good nor evil, they infest the waste places. And she . . . she is so beautiful. No mortal woman could so have tempted me." The tree bowed a little. "In sooth I became besotted, and for days have lived wild and crazed here in the Wood."

"But what made her turn you into . . . ?"

"I saw her bathing unclothed in the stream."

Wharton winced. "Ah. Right."

"You can imagine her anger."

"I'd rather not."

"They saw me and dragged me forth. Then—"

"Yes. I'm sorry. But look, I have to find her. Or at least Venn, and—"

The tree shivered. "You should not look for her. Now is the time she is strongest, when the sap is high and the leaves are green, when the hare dances and the owl hunts all night. Don't seek her out, sir, I beg of you."

"No choice, I'm afraid. Which of these three paths should I take?" Suddenly Wharton felt foolish. Was he going mad, asking advice of a tree?

"It does not matter. She will be at the end of all of them. Good sir . . ." The murmur came close to his ear. "If you gain her favor, ask mercy for me, I pray. My brothers will be so concerned. I am gone nearly a week now."

Wharton grunted, thinking of the ruined cloister at the Abbey, the hundreds of years that had passed since this poor crazed man had fallen foul of Summer. But he said, "I'll do my best."

"You promise me?"

"I er . . . well, yes. I promise I'll try."

The tree was silent a moment. When it spoke again he heard only the most desolate whisper. "But will God also forgive me? For I have longed for such deadly things."

Wharton had no answer to that. He turned quickly and walked into the right-hand path, cursing his own soft-heartedness for promising anything. Ask Summer for mercy! May as well ask the sun to turn itself off. He'd end up as a log or a stone himself. He was trying to imagine how that must feel, when a cloud of silvery butterflies came down and danced all around him.

He stopped.

Before him was an open clearing in the Wood.

Deep in its stillness was the hum of summer bees.

He knew at once that it was a trap. He knew that if he took one more step he would have entered the Summerland, and that he would see those slanted worlds again, and the temptation to turn and run was so strong, he almost heard it like a warning voice. But George Wharton, he thought bitterly, was no one's wimp. So he squared his shoulders, lifted his chin, and stepped in.

→→·←←

Instantly, he was in sunshine, and there was a summer-house.

It was a fragile construction, of gaudily painted trellis-work, and it was thatched with a complex iridescent thatch that glimmered like kingfisher feathers. As he came closer he saw it was, in fact, made of the wings of countless birds, all woven together.

The structure stood on a bank of wild thyme, the smell of the herb cloyingly sweet. Columbine grew there, and honeysuckle wreathed the tilted veranda.

The Shee came down around him in clouds. He watched how some of them stayed butterflies and how others transformed, wholly or in part, to the pale tall people he had seen before, their clothes now brilliant scarlets and turquoises and oranges. With soft rustles and crackles their bodies unfolded. Abdomen and antennae became skin and smile.

Wharton stood still, hands clenched.

Then one moved aside, and he saw Summer loung-ing elegantly on a wooden cruise-ship deckchair.

The Shee queen wore a short dress of shimmery gold, her feet were bare, a smile of delight lit her pert, pretty face. "George!" she said. "What a wonderful surprise!"

Wharton didn't answer.

He was looking at the man standing behind her chair.

Oberon Venn seemed taller, thinner here, his hair as blond as sunlight, his eyes cold as ice. Wharton was shocked at the change in him. Rumor had it Venn was half Shee. Well, certainly he was paler, somehow less solid. As if his human half was being sucked out of him, like bees suck honey from a flower. As if the curse on his family was coming true right now.

But his voice was still sharp as flint. "What the hell are you doing here, teacher?" Wharton stood his ground.

"I'm wondering that myself," he said. "Because when I tell you the reason, you probably won't even care."

→·←

Maskelyne walked quickly down into the black-and-white-tiled hall, crossed to the Bakelite telephone, and dialed. While the ringtone sounded, he glanced around, dark eyes wary.

A single black cat sat at the top of the stairs.

He turned away from it as she answered.

"Hello?"

"Rebecca? It's Maskelyne."

"Oh . . . hi . . ." She sounded breathless, sleepy.

"Did I wake you?" he said.

"It's the middle of the night! What do you think? Even students have to sleep sometimes."

He imagined her hair, all tumbled on the pillow as she sat up and said, "What's wrong? Is it the mirror?"

She could always tell a lot from his voice, he thought. "In a way." He stared unseeing at the open casement, where a frond of ivy was growing in. "It's Jake. He's been kidnapped."

"What!" He felt her shock.

"Someone came through the mirror tonight and took him. Sarah's gone too; it seems she followed them. Do you understand what I'm saying, Becky? They've *journeyed* and have no bracelet to come back with. They could be anywhere. It's a disaster."

Her breathing. Then: "I'll come straight back."

"Not if . . ."

"I'll come now. I'll be there in an hour."

"Don't wreck your degree. That's more important."

She said, "Writing essays on the past is pretty dull after *journeying* into it. And I can skip one lecture. How's George taking this?"

"Hard."

"Where is he?"

"In the Wood."

She seemed to laugh, uneasy. "Wharton-in-the-Wood. Sounds like a lovely little village. Why on earth is he—"

"He's gone to get Venn." Maskelyne's husky voice was quiet. "But, between us, I don't know if Venn even cares anymore. About Jake, about any of it. Venn is with Summer now. She has her claws tight in him, and this is her season. He's been changing. Becoming more Shee. He hasn't been at the house for over a week. I fear we've lost him, Becky, and with him any chance of saving his wife and Jake's father."

"I would have thought that wouldn't worry you too much," she said tartly. "If Venn loses interest in the mirror, you get it."

Silence.

Maybe she was sorry, because she said, "I didn't—"

"I deserved that. But the mirror is already mine, and always has been. And I am beginning to think that defeating Janus and regaining Leah are two aspects of the same problem." He smiled, weary. "Come as quick as you can. This eruption from the past has energized the Chronoptika. I hear its anger in the corners of my mind. That worries me."

She said, "I'll be there."

He nodded, put the phone down, and stood still. Then he crossed to the open window and tried to shut it. But the casement would not close. Ivy had grown thickly inside; already a long bine of glossy leaves had attached itself to the woodwork of the sill, leaving clinging fragments as he pulled it away.

He gazed at the leaves, then walked down and looked at the other windows. In the hot weather they were all open wide. Their hinges were clotted with greenery. In one, a tiny diamond pane had been cracked by a bramble. Moths fluttered around the hall.

Maskelyne turned and went quickly down to the kitchen.

Piers had the baby, Lorenzo, in one arm and was feeding him from a bottle. Horatio, Jake's cheeky little marmoset, was hanging upside down from the chimney among bubbling saucepans, spitting nut shells into the fire.

Gideon was eating biscuits dipped in coffee, savoring each mouthful intently, as if it would be his last.

"Is she coming?" Piers asked.

"Straightaway. Look at this." Maskelyne put the ivy branch on the table. Gideon's hand paused in midair as he saw it.

"The Wood is starting to creep inside. The windows in the hall—"

Gideon said, "I shut them every night."

"—are all open and the greenery is growing inside. As if the power of the Wood is groping and searching for someone. Or something."

Piers made a face and looked at Gideon, who stood, quickly. "She doesn't have to search for me. She knows where I am. I'll go and close them. As for Venn . . ." He shrugged. "Do you still know, in this century, the tale of the war between Winter and Summer? The Shee tell it often. They had a bet as to who was stronger—the test was to take the coat from a mortal. The icy blasts of Winter blew and the mortal merely held his coat all the tighter. But when the sun shone hotter and hotter, he had to take it off. It's a true story. Venn can roar and flummox all he likes, but when Summer smiles, believe me, everyone obeys."

He took a light step toward the door. But Maskelyne said, "Gideon. I smell a magic on you. Faint and strange. What might that be?"

"No idea," Gideon muttered. But as he pushed past the scarred man, he thought of the flower in his pocket.

And smiled.

→·←

Curled beneath the stifling layers of the Scribe's dusty robes, barely able to breathe, Sarah felt the wooden lid being lifted away.

She kept utterly still, listening.

For an hour the automata had been rocked and rattled on some cart halfway across the city, through turns and twists of alleys and streets and secret courtyards, over cobbles and bridges and a long graveled path. Now she smelled wonderful, exotic scents, the perfumes of flowers, cloying and sweet.

Footsteps pattered close. She saw the tip of a small,

heeled shoe. The voluminous robe of the automata made a purple tent around her, but if anyone lifted it off they would see her. Reluctantly, she again made herself invisible.

A thin, male French voice said, in English, "Astonishing!"

"This is the finest of the machines, milord, manufactured in London by watchmakers of the most delicate skill to delight your guests. It will answer simple questions and compute the answers to arithmetical problems. The ballerina will pirouette, perform a most wonderful dance. The Conjuror will entertain with magic."

"I love them. I love them, monsieur. I love them so much I could weep tears of delight. Let me see them move! Show me how they operate!"

"Certainly. Shall we start with the Dancer?"

Carefully Sarah edged away a corner of the velvet. She was dazzled by sunlight. Greenery crowded her, a tropical jungle of lushness she had never imagined; she slid down onto hands and knees and slipped into it, crawling out hurriedly. Vast leaves as wide as she was hid her easily, great tree roots and trunks that rose high over her into the glassed ceiling of an enormous hothouse.

In only seconds she was soaked with sweat; condensation dripped from the leaves and twining stems around her, splashed on the terracotta-tiled floor.

Hearing music, she crouched, lifted a fern and watched the men.

They stood admiring as the Dancer turned and bowed and raised her arms, pointing her toes with exquisite grace.

The Englishman was tall, bony, his clothes dark and plain, his hair straggly under a tricorn hat. There was something about him that made Sarah sure he had been one of the two men who had taken Jake. He watched the other man as beadily as a crow watches a likely worm, head on one side, his contemptuous smirk barely hidden.

The French milord astonished Sarah. He was tiny, his suit the pinkest of satins, his shoes buckled with diamonds, his hair a powdered wig of pure white. He circled the automaton with his palms pressed together in wonder. "I will be envied by the world," he breathed. "By the world."

The mechanical dancer stopped, bowed her head gracefully, sank in a curtsey among a fluster of white taffeta skirt.

"How does it work? The clockwork, the cogs, how are they . . . ?"

"This lever, milord, will produce the desired effect. But perhaps we should discuss the price before . . ."

"Of course! Come with me, good Englishman. I assure you, the Vicomte de Saligne pays his debts most promptly. Your gold is waiting in the château." The tiny man almost capered toward her; Sarah moved back hurriedly as they passed, their voices fading.

When they were gone, she crawled out and stood a moment in the astonishing heat. Then she moved to the nearest glass and rubbed a small running circle in the condensation, the warm water trickling over her fingertips.

She looked out.

And laughed aloud with surprise.

5

Where ever the mirror has been, men have used it
for their own needs. Janus is just the last of many. They
are all responsible. They have all desired its power.

Now it is a dark agony that is devouring itself.

Time is ending. Humanity is ending.

We are the ones who will see that happen.

Illegal ZEUS transmission

JAKE WAS PRETENDING sleep when the carriage finally rattled to a halt.

They had traveled for a long time; twisting and turning and sometimes rattling down alleys so narrow he could hear the paintwork of the coach being scraped on both sides.

Now the door was opened; he glanced at it from lowered lids, measuring the odds of escape. The big men climbed out, the vehicle swaying wildly.

"Hey," one said. "Boy! Wake up."

Jake followed them out. He swayed, as if dizzy with hunger and travel-weariness.

"Watch him," one of the men muttered.

Another laughed. "Nowhere to run."

Jake snatched his elbow from the man's grip and looked around.

They were in a dank alley. Even though the long summer twilight was only just beginning, it was already dark here. There were no streetlamps, just the pale sky-glimmer reflected in pools of water and stinking liquids that flooded the central gutter. Great dim houses leaned over him, their heavy gables darkly medieval. The stench of refuse and rot was worse than ever; rats scuttled openly between his feet.

He realized he must be in one of the lowest sinks of the city, some slum so lost and dark that he felt all hope of rescue go out in his heart like a candle.

Turning, he saw the men were lowering a long package from the roof of the carriage; they handled it carefully, as if it was precious.

"You, stand aside," one of the men snapped.

He didn't move.

They shoved him back, and the package, all corded in sackcloth, was carried past him. Tall as a man, a thin flat slab of something delicate and heavy. He felt a stab of fierce joy. *It had to be the mirror.*

They carried it down the alley, one man at each corner. The final man, the one with the pistol, nudged Jake to follow.

Fog lurked in the doorways. Smoke clung to the rooftops. Under his feet the cobbles were treacherous with slime. Halfway down, he passed a huddled, miserable tent of rags; a half-starved child peeped out at him, then darted back in alarm. Jake stumbled on, trying to think, but he was so tired now his brain was numbed and he had to force himself to keep his head up and take notice. There was nowhere too dismal for Jake Wilde. But he wished desperately that Sarah or Wharton were here. Wintercombe Abbey seemed a thousand years away.

The street sloped downward; the stench grew worse. Then he realized they were coming to the river. The Seine was a wide, black flood, its mud banks littered with refuse that a few beggars picked over for scraps of food.

"Down the steps," the man muttered.

"Not much of a talker, are you," Jake said. *Make some connection with the kidnappers. Get them to talk to you.* Scenarios from old books and films flitted through his tired mind. "That's the mirror, isn't it. But none of you are the two who came for me. And who's behind this? Who's paying you?"

The nudge of the pistol against his cheek silenced him. "Shut up. Get in the boat."

He was pushed down a set of creaking wooden stairs. The river lapped at his feet, sucked at his boots. He climbed quickly into the boat, the last man followed and cast off, and they began to row downstream.

It was a journey through a nightmare. To each side the city rose, its church pinnacles, its crowded slums and rickety tenements. Lights flared, a woman cried out. Drunken men laughed on the waterfront. Almost silent, the boat floated on, the ripple of the oars barely heard among the noise of the quays.

Once they passed below the shell of what had been a great palace, all its empty windows lit with flames, fires still burning in its courtyard, and Jake said, "Is this the Tuileries?" He knew that palace had been destroyed in the Revolution.

To his surprise the man beside him said, "Bloody cut-throats. Call themselves Citizens! This would never happen in England."

One of the rowers grunted in agreement. "Sooner we get the goods and get out of this crib, the better. Before all our heads get chopped."

As he spoke they came under a wharf, wooden piles rising around them. It stank so foully Jake put a hand over his nose and mouth and tried not to breathe. Looking up he saw a dilapidated sign swinging in the wind. *Le Chat Noir,* a dark cat with yellow eyes. The boat rocked as one of the rowers stood and thumped upward with the oar.

A dull thud.

Then another, answering.

A trapdoor crashed down.

Jake was hauled up. He found himself in a cellar, moldy with damp, its walls green with slime. "Up again." The man with the pistol gestured; leaving the others to unload the mirror, he pushed Jake up some stairs in the corner to a door, which he unlocked. "Go on."

Jake shook his head, uneasy. "You first."

"What, you think we've brought you through time and tide to top you? Bloody thick, are you? Why she thinks you're so . . ." He stopped. Then, angrily, "Get on."

Jake climbed the stair and opened the door.

To his great surprise he found a comfortably furnished room. His wet boots sank into a deep rug. A long table, laid with silver dishes glittering in the light of five crystal candelabra, each with branches of bright candles.

Plates of food littered the surface—roasted meats, steaming vegetables, sauces. Sweet, sticky confections of cream and sugar and cinnamon were piled haphazardly on delicate porcelain plates. A carafe of dark wine stood by a cask of beer.

Jake went straight for it. He drank some wine and felt its heat flood through him; then he sat, pulled up a plate, and ate with concentration and speed.

After ten minutes he felt a lot better. He took a breath, wiped his lips with a napkin, took another long swig of wine.

Then he looked up, and saw in the warped silver side of a tureen that someone was standing in a doorway behind him, watching him; a slim, dark, cloaked shape.

His heart leaped.

"Dad?" he whispered, in wild hope.

Venn's temper was so spectacular that most of the Shee had fled to the safety of the treetops. Now as he picked up a chair and hurled it into the bracken, so that the frail wood splintered against a tree trunk, even Wharton winced.

He had made himself tell the story of the kidnapping very clearly, and without emotion. Summer had smiled her pretty red lips throughout, even laughed a cold tinkle of laughter when she heard of Sarah's disappearance. Could she be behind this? He wouldn't be at all surprised.

Now she said, "Calm down, Venn. It's nothing that need bother us."

He swung on her. "Someone comes into my house through the mirror, kidnaps my godson—"

"You know very well the boy means nothing to you."

"Summer, he's David's son. That means something."

"Still?" She pouted. "Oh, that's so disappointing, Venn. I thought you'd got beyond all that."

"*All that!*" Venn came and stood over her. "David was . . . is . . . my friend."

"You don't have friends, Venn. You have tools. People you use for as long as you need them, and then discard. Or forget. Or ignore. That's the Shee in you, my sweet." She smoothed her dress, sat up, and swung her legs around, poised daintily on the edge of the lounger. "But if it irritates you, I can send my people to find Jake."

"Well, do it then." Sullen, he turned his back on her and glared at Wharton. "How the hell could you let this happen!"

"Me?" Wharton was astounded at the man's arrogance.

"You're the teacher. You're supposed to be looking after him."

"Now look bloody here." Wharton stormed forward, ignoring a titter of mirth from the treetops. "First, you're the boy's guardian. He's in your house. But you're not there, are you, oh no. You spend all your time out here, in this godforsaken wasteland with these flim-flam creatures. What's the matter with you, man? Has she got you under some spell, that you can't get control of yourself, do your duty, get yourself back on track? A few problems with the mirror and you're gone, bored with it. So much for Oberon Venn and his deathless passion, his love that won't accept the grave! Or is it that you don't want your wife back anymore? That you're quite happy with the one you've got?"

He knew he was blustering, red-faced, making a fool of himself, but he didn't care.

The Shee loved it. They swung down, became butterflies and finches, fluttered around Wharton in mocking excitement. One of them landed on his head; he shook it off, furious. "Look at you! You're turning into one of them! And that kid, Jake—yes, I know he's a total pain, but all he cares about is his father, and then there's Sarah, with all that weight of the future on her, you just leave them to it and . . . and . . . gad about here with that . . . that . . . creature."

He was stuttering with fury. *Shut up George!* But it was way too late for that. The Shee shrieked with joy; they made wild patterns and flew around him; some of them crumpled back into people-shape and fell into the grass giggling helplessly.

He stood among it all. Then he took out a handkerchief and mopped the sweat from his face.

That made them laugh all the more.

The racket rose until Summer clapped her hands and there was instant silence. She glanced at Venn. "What do you want me to do to him?"

"Nothing." Venn stood unmoving. His face was emotionless, but his voice was dark and brooding.

She put her hand on his arm. "I can turn him into the donkey he is."

He shook her off, as if a spider had landed on his

sleeve. "I said no. I don't need you to act for me."

She stepped back. Very slightly, the sun darkened. "Oberon . . ."

"He's right. I know it, he knows it. I've let myself lose hope. I've let you take it away from me."

Summer bit her lip.

The Shee fled. They melted silently away into the trees, flew among the leaves, hid in the undergrowth. A small breeze rustled the clearing.

Wharton watched, fascinated.

Venn turned and strode toward the Abbey.

"Where are you going?" she said quietly.

"To sort out this mess. To get the mirror up and running."

"You won't need to," Wharton muttered. "The kidnappers, whoever they are, did that. Maskelyne says its awake now with a vengeance."

Venn turned fast. His eyes were bright with interest. "Really?"

At once Summer tapped her bare foot on the ground. Instantly all the trees around the clearing seemed to link arms and pull together; a solid green wall of branches and boughs meshed in seconds.

"I really think you are taking a few things for granted, sweet," Summer said.

She stood among the flowery grass, a small, delicate creature, her dark hair woven with white daisies, and

Wharton felt the cold fear of her slide into his heart. They were at her mercy now. And she had no mercy.

"You see"—Summer brushed the slightest dust of pollen from her shimmering dress—"I haven't decided to let you go yet. Persuade me, Venn."

He was still a moment. Then he approached her. Warily, Wharton thought. Like a hunter circling a most deadly prey. He said, "I have to go back. Jake is in danger. Surely you see that."

"Ah, but what about Leah?"

His face darkened. "Don't say her name."

"Leah. Leah, Venn."

"Leah is dead."

"Not to you. I know whatever George here says, she lives inside you. Deep, deep down in some locked, steely place even I can't reach." For a second, so fast Wharton almost doubted he saw it, her features lost all their beauty, flickered through a transformation to some ancient stony hag and back.

Venn laughed his rare cold laugh. "Your jealousy's devouring you, Summer. What more do you want? You've surrounded my house, you invade my life, grow and tangle over all of it. You know very well I can never escape from you."

Silent, she gazed at him. Then she said, "I wish I knew what game you're playing, *Oberon*."

He shrugged, as if careless. But Wharton saw the

sweat under his lank hair, the tension in his eyes.

Suddenly Summer turned away. She twisted on her toes and clapped her hands. "Let's have some lemonade and ice cream!"

The Shee descended in a whirl of preparations; the cloth was whirled over a small tilted table. Glasses with stripy straws suddenly fizzed with drink.

Venn said, "I'm going."

He strode toward the hedge. A gap opened in its mesh, a mossy branch unfurled. Two lichened boughs creaked apart.

"Go then," Summer said, light as air.

Venn flicked a glance at Wharton. "Come on."

But Summer's smile was brittle. "Not him."

"What?"

"Dear George stays here with me."

Venn came back. His eyes were blue and curious. In the heat he seemed to shimmer, his pale coat dusted with damsel flies. "Why?"

"Because I am in love with dear George." She pouted at Wharton. "Because I would love to show him all the delights of the Summerland. And because you still have my pretty changeling."

Venn nodded, grim. "Gideon! I knew you'd get to him sooner or later. Well, he's not my prisoner, Summer, and he could come here anytime, but he won't. He's had enough of you. "

She smiled, showing small white teeth. "He's afraid. He took that girl into my very house and stole . . . Well, never mind what he stole. Until he comes back, dear George stays here with me." She turned to Wharton with an amused glance. "Look at him. He loves the idea."

Wharton was exercising every ounce of self-restraint he possessed. He'd faced down enemies and sorted hundreds of school brawls, knew how to quell uproar in a classroom with one glance. One small woman, however powerful, would not intimidate him.

But as Summer's tiny fingers closed over his, he felt only a shiver of complete fear.

He looked at Venn. He wanted to shout, *"Don't leave me here."* Instead he said, "It's quite all right. I'll be fine. Jake is what matters now. Get back there and find Jake."

He made himself stand tall.

Venn watched him a moment, then quietly nodded. He turned to the gap in the hedge and walked quickly through, then turned and looked back.

"You're a brave man, teacher," he said.

And was gone.

Wharton cleared his throat. Summer stood on tiptoes, reached up and kissed him on the cheek.

"You won't regret it," she whispered.

He had never been so scared.

Jake put down the wineglass slowly.

The figure moved forward. He saw, with a shiver of disappointment, that it was too small for his father, but still he dared not stand, as if sitting still kept that hope alive.

Then she said, "Not your dad, cully. Just me. Watch and learn, Jake, luv. Watch and learn."

Astonished, he jumped up, knocking the chair over with a smack.

"Moll?"

She never had so sweet a changeling.

Moll's diary.

JHS has tort me to read. I catch on fast, he says. He don't no the harf. So I'm starting a diary too, Jake, all for you, and locking it in my room so that snivelfacd creep Hassan can't read it and split on me.

Been a year now in this posh crib. Good dresses, a coat, boots withaht holes. No rozzers after me, no punks pinching my stuff. Warm bed, food, plenty of it. JHS likes his grub.

Working every day with the mirror. But you no what? No braslet, so nothing works .

Jake said he'd cum back for me. Swore he wood.
Cum on, Jake. Hurry up and get me.
I'm waiting, Jake.

Moll's diary. 6 months later.

Today *JHS nearly exploded with excitement. He's been writing to some scolar who says he knows where there's a bracelet just like the one we need. The letter came at breakfast; JHS came bursting into the kitchen (because I have to eat there with Hassan and Mrs. C since he met the* LOVE OF HIS BLOODY LIFE).

"My coat, Moll!" he says. "Quick!" His face was as red as a turkey-cock's comb.

Mrs. C rolled her eyes. She thinks JHS is for the Bedlam over the mirror. She hates it, won't even dust it. Says it's a black eye watching her and she might fall into it and go down and down and down, skirts over her head, still holding the feather duster.

Anyway, I grab his coat and we (me and JHS) jump in a cab.

"Where are we going?"

"The Ash Moleyan," he says.

"What's that?"

"What's that, sir. Why do I keep having to remind you of your manners, Moll!" He gets tetchy over that. Remember your place, girl, I thought. I kept shtum.

Till he says, "That's a museum, in Oxford. I've been corresponding with them, about the brace-

let, and they've got one, Moll! They've got one!"

"Just like Jake's?" I say, all quiet.

"From the description here it sounds absolutely identical! Silver snake swallowing its tail, the amber stone in the center . . ." He couldn't sit still he was so took up. "Just think, Moll, if it's what I've been searching for for years! As things stand, I dare not use the mirror myself until I'm sure I can return. But both Venn and David Wilde had such a bracelet; they were a pair, and a pair must exist in our time too, somewhere. They simply must!"

He went off into a mumble and then a dream and I let him, Jake, because I like looking out at the streets, all them crossing-sweepers and peelers I used to know. We drove past Hayes, the butchers what set his dog on me once and he saw me and stared and I waved like the Queen. Then stuck my tongue at him.

It's hard to get used to, being upper clars.

And why did the bracelets have to exist in our time? What if there was only one pair and they were the same ones all through . . . but then it all got too complicated and my brain went giddy.

You'd know, Jake, I'll bet . . .

At the station we got the 9:30 train for Oxford. I sat opposite JHS in First. A woman got into our compartment and looked at me through her specs like I was an ant with measles.

JHS read the letter over and over and then fell asleep with it on his lap. It fell off and I picked it up and read it. Lots of guff, lots of long words. But the bracelet sounds the same.

Won't let myself get all excited, though.

Won't let myself think about you, Jake.

At Oxford we got out. Gave the old biddy the finger. Doubt she even knew what it meant.

The Ashmolean is a big museum full of all sorts of junk, and Bill the Brick (they called him that because he could smash one with his fist), who used to fence my stuff, would pop his eyeballs at some of it. JHS made a fuss in the entrance hall and they got a little foreign-looking cully with glasses that made his eyes wide as an owl's, to come down.

"Mr. Harcourt Symmes? Good morning, sir. I have to say we weren't expecting you quite so soon."

Symmes shoved the letter in his face. "I came at once. This bracelet. It's exactly as you describe it?"

"I assure you—"

"Then let me see it, man, immediately. I can't tell you how much this could mean to the scientific research I am in the process of . . ." Blah, blah, blather, blather.

The long and short of it is I'm dragged after them through endless rooms of rust and dust and broken pots. Once I got a big shock and screeched and they both stopped and stared at me.

"What?" Symmes asked.

Couldn't they see? I pointed at the dead geezer in the painted coffin. Talk about a stiff.

"Oh for heaven's sake, Moll." JHS caught my arm and whisked me on. "It's ancient Egyptian. It's not going to hurt you."

He smiled a sort of ghastly grin at the other man. "My niece. I'm bringing her up, having rescued her from . . . a very difficult childhood."

Owl-Eyes stared at me, his lips as tight as a mouse's arse.

We got into a big gallery. Owl-Eyes switched the gas on and I saw long glass cases packed full of serious tin—silver, gold, diamonds.

He took out a small key and unlocked a case and lifted out a bracelet.

Me and JHS stared at it.

The silver creature crawled round and swallowed its own tail. An amber crystal glowed in its heart.

I would have recognized it anywhere, even

though I really only saw it for a few minutes, when you showed me after we got it back from the thieves at Skimble's.

Those were the days, eh Jake?

JHS cleared his throat and shook his big shiny head and made a big effort. "Ah. How unfortunate. It is not at all the same. Quite unlike. The whole design is . . . er totally different. Isn't that so, Moll?"

I nodded, deadpan. "Nothink like it, Uncle John, Your Honor, sir. Nothink like it at all."

➤＊➤

Oberon Venn stood before the obsidian mirror.

In it he could see his own reflection, his face all angles, a pale glimmer in the depths of the dark glass.

For a moment he could not recognize himself. The mirror showed him something insubstantial, wavering, a being caught halfway between existing and not existing. He wondered if it could see into his soul, into the fluttering indecisive thing he had become. That Summer had made of him.

Maskelyne and Gideon watched, the changeling standing, arms folded, in the heart of the malachite web, the scarred man seated at the control panel. The baby, Lorenzo, crawled unnoticed on the dirty floor.

Venn said, "And you're sure Sarah went after them unseen?"

"Piers says the cat says so."

Venn nodded, reluctant. "That girl . . . She really is a true Venn."

He came forward and gripped the silver frame, its unknown letters. As he closed his fingers around it, the mirror gave the smallest shiver; only Maskelyne sensed it, and he looked up and saw that Venn, as always now, was wearing the remaining bracelet locked tight around his wrist.

"Step back," he said quietly. "The mirror knows you're there."

"Does it?" Venn stared into his own cold eyes. "Does it know what I want? Does it know where they all are, the lost ones, Leah, David, Jake?"

Piers came running in, breathless. The little man wore his white lab coat, the pockets stuffed with papers and wires. In his arms he carried a tall pile of books with the marmoset balanced precariously on top of it. Seeing Venn, his gaze widened with alarm.

"Be careful, Excellency."

Venn was still, as if by his own despair he could conjure something, anything, from those black, heartless depths. When at last he did step back, his face was gaunt.

He turned to Gideon.

"Summer is holding Wharton. As a hostage for you."

Gideon folded his arms over his patchwork coat. The news was a shock, but he managed to keep his voice steady. "Then I truly feel sorry for him."

"The fool thought he had some sort of choice, thought he was being heroic, giving himself up." Venn's ice-blue gaze held the changeling in contempt. "I won't force you to go back. But don't you think you should . . ."

Gideon shrugged, calm. "No, I don't. Summer doesn't keep bargains. The Shee don't understand fair or unfair. If I went back, she'd still torment him and probably imprison both of us in some dungeon in the Summerland. It's a pity about him. But I'm more use to you here."

Venn nodded. "A cool judgment. You've grown very like them."

Annoyed, Gideon paled. "I don't think so."

"No? If Jake was in your place, he wouldn't hesitate. He'd be furious, reckless. He'd be storming into the Wood to save Wharton right now."

That was true; Gideon knew it. He felt the familiar stirring of self-hatred, of shame, but Venn turned away abruptly, and said nothing more.

Gideon breathed out. Then, seeing Piers's bright eye on him, he growled, "Keep your opinions to yourself, little man. You wouldn't go."

"Well no," Piers said, "I don't suppose I would. But then I'm not a mortal. I don't have to be brave and stupid."

He turned to Venn. "Excellency, this is what you asked for. Like I told you, I found it under a floorboard in Sarah's room—she had a stash of stuff there. She must have had the hiding place in the future time, when the house is ruined. If that makes sense." He fished a small gray notebook out of the pile and laid it on the workbench. "And this."

A black pen, with a capital Z on its cap.

Venn picked the notebook up and opened it.

He flicked through the messages she had written, and Janus's mocking answers. One of them caught his eye.

DO I HAVE TO SEND MORE OF MY TIME WOLVES AFTER YOU, DEAR SARAH? DO I HAVE TO HUNT YOU DOWN TO STOP YOU DESTROYING THE MIRROR?

NO, I DON'T. I CAN SIT BACK AND SMILE. VENN WILL DO MY JOB FOR ME. VENN WILL PROTECT THE CHRONOPTIKA BECAUSE VENN IS THE MOST SELFISH OF BEINGS. HE WOULD SACRIFICE THE FUTURE OF THE WORLD FOR HIS OWN HAPPINESS. AND SO HE WILL ENABLE MY TYRANNY TO BEGIN.

It stabbed him like a thin blade of fear in his heart, a sliver of ice. It was clever and mocking and it would have hurt her all the more because she would have thought it was true.

Bitter, he looked up. "Why did she communicate with him like this?"

"*Know your enemy,* they say." Maskelyne came and picked up the pen. "This is interesting. The notebook is just ordinary paper. The pen, however, is the device that coveys the message. It is some creation of the future. She must have brought it with her."

Venn took it from him and looked at the letter *Z* on the cap. Then he said, "It makes me think. What if it was Janus who took Jake? What if Sarah guessed that when she went after them? Who else can send Replicants across time?"

"We won't know, unless—"

"Unless we ask him."

Venn took the black pen and strode to the mirror. In huge, angry letters he scrawled a message over the black glass.

WHAT HAVE YOU DONE WITH JAKE?

→>·<←

Through the hothouse window Sarah saw a paradise such as she had never believed could really exist. She opened the door and went out and stared.

A great park stretched downhill before her, its green lawns perfectly smooth. Between neat paths, formal gardens were laid out in squares and rectangles, immaculate with parterres of white shell, dark cinders, crushed terracotta gravel. Box trees, cut in precise balls or tidy triangles, stood in containers. Great urns of roses perfumed the summer air, and as she looked up, doves rose in a cloud from the roof of the hothouse.

"My message was for you to wait inside!"

Sarah turned.

The thin Englishman was back; with a shock she realized that he could see her.

Behind him a château, a vast white sugar-icing palace rose against the blue sky, its windows perfect, its symmetrical steps leading up to a pillared colonnade.

He glanced around. Grabbing her arm, he hustled her back into the steamy greenhouse. "Bloody stupid girl!" He hurried to the Conjurer automaton and pulled a parcel from under its seat. "These are your clothes. Your contact in the kitchen is the woman called Madame Lepage. She's in the plot. Get changed, quickly."

She said, "But you. You're—"

"Long Tom. I'm inside too, with the metal puppets. You know all about the plan? You can do what we need?"

Baffled, she said, "Of course . . . But—"

"Good. Then hurry! Get dressed now."

He shoved the parcel at her; she took it and ducked between the giant leaves.

The Scribe automata watched her with its vacant glass eyes; she wished it could truly answer questions because she had absolutely no idea at all what was going on here. Opening the parcel, she found the dark plain dress of a kitchen maid, a white apron, a frilly cap. As she changed quickly, bundling her own clothes into the bag, she said, "You snatched the boy Jake, didn't you?"

"How the hell do you know about that?"

"I heard . . . talk."

"Yes, we got him." The tall man laughed. "Went straight in and kidnapped him from his bed. Arrogant brat too. Don't know why she was so keen."

Sarah paused, half buttoned. "She?"

"Some sort of twisted revenge, maybe? Some joke? You never know with our little contessa. Are you done?"

She hurried out, breathless.

"Why is your hair so short!" He glanced at her, anxious. "Well, maybe the cap hides that . . . Remember, your name is Adelie, you're madame's niece, just here tonight to help for the Midsummer Ball."

She said, "I don't know a word of French."

Long Tom swore a lurid oath. "Where in hell's dregs did they find you? Then just keep your mouth shut. *Okay?*"

Bewildered, she nodded. "Okay," she said.

As he turned swiftly toward the château, she said, panicking, "About the ball . . ."

He glanced back. "The vicomte's invited half of

Paris. You know what to do. The door in the moon has to be open by the stroke of midnight. Don't forget." He pulled his hat on, wiped his sweaty forehead with his sleeve. "Too hot here. Too dangerous. We must be mad."

Then he was gone, a flicker in the brilliant sunlight.

Sarah smoothed her dress with shaky hands. All right. Think. They—whoever they were—had mistaken her for some other girl. They could *journey*. They had the mirror, and at least one bracelet. And they were planning something for the Midsummer Ball, something that involved Jake.

Which meant, presumably, that they would be bringing him here.

To do what? What was this plot? To steal something? Murder someone?

She looked up. The glorious confection of the château stood serene under its blue sky. But a few miles back there, in Paris, the crowds were screaming around the guillotine. Blood was running in the gutters, and mobs roaming the streets. How long before the heedless aristocrats holed up here felt that wrath?

She had to find out more. About where Jake was, and about the mysterious *contessa*.

Not to mention, she thought as she set off for the kitchens, about finding a door in the moon.

7

At last the Abbot himself said, "I will enter the dark Wood and face the demons in my own guise. And if our lost brother is there, I will find him, and with God's grace and the protection of the holy saints, I will bring him home."

Wiser monks shook their heads and counseled him not to venture. Because they knew what fiends, what temptations, lurk'd in those desolate places.

Chronicle of Wintercombe

SHE CAME FORWARD, out of the shadows, small and smiling.

"Moll!" he said. "How can it—"

He turned, and stopped.

She seemed to transform. From a small dirty child to a girl, as if time accelerated before him. As she unfastened her hood and swung off the dark cloak, he stared with astonishment.

She said, "Time don't stop, Jake. I've been waiting an age for you."

He saw a girl of about fifteen, dressed in a gown of maroon-and-black velvet.

Lace gloves covered her fingers. Her hair, dark and

lustrous, was pinned up in an elaborate style. Earrings, glinting with diamonds, hung at her ears.

She was slim and beautiful and cleaner than he was.

His face must have shown only shock, because she giggled. "You should see your face, cully. Have I changed all that much, then?"

He swallowed. "No . . . but you've . . ."

"Grown up?" She came forward, her dress swishing on the floor, and he saw then that it was too big for her. "How long for you, then, Jake, since you went back through the mirror at Symmes's place? Five months? Six?"

"Six."

"Not long." She sat on a striped sofa and leaned back. "Not for you. Five whole years for me." She winked, a coy, knowing look. "Catching up with you, Jake."

He was devastated. The cheeky, bold urchin he had known was transmuted into a girl who had probably seen more of life than he had, and he felt bewildered. As if he was the child and she the adult.

He said, "They didn't kidnap you too?"

She giggled, gleeful. "Lord, there's no they, Jake, luv. Just me and the boys. Surprised?"

She sat on the sofa, demure, then tiring of that, swung her legs up and sat with them crossed.

Jake stared. "You mean . . . My God, Moll! I was scared stiff! He had a gun and—"

Moll laughed. "Empty, Jake. Wouldn't have had you hurt. But what a lark! I knew you'd love it. All that malarky with the gag and stuff."

He had no idea what to say. He had forgotten her wildness, her fearlessness. He was angry, furious with her.

She tapped the seat beside her. "Come on, Jake. No hard feelings?"

And then he saw, under the lace of her glove, a slim edge. Grabbing her hand, he slid the glove down and stared at the bracelet.

"Moll, where did you get this? Did Symmes . . . But no, we know that Symmes never had one, because in the end he entered the mirror without one, so—"

"You don't know zilch, Jake luv." She was looking at him as if she feasted on the sight of him.

He dropped her hand, realizing. "And to get me you'd have had to travel into the *future!* How is that possible? We've never been able to do anything like that yet!"

"I worked a few things out. You don't know half of what that black glass can do. But I do, Jake." She shrugged. "I've just about sold my soul to the thing to find out. Because I had to, cully, once I worked out that you was never coming back for me."

He sat, slowly, beside her. "Moll, like you said, it's only been six months. I would have come, I meant to, but things have gone crazy. I tried to find my father and ended up in World War Two—well, you won't know what that is—and then I did find him, but I lost him again." He shook his head, stabbed suddenly by the pain of that, his father in the frayed doctor's robe, the terrible heat of the plague-ridden city. Then, looking up, he stopped, because what did any of that mean to her?

For her it had been years.

Moll put her lacy fingers together and said calmly, "I waited, Jake. Waited and waited. And you never came. I was a kid from the slums back then, the lowest dregs of the street. All I knew was cheek and snatching purses and being fast on my feet. And then you came. All big and brave and handsome. You crashed in like a hurricane—you and Venn—and blew my life apart. Little girls have stupid crushes, Jake, luv. Mine was with you. The boy from the future."

"Moll . . ."

She ignored him. "I was so sure you'd come back. We'd *journey* off to some city of glass buildings and magic machines, and there'd be fun and adventures and food and friends. Symmes gave me some clothes and a bag and I kept it all packed ready, for weeks, Jake. Months. Before I started thinking you'd forgotten me."

"I never forgot you!" He jumped, up, paced. "For God's sake, it's only been six months, Moll. I will—"

She watched him, calm. "It's been five years. *And you never did come*."

That silenced him.

He said, "How did you get the bracelet?"

"Blimey. That's a tale. You'll have to read my diary. I'm going to leave it for you, Jake, somewhere you'll be sure to find it. Anyway, me and Symmes got hold of it." She laughed. "And that was too big a temptation, Jake. Once a thief, always a thief. Symmes needed money for the experiments—he got married to this stuck-up piece what hated my guts. So I left, and I took the bracelet with me. Set up on my own."

He sat back down. The room was shadowy, but he saw now it was sumptuous; hung with heavy drapes, its tables littered with lamps and precious porcelain, silver dishes and etched glass. A door opened and a manservant came in, powdered and silent in silver livery, and began to lay the table with fresh linen.

Moll took Jake's arm and cuddled up close. "Know what you made me, Jake? You made me the best jewel thief in all the world. Because with the mirror I can steal anything, all across time, and *journey* away and never get caught. Such adventures I've had, Jake, such close shaves! The Sultan of Oman's Yellow Opal, I stole that, and we robbed the Duchess of Lindsey in her carriage on the Dover road, and then there's the Charing Cross Bank job—ever hear about that one?"

He sat silent as she detailed amazing and daring exploits, as she jumped up and gleefully acted out how she'd climbed the wall at Chatsworth House, how her gang had tunneled under the vaults of Dublin Castle. And as he watched he saw that maybe he was wrong, maybe she hadn't changed, hadn't grown up at all.

The footman cleared his throat. "Grub's up, Contessa."

"Thank you, James." She stood, took Jake's hand, and led him to the table.

He said, *"Contessa?"*

"Got to have a moniker, Jake, for this con. Like the spread?"

He sat, surveying the silver teapot, the plates of cakes and scones and sandwiches. For a moment he felt as if he was at a children's tea party, the chairs too big, the food pink and sweet.

"It's all for you Jake? It's okay, isn't it?"

"Great, Moll."

"Go on, dig in. I know you'll be starving."

He was still hungry, but first he sat back and put both hands on the table and looked at them. Then he raised his head. "Why did you really bring me here?"

She buttered a scone. "You and me, Jake, we're going to pull off the biggest, most sensational, most daring heist ever in the history of the world. A real adventure. Just like in the old days."

"But—"

"Just listen, okay? On Midsummer Eve 1798, while Paris is all in riot, a bloke called the Vicomte de Sauvigne goes ahead with the Midsummer Ball at his château. He's the owner of a stonking great necklace called the Sauvigne emeralds—big heirloom, costs a king's ransom. At the ball, hundreds of guests, entertainment, fireworks, you name it. But that night the mob come marching out from the city and the château gets burned to a crisp. The Sauvigne emeralds are never seen again. Which is where we come in, Jake luv."

He couldn't believe it. "Are you crazy, Moll! All I want is to find my father, that's all I'm thinking about, and you snatch me here for some stupid, what . . . jewelry theft? In one of the most dangerous times in modern . . . ."

He petered out, because her face was so bright and excited.

"It's going to be such fun!" She dropped the knife with a clatter and leaned toward him. "It's not just the loot. It's you and me, out there, plotting and planning and escaping. I've dreamed of it, Jake, for years, and now it's here. We'll have such a time! And"—she sat back—"of course there's something in it for you. I've *journeyed,* Jake, been lots of places. Seen stuff. Found things out."

He stared at her. "You mean . . . . ?"

"Spot on, cully." She took a huge bite of scone. Indistinctly, through the cream she said, "You help me out. In return, Jake, I tell you where I saw your dad."

→→←←

Wharton was lying on a striped recliner on a pile of sand among the trees. On his right was a round table and on the table a glass of bright orange fizzy liquid, a knotted straw angled in it. Next to that was a plateful of sticky cakes topped with icing, and an ice-cream sundae.

He frowned.

"What?" One of the Shee that Summer had assigned to look after him darted immediately from nowhere. There were four of them. His jailers. "What? What's wrong?"

"My ice cream's melted."

The Shee, a pretty female in a brown dress as ragged as a moth's wings, stretched a dainty finger and touched the glass. A cold crackle of frost solidified it immediately.

"Better?"

The Shee, Wharton was beginning to realize, like children, took everything to extremes. They knew nothing about subtlety. He gazed at the impenetrable mass of ice and said, "Thanks for that."

The moth-creature looked relieved. "Anything you want, mortal, you just say." It turned sideways, became a patch of bark on a tree-trunk. Then he couldn't see it at all.

He wondered how many of them were all around, watching him. He reached out for the orange drink, and drew back. He broke off a lump of cake, crumbled it warily on the plate, and looked at it.

Best not.

All the folktales said if you ate the fairy food you were doomed to be in their power for all eternity.

Besides, the cake had the texture of mushy leaves.

He pushed it away. Lying back in the seat, he gazed up at the flawless blue sky and thought about that word. *Eternity.*

How long had he been here? Had years passed in the outside world? He dared not think that. To him it seemed like an hour or so, but nothing had changed; the sun had not moved by a fraction. Presumably he hadn't grown even a second older, though, which was one good thing. He was in a timeless non-place, with no past or future, just an endless now.

It must have been like this for Gideon.

He pulled a face. He knew there was little chance of the boy coming back. Couldn't blame him. No, he, Wharton, had to take charge of the situation. He was a prisoner of war. He'd seen all the training films. He knew what he had to do.

You formed an escape plan. You dug a tunnel, made

a disguise, fooled the guards. Made a run for it. He had to try something like that. Get a grip, think clearly, not be bamboozled by the bloody Shee.

Get back and find Jake.

Suddenly, the sunlight was blotted out. He opened his eyes, jerking awake from the surprising snooze, to find Summer smiling down at him.

He sat up.

"Were you dreaming, George? I couldn't quite see any dreams."

"You can see them?" The idea appalled him.

"If I want to. I like to peep into the dreams of mortals, George. They're so wild and whirling, so colorful and confused! I can flit and wander and crawl into the darkest, craziest corners. The Summerland has nothing on them." She tucked her arm in his. "Let's go for a walk. I want to show you my lovely country."

He was hot and worried, but it would be useful to know the lie of the land, so he stood up and said, "If you say so. I'm your prisoner, after all."

"My guest." There was the tiniest edge of steel in that word.

"Whatever. Lead the way."

Afterward, if there was such a thing as afterward here, he was not sure they had actually gone anywhere. It was more as if the world had moved past them, fracturing into a crazy kaleidoscope of smashed and splintered places, piled up around each other.

She took him through an empty Santa's grotto into the deserted spaces of a big store's furniture department, where some of the Shee were holding a wild dance, leaping hand in hand over the settees and beds and sofas, trampling the cushions and tangling in the curtains.

"Good Lord," he said.

Summer danced a few steps. "Join us, George?"

"I'm . . . not much of a dancer."

"You will be. Gideon trips a merry mazurka these days, I can tell you."

Then she whisked him through a curtain and he was on a boat, a cruise liner, and he was wearing a white uniform and a peaked cap and she was twirling a parasol on the sun deck and staring out at the blue ocean. "You know, George, it's not all dancing. We can go anywhere, do anything."

The breeze was cool and fantastic on his sticky skin. He took the cap off and wiped his brow with an immaculate handkerchief. "So I see."

"We could work together," she said.

"We?"

"You and me."

"How?"

"Venn is wasting the mirror. He'll never get Leah

back. If it was yours, you'd use it more wisely."

She had plucked the thought from so deep in his mind, he only recognized it with a shock.

"Well. Maybe. But—"

"Think about it." Summer leaned on the white rail. "Mortals get old, George. They get all wrinkled and crabby. Their teeth fall out. Their brains go. They end up as parodies of themselves. You don't want that, do you?"

He tried to smile. "Summer, you're leaving out all the good things about—"

"Old age?" She looked up at him. "Nonsense. What sort of old age do you face? Some cold and lonely little flat in Shepton Mallet. Just you and the television." She smiled, and her lips were red and full. "But what if you could live for as long as you liked? If you felt a bit bored, or weary, just go back a few years. A decade maybe. Or even to the time you were twenty. Think of that, George, being young again, but with all the knowledge and wisdom you have now! Think of having your life over again, but so much better!"

He knew what she was doing. It wouldn't work on him.

But, just for a moment, a fatal moment, he allowed himself to think of it. University. Well, he'd pick a better one than that flea-pit he'd gone to. And the exams! Easy for him now. Man of the world, confident, instead of that bluff, cringe-making idiot he'd been in those days. Women . . . well, he wouldn't make those mistakes again. That girl in Devizes. He closed his eyes in dismay.

Summer watched, sidelong. She said softly, "You wouldn't be a teacher this time."

"No way! Nor the army. I've always wished I'd gone into pictures."

"Pictures?"

"Paintings. Art. Not as an artist—I can't draw for toffee. But as a dealer. Had my own gallery. Bought and sold. Big money in that, and I've always loved art."

She nodded. Then she walked off the deck onto the sea and said, "Something like this?"

He gaped. They were in a room with white walls, and on the walls hung glorious Monets, a Rembrandt, some pastels by Degas, a van Gogh.

"Oh yes! Oh good Lord, yes. Fantastic! But where . . . ?"

"We're in a private house in New York. A collector's house. Do you like them, George?"

He stared at the riot of color that was van Gogh's *Irises*. "They must be worth millions," he breathed.

She put her arm in his and for a long moment they admired the painting together. Then, without taking his eyes off it, he said, "Just as a matter of interest . . . no commitment of course, just vaguely curious . . . what exactly would I have to do?"

She tugged him forward and with a small gasp of delight he went with her, and they walked right into the painting, and stood among the brushstrokes, the blue and gold and yellow.

She said, "Sarah has my half coin. The Zeus coin. She has it hidden somewhere in Venn's house. Get it for me, George. Just get it for me. And the mirror and all the time in the world can be yours."

8

The black glasse erupts from the deep heart of the erthe. Molten and twisted, it is as if hell itself hath bled and this is what emergeth. It is erthe's wound.

When I found it I wept with delight.

Or was this all a dreme the Mirror made me dream?

From The Scrutiny of Secrets *by Mortimer Dee*

Moll's diary.

So then. Me and JHS went across to this posh hotel opposite the museum and he ordered lunch. He said, "My dear Moll, we must celebrate!" and made the waiter bring champain.

We tapped our glasses. JHS took a swig, gasped a bit, and said, "We have seen our precious bracelet, my dear, and have given the fools that own it no sign of what power it holds. The next question, is how we get hold of it."

He looked at me, and raised his eyebrows.

I'd already been thinking, you can be sure of that. I sipped the bubbly—it goes right up your nose, Jake—and I said, "Well, it's a museum. We can't just buy it. Let's not mess about. You and I know it has to be nicked."

He got all aeriated. "Moll! I'm not a thief!"

"Well, we could argue that one. But I am. And I know plenty more. Right?"

JHS squirmed. "I can't say I find it a very ethical situation."

"So you want to leave the bracelet there?"

He almost went electric. "Of course I don't! Good heavens. To get my hands on it I'd pay a small fortune. But robbing the Ashmolean is not really something I thought I would ever have to do."

"You don't have to." The waiter had brort the food and I was stuffing it down me as fast as I could. "You don't have to do anything, cully. Just put up the dosh."

"Dosh?"

"Lolly. Ackers. Money."

"Ah."

"I sort out the rest. I know plenty of people—"

"I'm sure you do." He held up a flabby white hand. Nervous. "But maybe it's best if I don't hear any of the details at all, Moll. One of us has to stay clean."

I saw it all then. If we was took, he wasn't in on it, he wouldn't know anything, would shake his head all sad about me, and say, "I dragged up the urchin from the streets and did what I could for her, but oh, officer, look how she has repaid me."

Fair enough.

That's the way the world rubs, Jake.

So I said, "A hundred should do it. In cash."

He nearly choked on his guinea fowl. "What?"

Heads turned. I muttered, "Keep it down, JH. Think about it. It ain't the Bank of England, but we still have to get in. Breaking a crib like that ain't easy. I'll need a cracksman, a carriage with fast horses, two, maybe three strong-arm men. They don't come cheap."

He chewed a bit, thoughtful. Then he wiped bread round the last gravy, swallowed it, and said, "Very well. But not a penny more, Moll."

So much for the small fortune.

"And I must demand"—now he came over all hoity-toity—"that you ensure your friends do no damage. The hallowed portals of such a temple of learning . . . its exhibits, priceless to science . . ."

"They won't have time."

"And nothing else is to be stolen. I insist."

The waiter came. "Would miss like dessert?" Miss would. Miss ordered the most expensive one. When he'd gone, I sat back and gave it to the old sod straight. "Can't be done, cully. If only the bracelet is gone the rozzers'll ask about who showed any interest in it, and they'll be knocking on your door before you can say Wormwood

Scrubbs. Best take a few more bits and pieces too—gold, mostly. Just to keep the law thinking these were just thicko thieves."

"Ah. Yes. I see. Well. If you think so."

Dear old JHS. The poor old bird doesn't have a clue. He sipped his coffee and sat back, gazing round the big room with its waiters and la-di-dah diners. "If only they knew, Moll! That we were planning a robbery right here, and as a result of it we will journey far into the future!" His bald head glistened, his eyes were wide and greedy. "We will achieve such things, Moll!"

"Course we will," I said, folding my napkin on the table. Got to confess, Jake, luv, I was thinking of you.

Finding you.

> ⤞⤝

Venn stepped back; Maskelyne grabbed the black pen from his hand and stared at it with something like horror. "Are you mad? You have no idea—"

The mirror gave a great crack.

For a moment they all thought it had broken; then it sparked and seemed to ripple. Gideon leaped away, Shee-swift, sure it would explode. Piers gave a moan of terror.

The black glass was gone. Instead, inside the silver frame they saw a sudden endless tunnel into utter darkness, and the tunnel was hung with lanterns, a small flame guttering in each.

"What's going on?" Venn stared, fascinated. "This is not how it usually works."

Maskelyne seemed frozen with dismay. "You asked him a question."

"What?"

"Janus! You asked him. Did you think he wouldn't answer? He's coming."

And now Gideon could hear them, the footsteps, softly approaching down the tunnel that led to the future, could hear them coming calmly and resolutely, and somewhere tiny in the distance a shadow began to flicker past the lanterns.

Venn snapped, "Piers. The glass weapon!"

The small man swore and raced for the safe.

"That will only kill Replicants." Maskelyne ran to the controls. "Don't you see, maybe this is really him. If he gets in here, he'll have an open channel to send anything through. His Time Wolves and his distorted creatures. His Adjusted Children."

"Like Sarah?"

Maskelyne spared him a haunted glance. "Worse. You have no idea."

"What do we do?"

"Stop him. We have to stop him."

The scarred man was stabbing at the controls. The

mirror darkened; a few of the lanterns flickered. But the passage stayed open. A strange, cold draft of air gusted from it. Gideon took a step closer, curious despite his disquiet. He could smell the future down that tunnel, and it was a metallic, toxic smell, the smell of a bitter and windy November day, somewhere without sunlight. There was an absence in it, a lack of life that made him shiver.

Piers had the glass weapon. Venn took it from him.

"I told you that won't stop him!" Maskelyne's voice was bleak.

"Then close the mirror."

"I can't."

"Rub the writing off!" Gideon ran forward and lifted his sleeve, but then, if Venn had not grabbed him, he would have plunged straight in; the glass was a vacancy and the written words hung in the air, demanding an answer. And the approaching figure was clear to them all now, a small man in a neat uniform, his graying hair tied back, his eyes hidden behind round blue spectacles.

"Don't come any closer." Venn lifted the gun.

Janus kept coming. "Don't you want to know the answer to your question, Venn? I've done nothing with Jake. I have no idea where he is. Such a risk for such a useless answer."

"Stay back."

Janus did not even pause. He paced steadily toward them, past lanterns that flickered in his draft. In the lab, all the alarms triggered; lights flashed urgently on the panel.

A ripple ran through the Abbey walls; one of the columns shifted. Dust cascaded from the roof.

Piers clutched his hands together. "Do something! Excellency!"

"Shut up!" Venn swung a savage glare on Maskelyne. "You! This thing responds to you! Close it down! *Now!*"

Maskelyne was still. Only his fingers danced on the controls. The scream of the alarms was deafening; Gideon wanted to cover his ears in agony. Instead he grabbed a knife from the desk and stood shoulder to shoulder with Venn. His heart was pounding. Strange joy was surging in him. This was something he had never known in the Summerland. He felt terrified, exhilarated. *He felt alive.*

Maskelyne abandoned the controls and moved to the mirror. Pushing Venn aside, he grasped the silver frame with both hands. His whole body shivered, as if some current had passed from it and through him. It seemed to re-energize him. He stood tall, his dark shape blocking the portal.

Janus said, "You won't stop me, scarred man. I told you once you would never stand in my way again."

Maskelyne ignored him. He spoke to the mirror.

"Close! You must close. Don't let him through."

Janus passed the last lantern. They could see that the passageway was made of gray stone, and the wind that blew from its depths was icy. Small fragments of snow drifted on it. He was almost at the threshold. Around them, the Abbey creaked and shivered.

Venn, without turning, said, "Piers. Get the baby out of the house."

"But—"

"*Do it!*"

Piers snatched up Lorenzo and fled.

"You too, changeling."

Gideon shook his head, stubborn. "Summer's more scary."

Venn snorted, kept the glass weapon steady.

Janus said, "Stand aside."

"No," Maskelyne said, tense.

"I think you should remember how you came by that scar, my friend. You overstepped your ability then. You are doing the same now."

They were face-to-face at the threshold of the mirror.

Venn said, "Get out of the way. Let me fire."

"*No.*" Maskelyne's voice was husky. He stayed, blocking the portal with his body.

Then he began to speak.

It was no language Gideon recognized, but at once he felt the sorcery and secrecy of it; it made his skin prickle, he shivered with its silvery power.

"What are you doing?" Venn demanded.

Maskelyne did not answer. Instead the words he chanted became harsh, sharp-edged. He spat them out as if they were shards of glass, as if speaking them cut his lips and throat.

Peculiar purple light flickered down the edges of the mirror. The lanterns behind Janus died. The alarms stopped dead.

Janus stared, then hurled himself at the mirror, but the words were faster; it seemed to Gideon that they leaped from the silver frame, crowded and crackled in the air, became slivers of lightning that sent jagged sparks about Maskelyne's thin fingers.

"No!" Janus's cry was a yell of rage; he slammed against the sudden black surface, crashed his fists on it in fury.

But it did not let him through.

Maskelyne collapsed. He staggered and crumpled at the knees; instantly Venn threw the weapon to Gideon and caught him, easing him down.

Gideon could not take his eyes from Janus. The small man's rage was a cold threat; he screamed and the mirror bulged, its convex surface swelling outward, ballooning impossibly into the room.

"Get back!" Venn dragged Maskelyne away, hastily,

but Gideon stood his ground, lifting the weapon. If the creature broke through, he would finish it. Here and now.

But with a snap that made his whole body jump, the mirror was flat and hard and solid.

On the far side, Janus took a deep breath, controlling his wrath. Finally, with an effort, he shrugged.

"So be it. There are other ways, Venn. Maybe the door in the moon will let me in."

Kneeling by Maskelyne, Venn looked up, his eyes fierce. "Once I have Leah back, I'll come through and destroy you myself, tyrant."

Janus nodded. "What if getting Leah back is what creates me, Venn? What if your weakness and your need is what starts the whole end of the world?" He laughed, a soft creak of scorn.

Then the glass was black and empty.

For a second Venn didn't move. He stayed there, gazing at the mirror as if the words had been a poison he knew he should never have drunk.

Then he swung around and felt Maskelyne's pulse.

"Is he dead?" Gideon lowered the weapon and stared, intensely curious. He had never seen a dead mortal.

"Unconscious. Move those boxes."

Gently, Venn picked up Maskelyne's limp body, carried him to the cleared workbench, and laid him down. "He's barely breathing. Get up there and find Piers . . . he won't have gone far."

"I'm not going outside."

"Just hurry!"

Gideon ran to the door. As he looked back, he caught Venn's reflection in the dark glass.

He was staring at the mirror as if it were his enemy. Or as if his own reflection were.

When she couldn't get the car through the undergrowth any farther, Rebecca stopped the engine and sat there, hearing the sudden summer silence of the Wood. She opened the car door, slipped across the sticky leather seat, and climbed out.

The warm night smelled of honeysuckle. She breathed it gratefully, then rolled a plastic bottle of water from under the dashboard and drank deep, her eyes watching the tree trunks, their dappled bark, the motes of moonlight and tiny insects, the flitting secret bats.

Wiping her mouth, she turned.

The gates to the drive of Wintercombe Abbey were wide open. Not only that, they couldn't be closed, because ivy and clematis had smothered them, and tiny saplings of birch had sprouted vigorously in clumps just inside. The stone lions were blindfolded with green leaves, Piers's cameras lost deep in a mass of bramble.

It scared her. She grabbed her bag, locked the car, and hurried on.

The drive was a thin path, barely there. It had always been overgrown, but now, she realized with a small shiver of fear, the Wood had rooted into it, devoured it. A million stems and bines and threadlike mycelia were encroaching above and below the soil. Small trees erupted through the leaf litter. She edged around them in astonishment. How could this have happened in a few days?

She didn't know why, but she began to run. Her breath came short; she had to duck under leaves that brushed her neck like fingers. Somewhere the croak of nightjars started up like wizened laughter.

Rebecca stopped.

Before her in the gloom was a crashing, threshing rhododendron, its huge red flowerets massed with moths and beetles. They rose in disturbed flocks; the bush shook, and a small, white, anxious face peered out at her.

She gasped in relief. "Piers? What on earth is going on?"

He was breathless; as he came out she saw he was holding the baby, awkwardly, in some trailing shawl. She glimpsed a few of the cats huddled around his feet.

"Oh it's you!" The little man stared around, distracted. "I thought . . . They'll find me if I stay here."

"What's happened? Where's Jake and—"

"It's Janus! He's coming through!"

She didn't wait for more. She was already past him and running toward the Abbey, and he was scrambling after her, Lorenzo giving a tiny wail of hunger, Piers trying desperately to muffle the sound.

Fear like heat erupted inside her, a molten terror. If the mirror was involved, Maskelyne would be there.

He would do anything to save it.

And he knew Janus.

Sprawled roots tripped her, dark shadow confused her. She stumbled, picked herself up, realized she wasn't even sure where the Abbey was, until Piers hissed, "Left," and she ducked under a low branch and fell out into dazzling moonlight, the façade of the building a silver slant of stone. Dropping the bag, she raced up the steps and slammed into Gideon at the door.

"Where is he? Where's Maskelyne?"

His face was pale as ivory. "Inside. Rebecca—"

"He's dead. *Oh my God I know he's dead!*"

Gideon took her hand with spidery white fingers. His eyes were green, a little disappointed. "No," he said. "He's not dead. Not quite."

9

Revolution erupts from the despair of the poor
and the heedless extravagance of the rich.
Often the same men are responsible for both.

A History of the Late Revolution in France,
by Maxim Chevelin

SARAH STOOD IN the kitchens with flour up to her
elbows. As she kneaded the dough, she sneaked a rapid
gaze around.

There must be over fifty servants, hurrying in and
out, snatching up dishes, yelling in French. The tall-
est chef, a man in a white coat, tasted and basted and
broke into rages so incandescent she thought he would
explode. An entourage of minor cooks fled at his command like mice from a cat.

"Keep your head down, girl!" Madame Lepage
whisked behind her, half hidden behind a pile of linen
tablecloths.

The old woman was small and wizened and smelled
of onions. Her skin was olive and her eyes dark beads
of greed; she bore no resemblance to Sarah. So the aunt
story was stupid.

But no one here had time to care.

This kitchen, and the one behind it, and the dairy and scullery and ice room and larders were a tumult of cooking, baking, roasting, toasting, of crashes of dishes, slamming of plates, the roaring of the fires, the crackle of fat dripping from skewered hogs on the great turn spits.

She had never known such rich, mouth-watering, savory smells.

Crushing lumps of flour in her fingers, she remembered the gray world of the labyrinth, its carefully processed food, accurate in vitamins and minerals, blandly tasteless.

All afternoon she had nibbled and savored and eaten fragments of hot pastry, stewed apple, pork crackling, soft melted onion, crunchy salads, creamy lemon syllabub.

Her hair was coming undone and there was a floury smudge on her forehead. She was as hot as it was possible to be without fainting.

But she was actually enjoying it.

"All right. Wash your hands and come with me."

The small Frenchwoman was back, with another pile of linen. When Sarah was clean she said, "Your cap. We go upstairs now. Silence. No speech. No English."

"Yes, but—"

The linen was dumped in her hands. "Do as I say.

Follow, look, and watch. I show you the salons of the ball. Keep your eyes to the floor. Like a servant girl, not a robber thief."

Sarah wondered how much they were paying her. As she followed the woman between the tables, she whispered, "How do you know Long Tom?"

"Many years, in London. I was on the boards. I was the French Nightingale. I sang in all the gentlemen's clubs, the coffee houses. Tom and I, we are old friends in crime."

They slipped out of the warmth and into a drafty corridor. Sarah said, "So . . . who's the boss? Tom?"

"Of course not. The contessa, always."

Sarah felt a tingle of excitement. "Contessa?"

"So bold, so clever. A queen of thieves, that one. Beautiful, a child, but she laughs like a man. They say her heart was once broken, but I believe she loves only danger." Madame turned the corner and stopped. "Attend. No English now."

She led the way up a circling stair and suddenly they were in corridors of startling size, all hung with swags of white satin, decorated with huge chaplets of greenery. Servants stood busy on steps and ladders, and as she hurried underneath, her head demurely down, Sarah marveled again at how the scents of the past were so much more vivid than her own time. The lavender crushed under her feet was eye-watering in its pungency, the roses and honeysuckle and all the plants she didn't know exhaling glorious scents.

They came to a vast dining room, tinkling with glass chandeliers.

"This is where the guests eat their buffet. Come through."

She followed between the long tables. There would be hundreds of guests. Presumably at some stage there would be entertainment; the automata must be part of that—that was how Long Tom would get in. But what did this have to do with Jake? Unless . . .

A thought struck her so swiftly her eyes blinked. *Jake had* journeyed *before.* Not in this time, no. But he'd met people who had the mirror! Symmes, for one. And for another—

She whispered, "Madame! One more question please. Does the contessa have another name?"

The woman threw her a glance of disapproval. "Once, maybe. But we people of Mercury, we change our names like clothes."

"But once she did. Beyond the mirror."

"Ah. Well. Yes. She was known as Moll."

Sarah took a deep breath, understanding like lightning, but before she could even think about it, Madame Lepage opened the double doors and they were in the ballroom, an expanse of polished wood floor, among a dazzle of crystal chandeliers and sunlight, and the grand enfilade of rooms, lemon and blue and gold, lay in a straight line before her.

"*Et voilà!*" Madam Lepage said, pointing. "The door in the moon."

→·←

Jake sipped the wine, to ease the shock.

"Not sweet enough, Jake? There's plenty of other—"

"For God's sake Moll." He put the glass down with a rattle. "Tell me about my father."

He leaped up and paced about. The room was dim and quiet. It was hard to believe the river lapped at the feet of the ancient building, that Paris roared with riot around them. "Is he here? Is Alicia with him?"

"Alicia." She scowled. "Symmes's dotty daughter? No, she's not."

He came back and stood over her. "Tell me! In the old days, Moll, you wouldn't have wanted me to be unhappy. You would have told me straightaway."

"We were good mates then, Jake."

"We still are." He stepped forward, hands gripped. "But I've got to know, Moll. Got to see him. Or I won't raise a finger in your crazy heist."

She dropped her cutlery and stood, the rich maroon velvet of her dress gleaming. "Okay. We don't have much time. Tonight is midsummer. The ball starts at eight p.m.—four hours, Jake. If I show you where he is, you'll get the whole thing. Come on."

Abruptly she turned and opened a small door in the paneling. Beyond was a stair; she ran up it quickly and he followed, heart thudding with anticipation. If he could get his father back he'd steal anything from anyone. In fact, he'd often thought of being a master criminal. Wharton wouldn't like it, of course. But he need never know.

"Here we are, Jake. The inner sanctum." She flung the door open and went in. He saw an empty room, containing only a chaise longue, with a ragged cloak on it, and opposite a dark rectangle of glass, reassembled in its silver frame.

The mirror.

He stood staring into it. "You took this from Symmes's house."

"After I heard about the explosion. Silly old fool had thrown himself in." She sounded peeved. "I would have shared the bracelet with him, eventually. He should have known that. I wonder where he went."

"He went to the future. Janus found him."

Her eyes widened. "The future! Hell's teeth, he must've loved that! How far?"

"Right to the end." Jake turned. "Right to the end of time, Moll. But by about 1910 the mirror is back in Alicia's house, so . . ."

"So that means I'll replace it. In my future." She

laughed. "Lord, Jake, all this living backward. It makes you giddy, don't it."

"Moll. My father . . ."

She sighed, picked up the ragged cloak and a red cap, made a small adjustment to the silver bracelet on her wrist. Then, with a speed so sudden he gasped, she grasped his hand and pulled him into the mirror.

>·<

Rebecca stepped back from the sofa.

Maskelyne lay still and unmoving, his breathing a faint lifting of his chest. His head was flung back, his hair dark on the pillow.

"We should get him to bed," Venn said.

"No." She was firm. "We don't move him. He stays near the mirror."

"A doctor, then."

"What's the use? He's stable. He just won't wake up. It's not illness, it's sorcery."

It was as if his soul had gone, she thought. Crashed so far down inside him, even she couldn't make him know she was here. What had he done? Had she lost him for good now, this dark man with his strange secrets?

Venn prowled the lab. Maybe he felt guilty, because he said, "I'm sorry this happened. We need him . . ."

"Then do something! He stopped Janus for you—he can't do any more. It's up to you to find Jake and

Sarah." She glared around at them, at Gideon moodily tangling the malachite fibers, at Piers sitting staring at his boots.

The small man looked up, flicked a glance at Venn. "She's right, Excellency."

Venn turned, quickly. "Piers, play me back what happened when Maskelyne spoke to David, the last time, in Florence. He said something to him . . . Something about the amber stone."

Rebecca expected the little man to hunt out a recording but instead Piers put both hands together, stared straight ahead, thought for a second, and then opened his mouth. The voice that came out was not his own, but Maskelyne's; not a copy, but a recording so accurate it made her shiver.

"First, listen to me now. We found Dee's manuscript. What it says is important. He says Time is defeated only by love. *You must remember that! And the snake's eye on the bracelet. It opens. Use what you find inside."*

Venn nodded. He slipped off the bracelet and stared at it. Without looking at Rebecca, he said, "Did you know he'd had dealings with Janus?"

"Yes."

"And you didn't tell us."

"I trust him. And I don't know what went on. I don't know anything." She stared down at the sleeping man, while Piers brought a blanket and tucked it around him. "I just think that he comes from somewhere so far back in the past it's almost legendary. He's traveled all over time. And when he threw himself into the mirror without the bracelet, it was a terrible journey. It broke him to bits. His mind, his memories. He's all shards and slivers."

Venn came and stood beside her. "You should look for a human lover, Rebecca. He'll never make you happy."

She looked at him, straight. "You're hardly the one to give me that advice."

His laugh was dark and bitter. He lifted the bracelet, laid it on the bench. "Piers. Take a look."

The little man was there in a second. Lovingly he fingered the exquisite silver band, the snake's head and tongue. Then he touched the amber stone of the eye.

"Oh yes. Definitely. All sorts of odd currents. Not sure if . . . no. Well, maybe this . . ."

It opened.

Silently, on a minute silver hinge, the amber stone opened like a tiny door, and at the same time there was the softest chime of sound, so melodious that Gideon shivered, remembering the songs of the Shee.

He stepped closer, peered over Piers's shoulder.

The mirror rippled.

Maskelyne, deep in his coma, murmured a word and then lay still.

Venn said, "What is that?"

Inside the tiny cavity under the stone was a spiral fossil, an ammonite, marked with tiny numbers. They seemed to spiral inward, growing smaller and smaller, into the heart of the coiled creature, so impossibly infinitesimal that even when Piers prised it out and put it under the microscope and they took it in turns to stare in, there was no end to the sequence. Gideon looked up, dazzled. "It goes on forever . . ."

"Maybe it does. Maybe we're looking at infinity right there." Venn walked back to the mirror and stared at his warped reflection. "I saw it once before, in a bottomless crevasse on Katra Simba. White and deadly and never, never, ever coming to an end." He turned. "Can we use this?"

"Ooh, I think so." Piers was agitated with excitement. "Because you may not have noticed this, Excellency, but . . ." He ran over and dragged a stool to the mirror, stood on it, and examined the top of the frame. "*Yes!* Right here . . . do you see? There's a small cavity. I've spotted it before, but it's quite empty and I never had a clue what it was for. Maybe that little spiral galaxy would fit in . . ."

"Be careful!" Gideon muttered. Fear had made him nervous; it was that word *infinity* that had triggered it, his buried terror of being with the Shee forever and ever, coming back now like a pain in his bones and teeth. He hugged himself tight. He would not give in to it.

"He's right." Rebecca watched, uneasy. "It might do anything."

"Piers?"

"I think it will tell us things." Piers sounded almost greedy. "We've never been able to configure the Chronoptika accurately. As if there was always some component missing, something we hadn't done right . . . but now. We can be exact. Know where Jake is. Snatch Leah with seconds to spare . . . Please let me try, Excellency. Please!"

Venn hesitated. He said, "Why didn't Maskelyne suggest it? It may be dangerous."

"Maybe there's a price to pay for accuracy," Rebecca murmured.

"Or it could just blow the whole house up."

"Venn." It was Gideon's voice, so amused they all turned to him, surprised. "Venn, the house is being eaten. Devoured by the Wood. The doors and windows won't close, ivy is tangling inside, there are saplings sprouting in the outhouses, splintering the cloisters . . . If you don't do something, *there will be no Abbey*. No Dwelling. Just some ruin lost in the Wood, a place of legends, a place sliding into the Summerland. And Summer will rule here."

For a moment Venn looked at him. Then at Rebecca, who nodded.

Then he said, "All right. Do it."

Piers gave a squeak of delight. He took some tweezers and very gently lifted the ancient coil from the plate of the microscope, carrying it across the room as if it was a jewel of great price. At the door two of the Replicant cats watched, like sentinels.

He climbed on the stool, took a deep breath, and placed the ammonite in the space on the silver frame, delicate as a leaf.

It fitted exactly.

And the mirror spoke. It said, "Where are we?"

→·←

"Where are we?"

"Paris. Same date. Place de la Bloody Révolution, Jake."

She held his hand in hers and they stood together in the crowd of screaming, howling people. He had no idea how many were here but it must have been thousands, and as Moll dragged him through the crowd, it wasn't the dreadful smell that horrified him, the spattered mud and dung under his feet, even the hatred and mockery in the savage voices.

It was another sound.

A sudden, sliding *slice* of sound from somewhere up at the heart of the crowd, repeated with dreadful regularity, and each time followed by a raw, bloodthirsty scream that stopped his heart.

"Moll . . ."

"Quiet, cully."

"Moll, is that . . ."

She looked up at him, her eyes dark and fierce under the rakish red cap.

"Sorry to bring you here, Jake, but you had to know. That up there's what they call the guillotine. A machine for killing people. That's what's facing your dad, soon, maybe tomorrow, if we don't snatch him. You and me, Jake. Like in the old days."

He stared at her, too appalled to answer. And behind her, over the baying, clambering crowd, over their raised fists and tossed caps, he saw the blade being jerkily winched to the top of its wooden frame.

Blood dripped from its edge.

❧⟶⟵

The mirror darkened.

Venn looked at Piers, then Rebecca. "Paris. The Terror, 1792," she breathed.

10

Down hollow ways he followed her
Down ferny banks they came.
They rode as swift as summer storms,
the forest's fearsome flame.

They rode as swift as sorrow,
As fast as birds will fly.
Until he saw the door of death
Rise up against the sky.

Ballad of Lord Winter and Lady Summer

THEY WERE TREATING him well.

Very well, even.

He had to admit that.

But he was bored out of his mind.

Wharton tapped his fingers together. He needed to act. He needed to get the temptations Summer had put in his head, out. Because of course there was no way he was going to help her get the coin from Sarah, even though a small part of him was shocked and disappointed. Why hadn't Sarah told him she had the coin? Where was it hidden? And what if she managed to find the other half?

He couldn't let that happen.

He shook his head. Then he said, "You! Moth-creature."

The small Shee slid from nowhere and stood looking at him around an oak bole. "Mortal?"

"I want something."

"Anything."

"Anything at all?"

"That's our orders."

"Right. Come with me."

He stood up and marched out of the clearing along the path. It took a while to find the gnarled tree, the Shee flitting anxiously behind him, and in the end he had to call out, "Monk . . . er, Brother. Where are you?" before the quiet voice said, "Here."

The tree looked as contorted and velvety brown as before. Wharton stood before it. "How are you feeling?"

"Just the same. After all, you were here only a few moments ago. I should be getting back, because of Compline. I am so often late."

Wharton scowled. He turned to the Shee. "Right. If I can have anything, I want him turned back into his own body and sent home."

The creature raised a beautiful eyebrow. "Why?"

"Why? What do you mean, why! Because keeping him here is cruel and heartless, that's why!"

"He's quite happy. He doesn't even feel time passing."

Wharton planted his feet, stubborn. "I want him free."

"It's a mistake."

"Well, I don't think so."

The argument was attracting interest. He became aware of them rather than saw them at first, the side of a face peering out, a silvery hand, and then there they all were, lounging and leaning among the trees, a crowd of languid and vaguely interested beings, their clothes a patchwork of velvets and lace, of denim and leather, all the greens and grays of the summer woodland.

"Can you do it?"

"Yes. But Summer won't—"

"Did she or did she not say explicitly that I was to have anything I wanted. *Anything?*"

"Yes."

"Then I want him free."

The moth-Shee shrugged and consulted with a few others. One was very tall with hair like thistledown. Another wore a coat the color of cobwebs, and a pair of buckled biker boots. Their eyes were green and unreadable. They murmured together, soft as flies.

Under his breath Wharton said, "Don't you worry, Brother. I'll get you out of this."

"Thank you, my son. I'm getting a little stiff, standing so still."

Did he even know what they'd done to him? Wharton had no idea.

He watched the group of Shee divide. The thistledown one said, "We'll do it, but if she blames anyone it will have to be you."

"Agreed."

Summer scared him stiff, but he wasn't about to show them that.

They looked at one another. One giggled. "Fine," they said.

The moth one came forward and touched the tree lightly with a delicate finger. Three times it paced around the mossy trunk. Then it stood back.

"Is that what you want?"

Wharton saw the tree become a thin man in a worn brown robe. He almost swore with astonishment, because there was no transformation, no slow morphing like in the films. As if the tree had always been just a thin man in a brown robe, if you looked at it properly.

"Wow," he said. "Great. Yes. Thank you."

The monk stretched his fingers and then surprisingly, yawned. "Bless you, my son. I can go home now?"

"Well, I would. Fast. But—"

"I can't thank you enough. I must hurry, or I'll be late."

He bowed, his tonsure a bald patch in a thatch of

straw-colored hair; then before Wharton could speak he was gone, hurrying along the path.

The Shee took to instant flight, some as birds, some beetles.

"Where are they going?"

"To watch," the moth creature giggled. "Me too. It's always such fun."

A sudden, terrible dread entered Wharton's soul. He yelled, "Hey you! Brother! WAIT."

The monk was already out of sight. Wharton swore, and raced after him. He was sweating in the heat; the path twisted, he had to leap over tree roots. "Wait! You need to stop."

"I'm so sorry, but I'm already late." The voice drifted back.

"Hell," Wharton gasped. He turned a kink in the path and saw the edge of the Summerland.

He knew it was the edge because the sunlight ended in a straight line; beyond that the Wood continued, but to his astonishment it was still night out there, a mothy warm twilight. And before him, as if the Shee had deliberately twisted the path, was the wall at the edge of the estate, its stones crumbling and falling into the lane beyond.

The monk was climbing awkwardly over.

"That's not the way," Wharton yelled.

"No, but I'm a bit lost . . . It's a shortcut to the Abbey." As he spoke, he slid down the earth bank. Wharton came scrambling up, the Shee flitting and darting behind him. He yelled, *"Stop!"* with all his strength. But it was too late.

The monk's sandal touched the tarmac of the lane.

For a moment he was still there.

Then he was older, old, ancient, a skeleton.

Then he was nothing but a pile of dust on the roadway.

The moth-shee put its head on one side. "Oops," it said, gleeful.

Behind it another giggled.

Wharton stood frozen in horror. Then, just as he moved to get down there, one of the things caught his elbow with cool fingers. "I wouldn't, mortal." Sly green eyes watched him sidelong. "After all, you don't know how many centuries might have passed for you, either."

He shook the creature off. But he dared not climb down into the lane.

And into his heart came a whole new level of terror.

→>·<←

"I saw them take him to prison. I was doing a reccy for the heist." Moll crouched by the empty fireplace, her knees up under the dark skirt. The mirror leaned in the corner of the room, as if it eavesdropped. Jake was too shattered to care. Since they had come back through it, the ominous slice of the guillotine had been rising and falling like a heartbeat in his chest. Now he stood at the window, looking out at the dark flowing river, the wharves where fires had been lit.

Moll settled comfortably. "This is what happened. We've been in Paris a few weeks, setting up this crib, working out details. A job like this one takes a lot of planning, cully, you wouldn't believe . . . Anyhow, that morning I was tailing the mark—like I said his name is the Vicomte de Sauvigne." She said the name with great care. "Codename—SNOB. He's the one with the emeralds. Typical tyrant. Bleeds the poor dry—be a pleasure to rob. So I'm hitched up like, stealing a ride on the back of his carriage. And it stops at this fortress. These prisoners are going in. About ten, men and women, all aristos and scared stiff. They walk past me. The last one is a skinny, anxious-looking man with brown hair, in russet court dress, feathered hat, gold ring, the works. Looked kosher, but Lord, I knew, Jake, straight away. There's something about a *journeyman*. As if he don't quite fit in the world. Symmes described your dad to me often. And he looks just like you. The clincher was, I saw it. On the lace under his sleeve. I saw the bracelet, Jake."

Jake looked up, eyes sharp. "He still has it?"

"Did then. My eyes nearly popped, I can tell you. So I tried a trick. I shouted *David!* as loud as I could. He jumped like something had stung him. Stared round. Then he yells, *'Who is that? Is that you, Jake? Venn?'* Course I couldn't answer. But when they'd dragged him inside I jumped off and asked around. Seems this English doctor made a nuisance of himself. Wouldn't stop demanding justice and the like. Someone high up got fed up, and he's for the chop at dawn tomorrow."

He stared at her. "They can't just do that! Surely there must have been a trial."

"This time, this place? They've gone mad. Crazy like animals. Killing all the nobs, they are. Trial or no." She snuggled over to him. "But don't fret, cully. It's all sorted. I was only going after the gems at first, but we can do both, Jake. We can spring your dad too, I promise. Easy as kiss-me-hand."

He wondered then, for a bewildered moment, if any of this was true, or whether she just wanted him mixed up in her crazy adventures, and David was an excuse. He felt angry and confused, but one thing was sure. If he found his father, they would never be separated again. He would get him home. He would.

He said, wearily, "How, Moll?"

She scrambled up, ran to the table, and came back with a scroll of filmy paper, which she spread out on the dusty floorboards, weighing down the corners with apples. He came over and crouched down, staring at it.

"Okay," she said. "Look. This is a plan of the Château-

Snob's place. A big house, out in the Marais, just outside the city. These are the three salons, one leading into another. And this is the ballroom here, the dining room here, the kitchens there, the formal gardens. Upstairs, along this corridor, milord's *boudoir*."

He grinned at the way she said that, so she nudged him back, serious. "The Midsummer Ball is held every year, but a lot of people thought this year it would be crazy to have it, with all the hoo-ha kicking off in Paris. But this Sauvigne—he thinks he's safe. So there's dancing and fireworks and puppets and all sorts of games and sideshows. Long Tom—he's the cracksman—gets by bringing the automata into the house. You and I are inside already."

"Are we? How?"

She shrugged. "As guests, Jake! Crowd of hundreds, all masked? Nothing easier. The problem is, getting up to the private rooms. There are only two points of access—a secret door direct from the ballroom, and the main stair, which will be too heavily guarded. A few of the servants are onside, the housekeeper and her niece—we're paying them serious dosh to have the keys ready. We get to the boud—the bedroom, open the safe—"

"What if we can't?"

"Tom will. He's the best and it'll be a patsy."

"And my father . . ."

"Coming to that. At exactly midnight the fireworks go off. Lots of noise. Everyone staring at the sky. At the same time, a very important message arrives for Snob—top secret, read-it-all-by-himself jobbie. He dismisses the servants. Then the mob hit. Panic. We snatch him, stuff him in his own carriage, drive to the fortress. All under the summer moon. Use him to get us in and snaffle your dad out from under their noses. Can't go wrong."

He stared at the map with such despair that when a creaky little laugh escaped her, he was shocked.

He whispered, "Will it really work, Moll?"

Moll put her hand on his arm, and said pityingly, "Jake luv, I'm not that little kid anymore. I'm the contessa now, an adventuress across time and space. My gang, my people. My obsidian mirror. I know what I'm doing."

"I hope so." He closed his eyes. "Because I couldn't lose him again, Moll. I think I'd rather be trapped here forever than that."

She tapped his arm consolingly. "Time to get some shut-eye. We want you all fresh and arrogant and stroppy for tonight. And then Jake, all you have to do is watch the experts. Watch. And. Learn."

➤·←

By seven o'clock, Sarah was too tired to stand up; she had chopped and cleaned and mopped and sliced until her fingers were sore and her back bent. She found Madame Lepage and whispered, "I need to sleep, or I'll be no good to you tonight."

Madame nodded. She fished a small key from her reticule. "My room is the last in the attic corridor. Lock the door behind you. I'll come and find you at exactly nine."

The château was vast, and sumptuous. Sarah walked down the corridor, jostled and passed by footmen and valets, butlers and chambermaids, all carrying plates and dishes, the air a babble of French. She kept her eyes down and walked fast, once bumping into a maid carrying a box of oranges so that they all fell on the floor and she had to hastily help gather them up, nodding and raising her hand against the stream of foreign curses.

Breathless, she reached one of the tall windows, slipped behind the curtain, and sat on the white sill, breathing the summer twilight with relief, because the kitchens had been unbearably steamy.

She thought about what she should do.

Wait until the ball. Jake and Moll would come, but why would Jake get himself into something like this. Precious stones meant nothing to him. Unless . . . his father was involved.

She was sure, suddenly, that was what it was.

The window was wide; a soft breeze drifted in heavy with scents of rose and gardenia. As she sat there, she closed her eyes, and then felt the tiniest touch on her fingers.

A butterfly was perched there, its wings all metallic green and blue. For a moment she smiled, thinking it beautiful. There were no butterflies left in the end days.

Then she snatched her hand back and scrambled up, staring down at the green lawns.

The vicomte was walking there. An entourage of courtiers and dogs and ladies followed, but he was talking only with one man.

A small, neat man, his uniform a Hussar's green, with black fastenings and boots, a short sword at his side.

As his face turned toward Sarah, she breathed, "No! No." But there he was—the familiar small tidy beard, the blue round spectacles. She shrank back in astonished fear. *Janus? Here?*

She made herself take a second look.

It was him. The knowledge felt like a blow.

She watched the vicomte bow and move away with his group until Janus stood alone on the graveled path. At once, two of the Time Wolves came out of nowhere and paced at his heels, not icy now, but russet and flame red as if they were made of fire, their eyes black as coals, their shadows long in the twilight.

She could not have dreamed of a more terrible guest.

For a moment the very thought of it paralyzed her;

then she jumped up and ran down the corridor, searching desperately for a door to the gardens, not even caring if she met anyone, slipping past vases and statues like a ghost. Her heart thudded. There was something going on here that Jake knew nothing of, a trap for him, maybe for Venn too.

Finding an open door, she fled through it, jumped down the steps, and raced around the corner of the house.

The path was empty.

With a hiss of fury she ran down the gravel. In the heart of the formal garden, a fountain played, its spray drifting over her face like rainbow glints of warm rain.

Flickers of light dazzled her. And before she could stop she had burst through a gap in the hedge and there he was, the tyrant from the world's end, sitting calm and alone on a wooden bench. He looked up, saw her, and stood.

With the quickest of snaps, he clicked his fingers.

On each side, the wolves rose out of the grass.

"Oh my dear Sarah," he said, and she saw with surprise that he had expected to find her. "Do we meet again? At last?"

The King doth keep his revels here tonight.
Take heed the Queen come not
within his sight.

11

The Abbot stood stout and bold before the
faery creatures. "Wilt thou release my brother?" he
demanded. The Queen of the Wood had eyes like
shadows. Her laugh was as a ripple of rain.

"Not before Domesday," she said. "For where
he is, that day is already come."

Chronicle of Wintercombe

VENN STRUGGLED INTO the dark suit. It was black satin, and Rebecca thought it looked fabulous on him. Under it he wore a white shirt, the lacy sleeves covering the bracelet.

"Sword," he snapped.

Piers buckled it on him. "Toledo steel. Sharp as a razor."

"Boots?"

"Period leather. Take this too."

A small pistol. Venn shoved it into his belt. "Are you sure about the dates?"

"Absolutely." Rebecca looked up from the computer screen. "Paris was in a ferment. The Revolution was supposed to liberate the people, but it quickly degenerated into factions—anyone could be denounced to the Council and hundreds were guillotined."

"David among them?"

She shrugged. "There's no way of telling. His name is on no list that I've been able to find, but he could have given a false name, or just not been recorded. But this château—it was definitely attacked during the night. Midnight. You have to be in and out by then."

"Understood."

Piers stood back. "You're ready, Excellency."

Venn wore the flamboyant clothes with his usual easy flair. He looked as though he had been born to wear them, tall and elegant, his blond hair tied back in a black queue.

"How's your French?" Rebecca asked, amused.

"Adequate." He turned. "Now, Piers. The change-ling too."

Gideon stood pale and anxious by the bench. "This is impossible. How can I go? If I even leave the Es-tate—"

"We're going back before you were born, presumably. Anyway, technically you won't be leaving the Estate."

"You have no idea what's going to happen! I might just shiver into dust and you don't even care."

Venn made two urgent steps toward him. "Listen, Gideon. I can't do this alone. Do you want to stay cooped up here forever, afraid of Summer? I thought you said even death was better than that."

"I did."

"Then now's your chance to find out." Venn glanced at Piers. "Sort him."

"Oh, he's easy." Piers came and stood before Gideon. The boy was tall and thin. "All that Shee-stuff he's wearing can look like anything."

Piers put his hand out and touched the lapel of Gideon's patchwork coat. A shriek made them all jump; Horatio had swung in and was hanging tail-down from the dusky vaults, watching.

Gideon's clothes shivered into a dark green silk suit, knee breeches, boots, a waistcoat, a white shirt, a sword. He grinned, because being with the Shee had taught him to delight in textures, and the eerie shimmer of the watered silk was like sunlight on a stream. The clothes felt heavy and real; they swished and flowed.

He felt more human in them.

But Piers was grimacing, snatching his hand away as if stung. "What have you got there?"

"What?" Venn said, alert.

"Something on him. Magic."

Gideon stepped back. "No, there's nothing—"

But Piers was too quick, his small hand darted into the pocket of the coat, and fast as a pickpocket he had the small flower in his fingers; he held it up and they all looked at it.

It had not faded or crumbled or even creased.

Horatio screeched again. He fled to Rebecca and hid in her lap. She said, "It's a flower."

"No." Venn was staring at it with a strange attention. "No, it's not. Not at all."

He came and took it from Piers's fingers, and it lay in his palm, a little purple bloom, with four petals, fragile and yet eerily alive.

Venn smiled. It was a cruel smile. It made Rebecca uneasy. He said, "This is a very powerful piece of kit. It's steeped in magic; I can feel it radiating out. More powerful than anything even the Shee have." He looked up. "Where did you get this?"

Gideon flashed a look at Maskelyne, but the scarred man lay safely deep in coma, unmoving. So he shrugged. "I found it in one of the books in the library. Slipped inside the pages."

"No way!" Piers said, adamant. "I would have known."

"Maybe you don't know everything in this house, little man."

"Maybe I know more than some lost boy on the run from the Shee."

Gideon took a step forward, his hand on his sword, but Venn said, "Shut up, the pair of you. We have it and we'll use it. Or rather . . ." He turned, and handed the flower to Piers. "*You* will use it."

"Me!"

"Gideon and I are going after Jake. Rebecca has to stay and guard the house. You're all that's left."

Piers's face was as white as his coat. "But *I* should guard the house!"

"She can't go into the Summerland."

"I can't go into the Summerland!"

Ignoring his panic, Venn checked the bracelet. "You can, and you will. You take the flower, you go into the Wood. You find Wharton. Give it to him. If it's what I think it is, she'll give him anything he wants if he owns it. Then just get him back here."

Piers was roaming the room, wringing his hands in anguish. "King of Shadows, listen! There is absolutely *no way* I can do this . . . Those creatures of hers, they terrify me. They'll eat me up and spit me out. It'll take me centuries to piece myself back together. Or they'll spin me in a whirlwind down under the sea, then they'll—"

"Don't let them find you. Be fast, be silent. But you're going, Piers. That's an order."

Piers groaned.

Rebecca felt sorry for him, but then the worry of having to hold the house alone against the Shee swept over her. Not to mention the marmoset, the baby, seven cats, a sleeping man, and the mirror.

If only Maskelyne would wake!

But what if he got worse?

What if he died?

"Do you hear?" Venn said, iron hard.

Piers blew out his cheeks, looked around helplessly, and nodded. "I'll be there and back in forty minutes," he said in the smallest of voices.

"Good. Now get us on our way."

Venn beckoned to Gideon. He came and the two of them stood side by side before the obsidian glass. In its frame the amber stone shone with a strange gleam; as Piers came to the controls Gideon felt that the power of the mirror was enhanced, that there was a new focus in its silence, a new awareness in its slanting lean.

Piers adjusted the controls. He said, "Ready?"

"Ready."

"Then—"

But before Piers could finish, the mirror opened. The vacuum of its blackness came out to enfold them. Gideon gasped as he felt a terrible cold, a darkness that seemed to fill his eyes and mouth and throat, that swallowed him whole, that he knew in an instant must be death.

He cried out with the terror and delight of it.

When the mirror was silent and empty, Rebecca stared at Piers. "That was different."

"Yes. Indeed."

The roar of the vortex had been stronger. Even held tight in its fixtures, the mirror had jerked; one of the bolts that had held it was sheared, another half torn out of the wall. The malachite webbing was shredded to pieces.

"The stone has made a difference, not just in accuracy, but in power." Piers shoved the flower in his pocket, swiveled on his heels, and turned and faced the door. "But there's nothing more we can do for them now. So. Right. Let's do this. Come on."

She gave one glance at Maskelyne's still-unconscious form and followed him. They hurried along the dim corridor of the Monk's Walk, along the gallery, and down the main stairs.

Wintercombe Abbey was a house invaded.

Every window was open, every door wide. White moths fluttered, ivy crawled everywhere. The very walls seemed to be splitting at the seams, cracked by saplings and sprouting seeds, and as Rebecca looked out from the main door, she took a breath, because the night was sweet and close with the heavy scent of roses, and the Wood crowded like a sinister shadow under the silver disc of the moon.

Piers straightened his back and raised his chin. *"It is a far, far better thing I do,"* he muttered sarcastically, *"than I have ever done."*

"Don't be scared. Just find Wharton."

"You have no idea. It's a big place, the Summerland. Goes on forever and ever."

She patted his back. "Yes, but you're Piers! You're too quick and tricksy even for the Shee."

"Am I?"

"I've always thought so. What would Venn do without you?"

"That's true," he said, doubtful.

"And brave, Piers."

"Not—"

"Brave."

"Really?"

"Really. Just think, what we'll all think of you if you get Wharton out of there. If you outwit Summer. What a hero you'll be."

He puffed up like a robin in the cold. "You're right, Becky. Quite right. I can do it. No trouble. You take care of the mirror and Maskelyne. I'll be there and back in a flash."

And then he was gone and she saw only a small brown insignificant bird, drab in its summer plumage. A flick of brief wings and it had flown. A leaf shivered. A beetle buzzed in the moonlight.

Rebecca stood there alone, in the peace of the summer night.

But gradually, with a crawling of her skin, she realized that every leaf held green eyes and the eyes were watching her. Every moth glittered with strange metallic colors. Every bat flitting over the Abbey roof swooped too close and was too dark, too interested.

She stepped back inside quickly and tried to force the door shut.

But it wouldn't close, and from far in the house the baby cried, as if woken by spiteful fingers.

→·←

Sarah felt like screaming. It welled up inside her, a sob of rage and terror and she had to choke it down and clench her fists and say, "Janus. What are you doing here?"

He smiled. The two wolves padded toward her, slinking through the rosebushes.

"What makes you think I *am* here?"

She already knew it was a Replicant. It was older than the others she had seen of him, nearer the age he really was, there in that far future time when the world was dying and the black hole of the mirror was roaring with imminent explosion.

She shook her head. "How could you know . . ."

"If a man sits at the end of the world, Sarah, with all the records of past times under his hands, what doesn't he know? Of course I realized you would be here."

Her heart pulsed. She said, "Are you going to try and take me back with you?"

"Not try. I *will* take you back." He shook his head, a little sad. "I have all the others, you know, Max and Cara and all your rebellious foolish friends from ZEUS.

Those that escaped through the mirror with you and were scattered over the centuries of time. Patiently I have collected them all up, like a man who has spilled a purse of coins on the floor. All my shining children. Safely back in my Lab."

She didn't believe him. "Liar."

"Not so, I assure you. You are the last, Sarah. So I have come to take you home."

"To kill me."

"Well, all the world will die. The black mirror will consume you all."

"Not you?"

He shook his lank hair, the lantern light catching the discs of his glasses. "Of course not. I will enter the mirror first. I have prepared my escape route." He held out a hand. "Come on, Sarah. You must be tired of all this. Of Venn's coldness and Jake's arrogance. Of the loneliness of your life. You want to destroy time, but we all know that time is a mirror that can never ever be broken. Come home, Sarah. Come home like the wild geese at the end of the day."

Maybe she almost wanted to, then. Until he added, "Your parents will be so pleased to see you."

Pain slid into her soul like a silver knife, so sharp it made her shiver with anger.

"Not before I've destroyed you."

He grabbed at her, but she was running, hard and

swift over the smooth lawns, and behind her she heard the wolves howl, unleashed in the joy of the chase. Up the garden steps she pelted, and saw from the corner of her eyes that the wolves had swung away in a wide arc on each side, driving her away from the door, away from the safe path to the kitchens. She glanced left; the nearest TimeWolf snarled, its eyes like embers.

No way out. No right or left.

Only, straight in front of her a blank wall smothered in thick ivy and some purple creeper.

They wanted to trap her against it.

Tear her to pieces.

Breathless, she summoned a final dash of speed. She ran full tilt at the wall, threw herself up and leaped, grabbing at the branches. Her feet scrabbled against stone, wedged in a foothold. She hauled herself up.

Somewhere behind, Janus yelled an urgent command. The wolves arrowed in, flame-fast they hurtled at her—she had to get higher!

Sobbing and screaming she dragged herself, hand over hand among the leaves against her face, the cascades of long lilac flowers. Pollen in clouds made her eyes water, pigeons flapped out in terror, the buzz of angry bees wove about her head. Desperately her fingers tore foliage, petals, sepals.

Something hot seared her leg. She screamed, kicked, jerked upward.

Below her the wolf leaped again.

Its teeth snapped at her heels.

"Sarah." Janus's voice was near. She twisted a look down, saw he was below her, at the foot of the wall. "Come down."

"No."

"You'll gain nothing."

"I'll gain time." Her voice was hard, and she felt as if nothing could touch her now, as if her determination was as hard as the wall. She climbed, quick and light, rustling her way upward, but he reached out and touched the ivy, and the leaves nearest his fingers turned brown.

She hurried. Quicker still the bines withered, the leaves died, the wave of brown shriveled up toward her, as if he had killed everything with the cold of his touch, and she knew it would kill her too, if it reached her.

Janus spoke again, but now she was too high to hear and dared not look down. A stem of the creeper tore from the wall as she grasped it. She yelled and grabbed another, clinging tight, afraid that the whole mass would peel and crack away and she would fall and fall to his feet, her blood a pool on the paving.

Then, above her head a bird flew out; she saw the edge of an open window, wide in the ivy.

With a twist that made her gasp with the pain in her

side she jerked herself over toward it, and grabbed the sill. Warm stone crumbled under her fingers.

Dust slid into her eyes.

She dug her toes in, found a good grip, raised herself until she could peer over the edge, saw a bedroom hung with scarlet silks.

Empty.

At once she was squirming up onto elbows and over, tumbling breathless into the scented room over a window seat scattered with cushions, knocking a vase of roses flying.

She lay flat on the floor, winded, staring up.

Then she scrambled to her knees and looked down.

Janus, and the wolves, were gone.

The ivy was dead and withered. And the skin on the palm of her left hand was withered too, like an old, old woman's.

12

Three things that shine in Summer.
The diamond dew.
The emerald leaves.
The gold coin of the Moon.

Trad proverb

Moll's diary.

Three weeks later JHS opened the newspaper at the breakfast table and went absolutely still. Then he said, "Bless my soul."

I just sat there, eating muffins. They were hot and the butter was greasy round my mouth. Mrs. C makes top muffins.

All innocent, I said, "What's up, JH?"

His bald head was shiny and his eyes were wide behind his specs. He read a few lines, looked up at me, then read some more. I just chewed.

He said, "I don't believe it."

"Believe it, cully. Let's have a gander."

He read aloud what it said.

SENSATIONAL ROBBERY AT THE ASHMOLEAN MUSEUM!

Irreplaceable artefacts missing! Tragedy for the nation narrowly avoided!

Last night a daring raid was perpetrated at the famous Ashmolean Museum in Oxford. The miscreants entered with great cunning and no alarm was raised. The night watchman heard nothing. It seems however that the thieves had no specialist knowledge; they stole several gold and silver items from the jewellery cabinets and in their ignorance left behind valuable pieces of historic significance. The Curator of Antiquities, Mr. Solomon Fortesque Jones, said to this reporter, "We have had a most narrow escape. These were clearly low and unintelligent men, seeking items for a quick resale. I feel secure that the police will do their duty and promptly recover our artefacts, as no reputable dealer will"—he looked up at me—"fail to recognize ..."

I smiled, licking butter from my fingers. Letting my sleeve slide slowly down from my wrist. "Recognize what JH?"

His fingers crushed the paper. "Oh Lord, Moll! Oh my good Lord. What have you done?"

The silver bracelet was pretty on my arm. It glinted in the sun, its eye all amber and shiny bright. Symmes dropped the paper and reached out both hands, not even saying anything, so I took it off and dropped it in his flabby palm. "For us, JH. A little present. So now we can get on and find Jake. And never mind what your fiancée says. Okay?"

The poor slob was too stunned to speak. He turned the silver snake over and over. Finally he gasped, "How did you manage it, Moll?"

I looked modest. "Told you, I know people. It's sorted. Won't ever get back to you."

That scared him. He looked up in terror. "The police won't come here?"

"If they do, you knows nothing, cully. Bluff it out."

"My God."

"Nothing to you, JH! You're a seeker after truth, ain'tcha? A scientist. Ruthless, you are."

He tore his glance away from the bracelet. "Yes, I suppose I—"

"Won't let nothing get in your way. Famous, you'll be someday. Up there with Newton and . . . er . . . them others."

"Moll, you're quite right." He jumped up, started pacing up and down on the hearthrug, go-

ing on and on about what he'd do, and how hard he'd work, and his voice got that big ringing tone it gets when he's lecturing. So I knew then it was all right. Wind him up and set him off. Because whatever you think of old Symmes, he's a fanatic about the obsidian mirror.

I buttered another muffin, and bit into it. What he didn't know woz I had plans of my own. To find you, Jake. And the snatch from the museum had given me my big idea. To be a sort of Time Thief. Get rich doing the big jobs, and then slip back through the mirror and never get caught.

Easy as kiss-me-hand.

As Symmes prowled and spouted and brandished the poker like a good'un, I looked at the mirror and the mirror looked back at me.

With my own slanty little face, all bent and warped.

All sly.

→←

Jake lay sleepless on the thick mattress in the thieves' den.

Around him the wooden building creaked, as if the river rushing below its rickety timbers would sweep it away.

He was thinking hard.

Sarah. Where in this dark, dangerous city was Sarah?

What was she doing? Because he knew she would be using all her guile and cleverness to find him.

And the others—would Piers and Maskelyne have been able to work out where he was? They would have told Venn. Jake rolled over and stared up at the ceiling and wondered if Venn would even care. Venn was lost, lost in his own guilt and the snares and tangles of the Wood.

There was no chance this time of Gideon coming to the rescue either—he'd sworn he would never enter the Summerland again. And Wharton? Where was he?

Jake wriggled onto his side. The bed was hard. He was alone, weary, bitten by fleas. All the problems weighed as heavy on him as the scratchy blanket.

Being in the past didn't change some things. There were the same worries, the same dread. He had brought them with him, secret, in his heart. But his father was here, in this city, somewhere close, and that meant he had to put up with anything and go along with all of Moll's crazy ideas. He had to be alert and sharp and ruthless.

Because to get Dad back he'd risk anything.

Even his life.

"*Jake!*" A hissed whisper from the door.

What?"

Moll had her head around the wooden frame. "Time

to go, cully. Get into the togs. Tie your hair back and paint your beauty spot on. Cinders and her prince are going to the ball."

He sat up and looked over at the pile of clothes on the chair. A dark silk suit, a white flouncy shirt.

He was going to feel a real idiot in those.

When he was dressed, though, it wasn't too bad. He tied his hair back, looked at himself in the dirty, propped piece of looking glass, scowled, made sure the sword was straight, and marched out, ready to face Moll's mockery. But what he saw made him stand still with astonishment.

She was transformed. The urchin was gone; he saw a demure, shining creature, a young princess in a silver dress, her hair ornately piled, her ears glinting with hanging diamonds. A silver mask on a stick showed the face of a vixen, fantastically designed of white fur and pearls. She dropped a graceful curtsey.

"Wotcher, Jake."

He came in. "Moll! You look like a real princess. It's fantastic!"

She grinned, shy. "Maybe I am a princess. Stolen at birth, like."

Gallant, he swished an ornate bow. "I could believe it. But Moll, can you do the voice too?"

"*Impeccably,*" she said, with a cut-glass pronunciation that made him stare, because for a moment she was completely someone else, and he wasn't sure if he liked that.

"But being *la petite anglaise,* no one will know the difference anyway." She picked up a filmy wrap and tossed it to him. "Big on manners, this lot, Jake. Remember that."

He opened it and held it out; she snuggled into its white smoothness.

He said, "Is it all . . . Have you . . . ?"

She turned and looked up at him. "Everything's set. So stick with me, stick with the plan. We'll get him Jake, I promise you. Okay?"

"Okay," he said.

Moll grinned. She flounced extravagantly to the door. "After all. What can possibly go wrong?"

→·←

There was a meadow. It was heavy with soft waving grass, yellow with buttercups. Beyond it, misty green hills rose against a blue sky.

Fine.

But slashed into the corner of the field was a triangle of tarmac, and down it, as Wharton stared with wide eyes, a plane—no . . . *half a plane*—roared into land. It thundered by and was gone into nowhere, and the grass was not even shaken.

He stood there and wrapped his own arms around him because only they felt safe, real.

He was George Wharton, forty-nine, of Shepton Mallet.

He had to hang on to that.

The slanted worlds of the Summerland terrified him. They defied all logic and reason. He had seen a river that flowed up the side of a cliff into a lake at the top. He had seen a dignified red-brick building upside down in the wood, standing on its pointed roof with perfect balance, as if some Shee had played with it like a child's toy and then tossed it away and forgotten it.

He had seen an orchard growing in the sea, its apples falling and bobbing on the waves.

It was completely insane.

Now he turned his back on the corner of airport and saw a park bench with a litter bin next to it in the middle of the meadow. He set off deliberately to get there, hurrying, because there was no saying when it might change to something else. But the bench remained, waiting for him, and when he sat down it even seemed to wriggle under him, into a more comfortable shape.

He ignored that, stretched his feet out, and thought about the monk.

Of course the poor man had been dead for centuries, in a manner of speaking. But the shock of seeing him dissolve to dust had shaken Wharton to the core. It made it all the more urgent that he should get back. He might already have been here years. Decades . . .

He had a sudden vision of himself running up the drive to the Abbey to find a roofless ruin, or to see a middle-aged man come out and stare at him and he would whisper, "Jake?" in utter horror. Or an old lady with a walking stick who would be Sarah.

No. No!

Get a grip.

Think!

He had two plans.

The first was to make a break for it and flee farther into the Summerland—into that airport for starters, and then into wherever that led. But it wasn't an idea he liked. He could be lost in a series of mirror-worlds, one within another, literally forever, and never find his way back; he'd become some sort of eternal *journeyman,* wandering time and space.

For a moment that reminded him of Maskelyne. Was that how the scarred man lived?

The second idea—more dangerous, certainly—was to bribe or persuade the moth-Shee or one of the others to get him back into the Wood and then take a run for it from there. They'd be after him, but he could go to ground. He'd done the commando training. Mud-smeared face, dig a hole, wait for dark . . .

A butterfly landed on his knee. He brushed it off, quickly.

Crazy plan, but all he had really. And yet, what did

you use to bribe creatures that had everything and cared for none of it?

"Hey," he said. "Hey! You!"

Nothing happened.

He looked around. Were they really not here?

"Moth?"

The moth didn't come. But zigzagging along the top of the grass flew a small brown bird, its red breast barely noticeable, with a purple flower clamped tight in its beak. It landed on the brim of the bin.

Wharton said, "There you are. Is that you? Look. How would you like to take a look at the mirror? The famous Chronoptika."

The bird hopped nearer. It came to the arm of the bench and edged along, one claw after another.

Wharton bent closer. "Take me to the Wood, and I'll get you into the Abbey. Promise. You can—"

The bird spat the flower out onto the bench and said, "Are you a complete idiot? You can't bribe them like that. They do just what they want."

Wharton gaped. "Piers?"

"Of course it's me."

It certainly sounded like him. But in this place nothing was as it seemed.

"How do I know?"

"Because I bloody say so! If you think I'm showing my face here even for a second, you're stupider than any mortal I've ever known. And believe me, I've known a few."

The acid testiness was unmistakable. Wharton suddenly felt a lot better. "Venn sent you?"

"Yes." The robin looked around anxiously. "Listen. He's going after Jake."

"*Journeying?* Where?"

"It's not good. Revolutionary Paris."

It was all Wharton could do to keep his seat. "God in heaven! What—"

"Shut up and listen! This flower will give you some sort of power over Summer. I don't know what it can do but Venn almost purred when he saw it, so it must be good. You should—"

Abruptly, the robin gave a strangled chirrup of terror and fled away.

Wharton looked up.

Summer was standing twirling a parasol at the far end of the bench. "My dear George," she said quietly. "Are you talking to yourself now?"

He hadn't a clue how to answer, so he just laughed, a ghastly parody of mirth.

And slid his fingers over the flower.

She didn't seem to notice. She closed the parasol, sat on the bench, and slid up alongside him, crossing her bare ankles in the buttercups.

"No sign of Gideon coming back," she said. "So it

seems I'll be keeping you here a little longer. Have you thought any more about my offer, George? I know you're tempted."

He couldn't stand it anymore. The anxiety that had built up in him seemed to explode in a silent, cold terror that made him reckless.

He picked up the purple flower.

"What's that?" she snapped, but before she could freeze him or snatch it, he had put it in his buttonhole, with shaky fingers.

Suddenly she was looking at him as if she had never seen him before.

"George," she giggled. "What's happened to you?"

For a moment then his dream flashed through his mind; he felt his head and ears with alarm but they were all as normal and he seemed just the same.

"Nothing. Why?"

Summer's eyes were dark as night. Her red lips twisted into a smile, and somehow its usual power to make him afraid had been doubled. "Because you're so handsome. So . . . strong. I feel as though I've been woken up, George. By a dark angel."

He felt himself going red. "What—what about Venn?" he stammered.

Summer shook her head. "Who cares about Venn?" she murmured.

She reached out and took his sweaty hand.

—→∙←—

The baby, Lorenzo, had a cot, made of white wood, and all around the cot Rebecca had hung metal implements—scissors, shears, spoons and saucepans, like some crazy force-field. She finished feeding him now with the last of the warmed milk, then laid him on her shoulder and tapped his back. She had seen this done on TV but had no real idea what it was for.

Lorenzo made a small burp.

"Good. Okay. Listen, I need you to go to sleep now."

She laid him back in the cot. He looked up at her with dark, serious eyes. A baby born over seven hundred years ago. David's son. Jake's brother. It was all so weird.

But she didn't have time to think about that. She turned to the cats. "I want at least two of you here watching him at all times. Got that? If Summer gets her hands on him, there'll be hell to pay, and I've got the whole house to look after.

The Replicant animals regarded her with seven green stares.

She turned and hurried out.

There was no way she could safeguard the whole Abbey. So she had brought the baby down to the Monk's Walk, together with a supply of food, all the water she could carry, the med kit, the radio, her phone—though there was no signal—and any weapon she had found in the house. Which was an old sword, a poker from the drawing room, and a set of kitchen knives.

Now, as the slow summer twilight descended, she made sure the lab door was securely locked, and went and stood over Maskelyne.

He lay still, his eyes closed.

For a terrible moment she thought his breathing had stopped, but then the dark cloth of his jacket lifted and fell, and she blew out her cheeks in relief. His temperature was normal, but nothing would wake him.

She should get help.

Get him in the car. Drive to the hospital, take the baby too.

And leave the mirror exposed to its enemies?

She sat down, helpless.

As she did so, all the lights went out.

For a moment her terror froze her; then she jumped up, fumbled her way across the pitch-black lab, and groped for the switches. When she found them she clicked them rapidly. Nothing happened.

There was a flashlight among the stuff from the kitchen; when she found it and switched it on, it gave only a narrow jerky cone of light that made everything outside it even darker. It flashed across some yawning emptiness in the corner. With a gasp she turned back, but it was only the mirror, a leaning darkness that took the light and swallowed it and gave nothing back.

She turned her back on it, but it was still there. Like an unlocked door into the house.

There were three candles; she lit them and stuck them around—one by Maskelyne, one on the bench, one by the monitor. The screen was dark, all the controls off. No images appeared in the mirror, and she had no way of knowing how things were with Venn.

Was this some sort of power cut, or had the Shee done it? In either case she couldn't sit here all night in the dark.

The backup generator.

It was out in the cloister. She would have to go out into the Abbey, along the gallery, down the main stairs, along the kitchen corridor, and out through the east door.

The thought of creeping all that way with only a candle was terrifying.

But what else could she do? They needed power.

"Right. I'm risking it. You stay here." She stuck a knife in the belt of her jeans and picked up one of the candles.

The cat Primo sat by the cradle; it mewed, but she had no idea what it said.

➤·≪

The Monk's Walk was quiet, the river far below running softly. From the arched windows she saw that the full moon had risen over the trees of the Wood, and she wondered where, somewhere out beneath it, Wharton was held prisoner.

She unlocked the door, slipped through, and locked it tight behind her. Then she hung a pair of metal shears on the handle.

The Abbey was dark and silent. She crept along the Long Gallery among the flickering of shadows, and every window was open. Moths and bats flitted down the corridors, the curtains drifted in the warm night. Slants of silver lay across the floor, and as she passed the doorway to Venn's room she saw that it too was wide, and creaking very slightly in the draft.

She peered in.

The bedroom looked more like a forest.

Ivy had broken in through the windows; it festooned the bed like glossy green curtains. Venn's clothes lay there. Already they were webbed in branch and tendril, and even as she watched, she saw that spiders, hosts of them, were matting the chandelier and the dressing-table and all his wife's things with gray web.

She looked up. The portrait of Leah was a mass of ivy. The creeper curled thickly, spitefully over it, and all Rebecca could see of it were the woman's dark laughing eyes. Suddenly furious, she crashed in, sending moths flying, dragged a chair over and tore down the ivy, flinging it in armfuls to the floor, not stopping until most of the painting was clear, her heart thudding with an anger that surprised herself.

"Leave us alone!" she yelled.

Then she stalked back out and down the corridor.

But her anger slid quickly away into fear. As she descended the stairs, small drafts moved around her. The candle guttered, sending eerie shapes up the wall. And the great house was not silent; it stirred and murmured, and through all the open windows, night creatures came and went.

But she ran quickly down, through the kitchens to the cloister, and saw the dim shape of the generator in its cobwebbed corner.

Would it even work?

There was a hand lever on one side. She took hold of it and forced it down.

A judder and a hum started up in its depths. A weak light flickered from a bulb overhead.

Rebecca grinned. Sorted. Getting back should be easy.

But as soon as she came back into the hall she knew that the fear had only been waiting for her. She slowed, almost unable to climb each stair, her limbs heavy, her heart thudding.

Halfway up, she stopped, wanting to crouch by the banister and curl up and just keep still.

She should never have yelled like that. Because the Shee were certainly close around the house.

As if the knowledge had slid back some filter over her eyes, she looked over and saw them, tall silvery people, whispering and peering in at the windows, peeping in at the open front door, dancing and laughing and gathering in hosts out there on the weedy drive, and she shrank back against the wall and dropped the candle and stood only in the pale light of the moon.

Their eyes and clothes glistened like the wings of beetles. Their voices were the buzz of bees, the rasp of crickets. Then one of them raised a fiddle to its chin with spidery fingers, and began to play.

Music broke over her skin like sweat.

13

Another thing that is remarkable about Venn is
that he is expert at changing his appearance. He has a
chameleon quality that can be uncannily convincing.
In Tibet he lived as a native of the country for two
years and was never discovered by the authorities.

For a blond, blue-eyed Westerner, that is so
unlikely it could almost be said to be magic.

Jean Lamartine, The Strange Life of Oberon Venn

T HE GUESTS BEGAN arriving at twilight, and just
after, Madame Lepage knocked softly on the bedroom
door. "Time," she whispered.

Sarah dressed and hurried down. She slipped through
the servants' entry and positioned herself discreetly behind a painted screen to watch the carriages roll up.
The night was flaring with flambeaux held by a line of
footmen in powder and gold-and-purple livery, the red
flames cracking and sparking all down the mile-long
drive.

There was no sign of Janus. But she knew, with that
strange inner link that bound her to him, that he was
still here, somewhere.

Behind her, in the first of several reception rooms,

the tiny vicomte, pale with anxiety, fussed over the piled sweetmeats, while the musicians warmed up with deep notes and quick arpeggios. He was dressed in sumptuous cream and more frills than Sarah would have thought possible.

A jog at her elbow made her turn, fast, but instead of Janus, she saw Long Tom. His narrow face was rouged and powdered. He winked at her with a sly eye.

"All set?"

"Yes, but—"

"At the stroke of midnight the fireworks start. Open the door *at once* and wait behind it. Don't go in."

"Yes, but you have to listen to me! Janus is here!"

"Janus?"

"He's a *journeyman*. An enemy. You have to tell Jake! Jake will understand."

Tom muttered a few swear words and shrugged. "Can't do it. I have to be with the automata. Is he from your time? Is he trouble?"

She laughed, harsh. "You have no idea!"

"Well, deal with him, girl! A cutpurse like you should know the ropes."

As he slid away toward the summerhouse she wondered what *deal with him* meant. There was no way of dealing with a Replicant. Let alone the wolves.

Then she straightened, and took a sharp breath of awe. Low on the horizon over the roofs of Paris, round and silver and beautiful, the full moon was rising. And under it, winding away into the dark, a long procession of carriages, black and gilt and gold, was rolling toward her like a dry, creaking river.

→·←

Venn said, "Here they come. Get ready."

Gideon, crouching among the heady flowers of the rhododendrons, nodded.

The carriages were drawn by sleek horses, their heads plumed, their eyes blinkered. He gazed at them in fascination, at the postilions in garish coats, the footmen riding in pairs at the back.

Venn waited until several coaches had galloped by; then the line slowed and closed up, the drive choked with vehicles.

"Now," he breathed.

He slid out, keeping low, and moved through the dark undergrowth to the back of a coach with huge wheels, painted gold and scarlet.

Only a single footman stood guard.

Venn hissed a few sharp words in French. It sounded to Gideon like some sort of appeal for help; certainly the footman looked sharply aside, then, as the carriage was now stationary, jumped down and came quickly toward them.

Venn jerked his head. Gideon stepped back.

As soon as the man ducked under the bushes, Venn

grabbed him and whipped a hand around his mouth; he grabbed the man's arm and jerked it up behind him. In his ear he hissed, "Not a word, monsieur, not a cry, or your throat is cut. *Comprenez?*"

A slant of moonlight lit Venn's sharp face, his hard ice-blue eyes. The footman nodded so vehemently his hat fell off.

Venn glanced at Gideon. The boy already had the silk handkerchief out of his pocket; he whipped it as a gag between the man's teeth, and tied it tight. Then Venn flung the man on the ground, dragged his coat of livery off, and hurriedly they trussed his hands and feet with his own belt and garters.

Venn crouched, his lips close to the servant's ear. "A few hours' sleep in a warm garden won't hurt you. Lie still, and don't struggle. Forget you ever saw us."

Standing up, he shrugged the livery coat on over his own and clapped the man's hat on. "Move," he said. Then he was out and striding back toward the coach, just as the driver glanced back and asked some question in French.

Venn shrugged. *"Ce n'est rien!"* he snapped, and jumped up onto the coach, Gideon a shadow behind him. "Don't let them see you," Venn muttered.

There was a dark space at his feet, maybe for luggage. Gideon slid into it, curled up, and felt the vehicle jerk awkwardly into motion.

The wheels rolled.

Venn stood tall and stared forward at the glittering château. Looking up, Gideon saw how the man's face was lit with flame light and energy. He was transformed—this was not Summer's bored lover but an adventurer heading full tilt for danger.

Gideon smiled a secret smile.

They made their slow, jolting way up the drive.

Twenty carriages behind, Moll knelt on the velvet seat and gazed back through the rear window. "Bloody long line, Jake! Nearly a hundred, I reckon. Plenty of aristos still in Paris with no idea what's coming down on them."

He thought again of the guillotine blade, slicing the air.

"Sorry." She slid back, patted his arm. "But don't you worry, Jake. This is my operation, and the contessa never gets it wrong."

He didn't want to think about his father in some dungeon, terrified, so he said, "How do you know so much history, Moll?"

"Research. Lord, Symmes was always bloody big on research. It was him taught me to read, Jake, and it was like a light came on in my head! All that stuff in books! I never knew about any of that. So now I always cram up on the history before any heist, though I have to say a lot of it is written by old geezers that could make you cry with the boring, dry-as-dust plod they make of it."

She giggled, squirming around. "Maybe when I give up the big game I'll be a writer Jake, and tell it like it is and people will read it and said, *Lumme, it's like she was really there . . .*"

The carriage jolted. He couldn't help laughing, even through the dull ache of anxiety about his father. "You're crazy, Moll."

"Only way to be, Jake." She turned, adjusting the delicate white skirt. "Got your pistol?"

"I prefer the sword." Seeing her quizzical glance, he said, "I was school fencing champion. So look out."

Before she could answer, the carriage stopped.

Moll sat upright, shoulders back. "This is it, cully. Success, or die trying. Agreed?"

"Agreed."

"Chin up."

The door was opened, the footman handed her down. Jake climbed out beside her and was instantly blinded by the rows of flaming torches. The twilight was heavy with the scents of roses and honeysuckle and perfume and smoke; rearing against the sky he saw a château of staggering beauty, white as a wedding cake, its windows and door wide, spilling light. Gorgeously costumed men and women wandered its terraces.

"Mask," Moll hissed.

He took it out quickly and fastened it on—a black highwayman's mask—and he felt that familiar tingle of daring, of becoming someone else.

Moll lifted the silver vixen face with a languid hand and peered through it. She put out her arm and he took it. Together they climbed the steps and entered the ballroom.

Maskelyne's dream had come late and slowly, and yet it was one he knew only too well.

He dreamed of falling.

Down and down and down, endlessly, through stars, galaxies, through dark seas and deep wells. Head first, hands reaching out, his whole body a silent scream. If he had wings they were broken. If he had come from some great height he had forgotten it. All he knew was the fall.

And he would never land, because the universe was without end and infinity a bottomless abyss.

He opened his eyes.

A gasp went through him, a great, painful in-drawing of air that made him shudder. His heart thudded as if he had come back from the dead. His hair was in his eyes.

He brushed it back, looked around.

"Rebecca?"

She had been here. He knew the scent she used, the taste of her on the air. But the lab was quiet and dark, only one candle had been jammed in a jar on the bench. A small movement made him turn his head; he saw the cats, all seven of them, sitting in a protective circle around the cradle, where Lorenzo slept peacefully.

"Rebecca? Where is she?" he said. "Where is everyone?"

The cats were listening, but not to him. He saw now that their fur was prickled in alarm, their sensitive ears alert, their heads angled to catch some distant sound.

Then he heard it too.

It came from somewhere in the house. The faintest, sweetest music.

He leaped up, flung off the blanket, raced to the door. As he passed the black mirror, its leaning vacancy jutted into his mind; he said, "Wait! I'll be back. Wait for me," but hurrying down the dark cloister of the Monk's Walk, he saw in alarm how much time had passed. Now the moon flickered beside him from window to window, snared in the black branches of the Wood, and in the Long Gallery he saw that this dwelling was broken—despite all its protection, it was prised and cracked open, infiltrated by the heat and the scurrying, scuttling, web-weaving creatures of summer.

He came to the head of the stairs and looked down.

Rebecca was standing quite still, listening to the fairy music. He knew that stillness. It filled him with a sick fear.

"Becky!"

She didn't hear, or move.

He fled down, a shadow among shadows. He felt the music like a prickle on his skin, a bramble-scratch, a nettle-itch; as he caught her arm they both jerked with the pain, as if with a wasp-sting.

Her eyelids flickered. She saw him.

"Cover your ears!" He did it for her, clumsy, grabbing at her hair. "Don't listen! Never listen to them!"

Startled, she said, "I've only just come down here—"

"That's what you think! Maybe it's been hours. They do that. They hold you like a fly in a web. Come away Becky, quickly."

But she didn't move, astonishment and joy coming over her as she realized he was there, awake, alive.

"Quickly!"

As he hustled her up the stairs she felt giddy and strange. How long had she stood there? The green twilight that had infested the house seemed to have crawled into her too. She felt hot, irritated, wanted to stop, scratch, fling off her annoying clothes. And always, somewhere below her hearing, under her skin, the soft music teased and lingered, and it was sweet, so wonderfully sweet, she could have cried with it, and she knew she would never, never get it out of her now, out of her mind and memory, out of her heart.

At the top she stopped, bumping into Maskelyne. She peeped around him and stared, astonished.

Perched on the banister rail was a small wooden bird with one eye made from an old bead. And yet it not only moved, but spoke. Tipping its head on one side, it said, "Hi. Look. Sorry to bother you. Do you happen to know where a mortal called Sarah is?"

14

Moll's diary.

Some nights, Jake, when the crib's been cracked and we're sitting on a bench in the Dog and Duck drinking porter, and Long Tom is wasted with his arm round the barmaid, I look up and see the moon peeping in. And I think "Jake's seeing that. Whenever he is."

Always makes me grin.

As if you're not that far away at all.

Really.

Jake had never seen such luxury.

As he strolled in with Moll on his arm, through the crowds of men and women and children, he thought again that the past was more than a different place. It was as if the world moved here at a slightly slower speed, with subtly altered colors, a curious sheen. As if he had somehow gotten inside a film, or among the characters of a story, and though he heard them talk and felt the draft of their passing, there was a fine mismatch between them and him.

Had his father felt like this? And did it fade away the longer you stayed, fade away to nothing, because in Florence his father had been married and had a son, and that had to be a real relationship, hadn't it?

Moll said, "Clock that?"

Startled, he turned. "What?"

"There. Room one on the plan. Pay attention, Jake."

Smoothly she steered him into the vast salon, and he took a drink from a tray as he passed the footman at the door. Moll took one too and sipped it.

"Champagne! Not bad either. Right. Check this out. Open doorways to the terrace on your right. When the fireworks start, everyone'll all go gallivanting out there. Straight ahead, three reception rooms. Each leading out of the other. Each one bloody bigger than the one before. Shall we?"

They entered the first. It was a confection of pale blue paneling encrusted with gold-leaf everywhere. Amazing, Jake thought, but cloying.

Moll spun around, her dress swishing. "Plenty of diamonds, Jake. On all those pretty white necks."

Vast chandeliers dripped from the ceiling. The room was filling with people, already hot. The wave of perfume and sweat made him feel sick. Restless, he said, "How long to go?"

"About half an hour. Make out you're loving it, Jake."

They promenaded through the crowd. The second salon was yellow and gold, the third white and gold. Finally they entered a vast, emptier space with a gleaming wooden floor.

He took a deep breath of relief. "The ballroom."

"Spot on, old thing. Musicians in the gallery above. Only way out of here the way you come in. Except for servants' entries behind the screens. And our little secret."

She was loving this. For him too, a growing sense of excitement gathered like a knot in his stomach. His senses sharpened. "Secret? What secret?"

She fluttered her fan. "Behind you, Jake."

He gazed and saw the paintings.

"Wow," he muttered. "Impressive."

The ceiling of the room was pure glass, brilliant with stars. The great wall below the musicians' gallery was painted with a vast mural of gods and goddesses—Zeus and Hera and Apollo and Aphrodite—sitting in a celestial heaven, under their feet images of planets and stars, sun and moon. Real stones were studded in the wall; as he stared he caught their glitter, rubies and emeralds, sapphires and opals.

The contrast with the stinking streets of Paris was hard to believe.

"This is crazy! Does any of this survive?"

"Burned down by the mob," she said softly. "To-night."

It chilled him. All these people, all this world, and in hours it would be gone, never to come again, and only he and Moll, in all this crowd, knew it would happen. He wondered for a crazy moment if anything they could do now would change things, if some word over-heard, some accidental brush against a stranger's elbow might trigger a series of events that would twist fate a different way.

Moll said, "See it? The secret way in."

For a moment he didn't. Then, as she pointed dis-creetly, he saw that between the feet of Ares and Her-mes, rolled there like a discarded toy, was the round silver-painted surface of the moon, all cracked and shimmering. And cut into it, so tiny and perfectly fit-ted it was almost impossible to see, a small doorway.

"That's where we go," Moll whispered in his ear. "Stroke of midnight."

The music began.

Jake bowed. Moll giggled and bobbed. They danced away into the crowd.

It was now or never. Wharton had no idea how long Summer's infatuation with him would last or how safe it was in either case. But he had to make use of it.

As he leaned on his elbow in the grass she tipped his head and examined his graying hair.

"Would you like to look younger, George?"

"No. No, I'm fine, really."

"But I want you to."

"I'm fine. The mature look . . . it suits me." He sat up. When had his clothes become this white linen suit? "Summer, look, there's only one thing I really want. I want to find Jake. Is that so hard to understand? Just to go and help Venn find Jake."

Summer lazed back. She regarded him with an unnerving silence, and just as he was starting to sweat she put her beautiful red lips together and whistled.

A male Shee as thin as a beanpole lowered itself upside down from a branch above.

"Do we know where he is?" Summer demanded.

"No problem." It slithered lower and whispered in her ear.

Wharton risked a quick look around for Piers. The clearing seemed empty.

Summer laughed, a peal of pure delight, and clapped her small hands. "Oh that's perfect! Let's go, George!"

She grabbed Wharton, hauled him up, and began

to drag him through the trees. "Everyone! Come on!"

He gasped, anxious to keep up. "Wait, Summer. Listen. I don't want them *all* coming!" He had a sudden nightmare vision of the host of the Shee crowding and cavorting into the Abbey, and it would have been his fault, he would have brought them there.

This wasn't what he wanted at all.

Summer laughed a heedless silver laugh. As she tugged him on, her fingers had the strength of roots and bines, as if they grew into his. He crashed through the Wood, snagged by brambles, torn by briars. His linen suit slithered and transformed around him, became breeches, a white satin coat, shoes with buckles. He had to grab the purple flower and hold it tight, stumbling over roots out into the graveled drive, running now between a line of men holding acrid flaring torches, while before him Wintercombe Abbey rose against the sky.

Only . . .

He stopped.

This was not Wintercombe.

It was a frothy confection of a building, a palace streaming with light, crowded with carriages, and all the Shee, in their coats and cloaks of metallic blues and greens, their starling eyes black with eagerness, were streaming past him and up its curved steps.

So much for her obliging his every whim.

He said, "I thought . . ."

Summer squeezed his fingers. "Surprise! You want to find Jake—well, Jake is here! And it can be our wedding ball as well, George! How perfect is that?"

He stared at her dress of red satin, her delicate white feet.

"Er . . . fantastic," he managed.

She took his hand and led him in past the flunkeys, and no one even saw them.

Far behind, deep in the shadows of the undergrowth, a small figure in perfect camouflage peeled himself from the bark of a tree and shook his head in despair.

"Give me strength!" Piers remarked to no one. "I cannot believe how stupid these mortals are."

Sarah was on the prowl.

She slipped open the door to the housekeeper's room, slid inside, closed it behind her.

Quickly she crossed to the wall, opened the third cupboard on the left, and found them hanging in lines, just as Madame Lepage had said.

The keys.

Big, small, ornate, simple. For diaries, presses, armoires, desks, each numbered and with a small white label above.

Number 46 looked ordinary. A small copper key

with a looped top, a snatch of faded red ribbon tied to it.

She took it out, closed the cupboard, was across the carpeted floor and at the door in seconds.

She waited.

A quick double rap.

She slipped out and was walking beside Madame Lepage, down the corridor among the hurrying servants.

"Got it?"

"Yes."

"*Bon*. Clever girl. Now get in position and wait for the clock."

→✴←

At the doorway of the blue-and-gold salon, Venn was watching the noisy crowd.

"We'll never find him in this," Gideon murmured.

"He's got to be here." Venn's eyes noted each passing dancer, but the swirling patterns and the grotesque masks made it difficult. A servant came by and offered them each a black mask; Venn took one and slipped it on. Gideon did the same. His green eyes surveyed the scene through slanted eyeholes. He was used to the riotous dances of the Shee, but this was different, a chamber of hothouse smells, of flowers and glass, of more mortals than he had ever seen together, chatting, laughing, drinking—preening men, slim girls, older women behind a fluttering wall of fans, the colors of their clothes more muted than the Shee's, the fabric more heavy.

He took a glass of wine, tried a sip and found it sharp as fire.

"We'll split up," Venn said. "You take the right-hand side of the room, I'll take the left. Work through, then into the room beyond. If you find Jake, get to him. If they're guarding him, find me. Whatever happens, remember we need to be out of here by midnight." He took the glass from Gideon's fingers and threw the wine into a vast arrangement of flowers. "Don't drink. You're not used to it."

Gideon was annoyed. The liquid was a wonderful glow in his face and limbs, made him feel light and scornfully amused at the heavy, clumsy crowd. But Venn was already gone, so he slipped between the dancers and moved, Shee-silent and elegant, to the edge of the throng. All along the wall, ranks of chairs held women, chatting, fanning, glancing at his slender elegance with interest. Gideon smiled back, bowed, walked quickly, head up, watchful.

The dancing crowd met and parted in complex patterns; he saw dozens of young men the right height for Jake, once even catching hold of one and turning him, only to find a foppish white-painted face that stared at him in disbelief.

"Pardon, monsieur." He copied Venn's words and backed off, quickly.

By the third salon he had drunk a glass of wine and was sweating. The music was tearing at his nerves; it was scratchy and raw with none of the sweetness of the Shee's. But glancing up at the musicians' gallery gave him the idea. If he could get up there, he could see everyone.

He slipped quickly behind a group of card-playing men, found a screen and a small metal stair. Ignoring the protest of a footman, he ran lightly up and stood behind the viola players.

A sea of pomade and wigs surged below him.

He looked at them with the sight the Shee had given him, the keen unblinking stare of the adder, the close scrutiny of the owl.

He saw every masked eye, every gloved hand, every bare shoulder.

Diamonds reflected in the green of his eye.

And he saw Jake.

He recognized the back of his head, his jerky, awkward movements, always a little too sudden. Jake was dancing with a masked girl in white. There seemed to be no sign of any kidnappers.

Gideon shook his head. What was he playing at? He turned to go down.

And stopped.

Between one note and another of the music, even with his back turned, he felt the change in the air with a prickle of his skin. A shiver ran up his spine.

Slowly, he looked back.

Through the double doorway, their clothes glittering like a host of dark butterflies, an enfilade of dancers was entering. Astonishingly beautiful, frail and tall and languid, their narrow faces masked in green, their hair silvery and caught up in elaborate coiffures, the Shee swept in and with them all the muskiness of the Wood, a scatter of bees, a drift of cobweb.

Appalled, Gideon shrank back into shadow.

Some of the crowd turned, staring at the newcomers.

And at the end of the line, Summer, in a red dress, bowed haughtily on the arm of a sweating mortal in a white suit.

Could it be?

Gideon's eyes opened wide. He had seen many crazy things with the Shee. But *Wharton?*

He glanced at the clock, felt a shiver of panic. The hands stood at ten minutes to midnight. He plunged down the stairs, threw himself into the crowd, and shoved his way urgently toward Jake.

→»·«←

Hidden safely behind the servants' screen, Sarah narrowed her eyes. For a moment, as the throng of dancers had opened and closed, she had felt sure she'd glimpsed beyond them a tall fair man, incredibly like Venn. But only for a moment. Now he was lost in the crowd.

Six minutes to midnight.

Jake must be here. He had to be here.

A murmur of laughter and excitement made her put her eye to a crack in the screen and peep out. Long Tom, among a crowd of jugglers and card players, had wound up the automata and set them working before an admiring audience, the Dancer spinning gracefully, the Conjuror uncovering the three balls, the Scribe writing sentences with jerky movements. There was a spatter of applause.

Too nervous to keep still, Sarah crept to the other end of the screen; above her the sandaled feet of the gigantic painted gods seemed poised to trample her down.

In the painted moon, the door waited.

Five minutes to midnight.

Then, with a jolt of absolute astonishment, she saw George Wharton.

And he saw her.

→⚹←

Wharton dropped Summer's fingers, and gasped.

"What? What is it?" Quick as a snake, Summer turned, following his gaze.

Sarah couldn't move. Her eyes met Summer's. A

spasm of spite crossed the faery woman's face; she raised a white finger ready to stab, a terrifying, lethal threat, and then Venn came out of the crowd and grabbed her hand.

"Don't do that," he said.

For a second the two of them, the tall man, the small woman, stood still and silent among the surging crowd. As if time stopped, Sarah thought. As if they were all held, suspended, in the endless reflections and possibilities of the mirror.

Then everything happened at once.

The music stopped.

Clocks in every room began to chime, a delicate medley of bells and tinkles. Outside, the first firework exploded, a crack of light illuminating the windows and slashing the lawns white.

The dance broke up; with an excited murmur everyone rushed to the windows, hiding Venn, sweeping Wharton along with them.

Sarah leaped back, into a girl who whispered in her ear. "Got that key, luv?"

She spun around.

She saw a dark-haired girl in a white dress, her eyes sharp with mischief. And behind her was Jake.

He looked amazed. "Sarah? How in hell—"

"No time." She moved to the tiny lock, slid the key in, and had the door open in seconds, a dark rectangle in the gold disc of the moon. Moll—*so that was Moll!*—was through in an instant.

Long Tom came from nowhere and darted in behind her.

Jake said, "Come with us."

"Can't." Sarah grabbed him, her face close to his. "Listen, Jake, Janus is here. And Venn's come for you. It's okay. You don't have to—"

He shook his head.

"Sarah, I'm here to save my father. Find Venn and get out. The mob is on its way—this place will be burned, be in ruins by morning. There's a house in Paris, a place on stilts, over the river. Le Chat Noir. Find it and wait for me there. That's where the mirror is."

"Jake—"

He smiled. "I'm glad you're safe."

Moll darted back, grabbed him. "Move, cully!"

The door slammed behind them, in Sarah's face. She gasped with frustration.

Reflected in her eyes, the night outside exploded in a shatter of green and gold.

15

We exist in a regime where dreams are forbidden,
where magic is outlawed, where wonder is lost.
But there is no tyranny that can close down the
imagination. We still dream of freedom, and that there
will be a future. Beyond the black hole.

Illegal ZEUS transmission

"YOU'RE NOT A real bird. For a start, I mean, you're not alive—" Rebecca stopped, wondering what exactly she did mean.

The flimsy creature ignored her. They had carried it down to the lab; now it perched on the edge of a filing cabinet and stared in fascination at the mirror. "So that's the famous Chronoptika! Wow. I can't tell you how much Summer wants to blow that thing to bits. When she gets to thinking about Venn bringing his wife back with it, she gets into *spectacular* moods. If she had had any idea that the half coin was . . . well, you know . . ."

Maskelyne flicked a glance at Rebecca.

She said, "We don't know. I think we should."

Maskelyne leaned against the bench, rubbing the

back of his neck as if it was stiff. She said, "Are you all right?"

"I think so. A little dizzy still. How long was I . . ."

"A few hours." She glanced at the digital clock on the screen and frowned. "It's ten minutes to midnight. They've been gone over four hours."

He nodded.

She said, "Piers told me Janus would have come through the mirror if you hadn't done . . . whatever it was you did. You really knew him well, didn't you?"

He stood and paced, restless. "I told you, we worked together. I had no choice. I'm not a traitor in your midst, Becky."

She hadn't thought that. But it scared her, that there was so much of his endless life that she knew nothing about.

The bird said, "Well look. If Sarah is really gone and you don't know where she is, then maybe I should tell you about the half coin . . . the Zeus stater. Only, it isn't lost, you see. And Summer hasn't got it. I stole it back from her for Sarah." It preened a fake feather complacently.

Maskelyne's whole body stiffened. "You did *what?*"

"Stole it. Took my life in my hands, but—"

"Where did she put it? For God's sake tell me where it is." He was across the room and crouched, his face on a level with it.

The low, terrible urgency in his voice made Rebecca shiver.

The bird's bead-eye considered him. "You're a sorcerer, aren't you."

"I have some abilities."

"Cast-iron A1 as far as I can see. Can you turn me back?"

He shook his head. "Summer's spell is too strong."

"Tell me about it." The bird sighed. Then it said, "All right. I'll tell you because if the Shee get in here, we're all finished. The half coin is stashed up on the roof."

"The roof!"

"In one of the gutters. Under a continual flow of running water. That was the theory. We—the Shee—don't like running water, so Sarah reckoned it would be safe there. Trouble is, it hasn't rained for weeks."

Maskelyne stood. He looked so deeply troubled Rebecca went to him. "This coin. What is it?"

He turned his scarred face to her, and his eyes were dark as the night.

"The only thing that can destroy the mirror. In all time and space. If the two halves are ever reunited."

She stared. "So who separated them?"

"I did," he said.

➤⦁⬅

Inside the door to the moon was nothing but darkness.

Jake whispered, "Moll?"

"Right here, Jake."

Her voice echoed. A light flared. He saw her fingers touch a quick flame to the wick of a lantern. "Okay, Tom. Get on it."

The tall man was already ahead, hauling his coat off, pulling out slim tools from sleeve and inner lining. Moll caught Jake's hand. "Step out, cully." *Two minutes to midnight.*

Beyond the walls he could hear the fireworks exploding. Sarah's words rang in his head. How could Janus be here? And Venn?

"This is it," she hissed. They had come to a set of spiral stairs winding around a gilt railing—they raced up, burst through a small door at the top, and found themselves in a silken boudoir where every surface, or so it seemed to Jake, was draped in chiffon and velvet.

Moll swept them straight to an iron door in the paneling.

"There's the safe, Tom."

He was already working at it, expertly sliding the tools into the lock. "Kid's stuff this, Moll," he muttered. "Not even sweating."

"You may not be," Jake muttered. He had taken up his place at the door, sword in hand. His heart thudded with every crack of the fireworks.

"Relax, Jake," Moll said, arms folded. "Not long

now. Straight to your dad when we're done, Jake. I promise you."

He looked back at her.

"What's wrong, cully?" she whispered. "That girl down there?"

He shook his head.

"Don't like the stealing, eh?"

"Not really. You're better than this, Moll. You could be . . ."

She lifted her white skirts and held them out. "What else does a kid from the gutters know, eh Jake? A girl too. Can't be anything except a thief or a trull. Can't have a brain. Brains are for men. That's the way it is in my time."

"Not in mine," he whispered.

Her eyes met his. She stared at him.

"Got it." Something metal cracked. Tom swung the door open.

Moll turned. His gloved hands were already groping among the papers and documents. He drew out a scatter of gold and diamonds, a bag of gold coins, then a case of red leather and flipped it open.

Moll gave a hoot of delight.

The Sauvigne emeralds were a glittering green dazzle, a great supple collar of stones with matching earrings. She lifted them on her gloved hands and held them up for Jake to see. "Dosh, Jake. That's what the world is all about. Them that has it, survive. Them that don't, starve."

A sound outside.

Instantly she thrust the jewels in a bag under her skirt and flattened herself against the dressing-table; Jake stepped back behind the door, sword ready. The hilt was sweaty in his hand. This was it.

The door opened. The tiny vicomte scurried in. "*Ma chére*, I had your note but this is no time . . . surely . . . my guests . . . the fireworks—"

He froze. The tip of Jake's foil gently touched the folded skin of his neck. He saw three masked figures in the darkness.

"Do you understand English?" Jake said softly.

Silence. Then "A little."

Jake nodded. "Good. Please listen carefully. We now all go downstairs, together. We go to the front steps of the house—not where the guests are. You have your coach brought round. We all get in. Do you understand?"

"Do you think to kidnap me! How dare—"

The sword point pressed harder. The tiny man swallowed.

"Just do it, luv," Moll's voice said pityingly from the dark. "And be thankful. Without us, you'd be carted off to the guillotine with all the rest of them."

→✳←

The guests streamed onto the lawn. Among them the Shee flitted, under cascades of shimmering gold and explosions of turquoise flame.

Sarah, shoving her way among them, cannoned into Gideon. "I saw Venn. And Wharton. Where are they? Where?"

"I don't know. We have to leave here, Sarah!"

But he knew it was too late. Already his keen hearing could hear a new sound, the low tread of many marching feet, the mutter of angry voices.

"There! I see him!" Sarah turned away; in an instant she was a dark shadow among the bright dancers. Gideon cursed and pushed after her. "Sarah! Wait!"

But she had struggled out of the crush to an empty expanse of lawn, and racing by a fountain of gold and scarlet, she found Venn. He was surrounded by Shee; Summer was there too, clutching Wharton. The Shee crowded close, greedy. But as Sarah walked among them, they fell back and let her through, gazing at her with the cold, bright curiosity of infants.

Venn turned. "Sarah! At last! Where's Jake?"

"With Moll."

"Moll!"

"He's caught up some plan to find his father." Her eyes flicked to Summer, hanging possessively tight to Wharton's arm. The big man looked thoroughly embarrassed.

"Hello, Sarah," he said. "Thank God you're safe."

"Yes. How lovely," Summer said in a voice of pure venom, "to see you again."

"This is ridiculous," Venn snapped. "Let that man go."

"Not until I have my changeling back. Where's Gideon, Venn? Isn't he here? Can't I hear his breathing?"

Sarah looked back. Gideon was nowhere to be seen.

But she saw something else. Roaring in like a dark tide of ragged shadows, the poor of Paris were invading the party. The cry they made as they came chilled her; it was a barely human murmur, a low deliberate threat, the growl of the starved and the forgotten, a raw blood-lust for revenge. There were armed men at their head, red-capped in some ragged attempts at uniform—all had muskets and pikes and crude clubs, even the women.

Venn took one look and whirled on her. "Where's the mirror? *Where, Sarah?*"

She stared at him, aghast. "I don't know! Somewhere in Paris. It's not here."

"Poor Venn." Summer turned calmly away, leading Wharton with her. "You'll just have to stay and see all the fun. The rest of you—home! Now."

The Shee dissipated like cobwebs in the wind; they scattered like starlings before a hawk. Wharton's look of despair struck Sarah to the heart.

"No!" She leaped forward. "Wait. You can't take him back there."

"Really?" Summer smiled. "Do you have anything you could exchange for him?"

There was only the half coin. Sarah was silent.

"No, I thought not." Summer shook her dark head in mock sorrow. "These are supposed to be your friends, George, and they won't even help you. Believe me, you're better off with us."

"Don't worry about me," Wharton muttered, defiant. "Just find Jake."

"We will," Sarah began, but Venn pushed her aside and said, "Summer. I thought we understood each other."

Summer laughed up at him and pulled Wharton closer. "Too late. I have a new mortal now, Oberon."

She turned away.

And came face-to-face with Janus.

He was wearing a blue uniform jacket slashed with a tricolor sash; a red cap covered his tangle of greasy hair. The scrutiny of his blue lenses was calm and close.

Summer did not flinch. "So! It's you! The fascinating tyrant from the end of the world!" she said with cool amusement.

He bowed to her. "And the beautiful Queen of the Midnight Court."

Summer raised a perfect eyebrow. "You know all about us, it seems."

His eyes behind their blue spectacles stared at her curiously. "On the contrary. I know very little. I think I told you once that there are no Shee in my world."

Summer tinkled a laugh. "That's what you think."

"I assure you. Any magic there belongs to me."

Summer glanced at Venn. "Hear that, beloved? What a future the world faces! Nothing left of the Wood and the Wild. And all because one man owns the mirror, and feeds it with his own greed and his own darkness until it becomes a monster."

Venn's stare was bitter.

She turned back to Janus with dark disdain. "Not that it worries me. There is no world where we're not hidden somewhere."

Janus frowned. Behind him revellers fled. A woman screamed. Red flames began to lick the eastern façade of the château; Sarah smelled the drift of smoke. Guests were running, many being rounded up and forced into their carriages at sword point.

Then, before anyone could realize what he had done, Janus reached out and took the purple flower from Wharton's buttonhole. He twirled it in his fingers. "How strange this is. A flower that doesn't die."

Venn took a breath; his hand reached out to snatch it, but Janus drew the flower close. Wharton's face was white.

Sarah had no idea what the artefact was, but she saw

clearly its effect on Summer. The fey queen's face flickered; as the small man slipped the flower into the gilt braid of his uniform, she stared at him with slowly considering eyes, her disdain seeming to kindle into a new fascination.

Venn whipped out his sword. "Give me that."

Janus smiled. "I see it has more power than I thought."

Venn moved; the sword jerked up, but the Replicant laughed as the blade sliced through him harmlessly. Then he shouted, a great cry in French. Venn roared in frustration but already the mob was on him. As Sarah gasped, two men hauled him back, snatched the weapon away, and then began dragging him, kicking and struggling, toward the sobbing prisoners.

"*No!*" she screamed. "Let him go!"

Wharton too was yelling, but Summer's small fingers held him, a tight vise. As she turned away he managed to yell, "Sarah! Get that flower!" and then he was gone with Summer into the acrid smoke and the moonlight.

Sarah took a breath, twisted between the men, and threw herself at Janus. The Replicant was startled, for a moment almost off-guard, but then it grabbed her wrist, and its grasp was like a manacle of ice.

"Venn!" she yelled, terror bursting out of her in a scream.

Venn saw, struggled, but he was struck down and

dragged away, and now the tyrant's grip was an agony, and she was sobbing with the pain of it and she knew he would take her back with him, back to the end of everything, and the world would be lost in the black hole of the mirror.

"*Let her go!*" Gideon was there. He came swiftly out of shadow like a flicker of green leaves. Without a word, he leveled the glass weapon at Janus. The Replicant released its grip.

But Gideon fired anyway.

The flash was brilliant, stunning, like another huge firework. For a moment it dazzled them both. When they could see again, only gray smoke drifted across the empty lawns.

"Did I hit him?" Gideon whirled around. "Is he still here?"

All about them the night was a panic. The château was ablaze now, its windows roaring with flame, its white classical columns blackening and cracking in the heat. Servants and musicians and cooks and entertainers fled in terror, the mob smashing every window with delight.

In a crash of sparks, part of the roof collapsed.

Gideon grabbed Sarah and pulled her back. She held her seared wrist; stared around. "Where's Venn?"

"They've taken him. With a lot of others. The carriages—"

She broke away, raced to the drive, but already the carriages had rattled away, the horses whipped to madness, the terrified coachmen fleeing.

Helpless, she stood with Gideon and watched them go. Toward Paris.

→»·«←

Wharton watched too as Summer led him away from the blazing building. At the edge of the dark lawns they stopped.

"That man Janus," he said sourly. "He's your real enemy."

Summer looked at him as if she had forgotten who he was. "You think so? Actually, Janus is what I call a really *interesting* mortal."

As she led him into the Wood he looked back, and for a moment thought he saw the small dark form of the tyrant silhouetted against the flames, staring up in calm satisfaction, and two great beasts, like dogs with eyes of burning coal, racing in and out of the inferno, the flames leaping harmlessly down their backs.

Nor doth this Wood lack Worlds of company.

16

I will not let you go, my lord.
I will not let you flee.
My chains are frail as cobweb,
Strong as ivory.

I will scorch your fevered brow,
Melt your heart of ice.
You will forget the love you lost
and all the world besides.

Ballad of Lord Winter and Lady Summer

JAKE HELD THE sword comfortably on his lap as the carriage jolted. He watched the small man sitting opposite.

The vicomte was in a perfect sweat of terror.

"Monsieur Englishman," he said at last. "Listen to me. I will give you ten thousand *livres* in gold for my release. More than that, I will—"

"Save your breath, chum." From her corner of the carriage, Moll was curled up in satisfied calm. "You ain't got as much as a church mouse left by now. Not when that mob get into the house." She grinned at Jake. "Timed it to a whisker, Jake. Spot on."

He nodded, silent. Her ruthlessness chilled him, but he knew something of it was in him too, and if he could find Dad, all the aristocratic houses in Paris could go up in flames for all he cared. And yet the stench of smoke, the terrible scorch of flames against the sky, crackled in his memory.

"They were there," he said, bleak. "Venn, Sarah. All of them."

"Well, we can't do anything about that now. Got to stick to the plan, Jake. Got to get your dad. They can look after themselves, that Oberon Venn can, anyway. But, blimey, who was the looker in the red dress? Wouldn't want to get the wrong side of her."

"That was Summer, Moll. She's"—he shrugged, despairing—"what you might call not quite human."

Her eyes widened. "Straight up? Lord, Jake, there's some loopy stuff goes on in that century of yours! *Not human* meaning from some other planet?"

"Oh, she's from this planet all right." He had no desire to talk about Summer or let worry about Sarah or Wharton distract him, so he glared again at the Frenchman and said, "When we get my father, what happens then?"

"You take him home."

"How?"

"Well, through the bloody mirror, Jake, how else?" Suddenly she uncurled and wriggled over to him, ignoring their prisoner. "What's the matter, cully? Ain't everything going to plan?"

"So far." He stared into the dark. "It's just that . . . I've been thinking. To snatch me you had to come into the future. How is that possible, Moll? For us to *journey* backward, well, this world already exists. Or had existed, once. But how can the future be there ready to go into if it hasn't happened yet?"

"Don't know and don't care," she said. "When you go home you go forward, don't you?"

"Yes . . . but that's different, because—" He stopped. Was it?

Moll shrugged. "Maybe all the time there ever will be is in the mirror, all at once, and we just get off and on like stops on the trolley bus. But if you're fretting we can't do it again, then don't, Jake, because like I said, me and Symmes, we worked hard on the Chronoptika. And if the silly old coot hadn't got married and wasted a few years with some hoity who only wanted his money, we might have done more. Trust me. I'll get you and your dad home."

There was a stubborn, determined edge in that that made him smile at her. She had unwound her hair; now it was an urchin's straggle again. To the vicomte's interest and astonishment she had pulled on dark trousers and boots and wriggled out of the white dress, replacing it with a ragged coat and a sash with the tricolor colors as soon as the carriage had left the drive of the château. Now she looked more like the Moll he had first known, small and fierce and reckless. And more than a little sad.

"What you said about girls in your time. What's it really like, Jake?"

He shrugged, rocked by the rapid motion. "They can do what they want."

"Just like boys?"

"More or less." He had never really thought about it. "At least . . . in some countries they can."

Wistful, she curled a scrap of hair around her finger. "Get educated?"

"Of course. And for free."

"Bloody lucky them. But not much of a place for pirate-princesses, I don't suppose."

He wanted to say "Come back with me, Moll." He had promised her that once. But somehow the words wouldn't come, as if he sensed danger in them. So when the carriage slowed and Long Tom leaned down and yelled "We're coming up to the city gates," he was almost glad of the distraction.

If Moll noticed, she didn't show it. She sat up and fixed the vicomte with a glare. "Okay. Don't make a murmur."

The marquis nodded, licking dry lips.

Horse-bits jangled. The carriage stopped; there was

a murmur of voices outside, a few barked questions, Tom's laconic answers.

"Sit tight," Moll breathed.

The door was wrenched open.

Some sort of citizen guard in a dirty tricolor sash stared in, at Jake, Moll, the vicomte. A slow grin spread on his face. "New prisoner?" he said.

Jake nodded. "Our orders are to get him to the Conciergerie prison. So don't keep us waiting."

The man eyed him. Jake's hand closed slightly on the sword. The words had been right, but he knew his accent must sound all wrong.

But the man just nodded; the door was slammed and the carriage lurched on.

The vicomte took out a silk handkerchief and wiped his face. *"Sacre bleu,"* he whispered.

Jake breathed out.

Moll edged back the blind and peeped out. "Sweetly done, Jake. We're back in the city."

When Rebecca had fed the cats she made some tea, grilled three sausages on a makeshift gas burner, put them on a tin plate, and took them to Maskelyne.

The lab was quiet and stuffy. Small green lights winked on the monitors. The mirror, tethered like some monster in its malachite web, reflected only blurs and warped shadows; her hand, her twisted shoulder.

One cat on guard watched her as she tiptoed past the cradle where Lorenzo slept. On a shelf safely above, head under wing, the wooden bird seemed to sleep too.

Maskelyne sat at the workbench, facing the mirror. She paused, watching him. He had his fingers wreathed together and he was staring into the darkness, lost in some deep reverie, or maybe in memories of past lives that she could never be part of.

Stupidly, she was jealous.

She came and put the plate down with a noisy clatter. "You need to eat."

He looked up, startled. "Oh yes. Thank you."

"It's not Piers's cooking, but it's all I can do. The supplies down here are limited." She glanced at the mirror. "Still no sign of them?"

"None." He brooded. "Not even a murmur. As if, on the shortest night of the year, the mirror sleeps. And yet maybe the mirror too has dreams."

She sat down. "You can feel them?"

"Barely. Mere colors and smoke drifts. Fleeting like clouds over the moon." He cut the sausage in half and ate it as if it had no taste at all.

She said, "I want you to tell me about it. What you remember."

He shook his head, and the scar down his cheek moved in and out of the light. "When I threw myself into it without a bracelet I was scattered, Becky. My whole body and soul, broken to its atoms, split like a swarm of fish when the shark comes. Only now, after years, do I feel I am coming back together. What I was before, what I did, those things are like fragments of a smashed window, a kaleidoscope pattern. My mind works on them obsessively, but they no longer fit together."

"You did create it, though, didn't you?"

Maskelyne managed his rare smile. "I found it. Long ago, I went searching for it. For years. I climbed mountain ranges, explored the valleys and peaks of the world. I found much obsidian, but never the piece that would be good enough to make my mirror. Until one day, on the slope of an extinct volcano, I entered a deep cleft in the earth, a path that led down and down until I feared I would come to some Underworld, some dark Hades. Then, turning a corner, I came face-to-face with my own dark image and realized I had at last found what I longed for, a slab of obsidian that was perfect, without flaw or blemish, tall as a man, thin as a wafer. So I had them take it to my secret palace."

"Them?" she asked softly.

He shrugged. "My servants. My slaves."

The word shocked her. But as if he was feeling along the most delicate thread of memory, so frail that a question might break it, he went on quickly, his husky voice a whisper in the buried room.

"How many years it took, Becky! How much ambition, how much obsessive greed. To polish it, inch by inch, grain by grain, to perfection. No one else was allowed to see it. I kept it in the darkest and most secret chamber, down a labyrinth of passageways. No one knew the way to it but me, and at night, every night, when all the people slept, I was alone with the mirror. My eyes so close to it, my breath misting it. And slowly, so very slowly, I saw my reflection begin to form, appearing on its blackness, my eyes, my hair, my face, until I knew that the long work was done and the glass was ready for my spells."

She kept quite still. The food was cold and the mug of tea in her hands no longer steamed.

She said, "When was this?"

He looked up at her, eyes dark, as if he was blinded by memory. "Long ago. Too long to remember who I was then. A prince maybe, and a sorcerer. In some desert land far away."

She wondered swiftly about Egypt, about the Aztecs, about the lost civilizations of Sumer and Ur. Because she knew now that he must have lived many lifetimes, this ghost of hers, long lifetimes always moving in time. Fleeing Death.

"And then?"

"I can't tell you."

"Can't?"

"Won't." He ate the last bite of cold sausage. "There are things that shouldn't be told. I was a different man then, Becky. You would not have liked me. I sacrificed everything to the fascination of the mirror, put all my greed into it, all my pride and energy. It became my own dark image." He looked up. "I was an obsessed and evil man."

"I don't believe that."

"You should. I've spent an age atoning for what I made. And I've paid, in pain and fear, and all I want to do now is take this . . . . thing . . . back to where it all began, where no one will ever find it."

Watching him, she saw how his meshed fingers clenched. "And the coin?" she said. "What about that?"

The mirror rippled.

She felt it happen, a disturbance in her teeth and bones.

The cats, as one, opened their eyes.

Horatio gave a low chatter and swung down into her lap.

Maskelyne stared at the black glass.

"Venn?" she whispered. "Jake?"

"Neither. Sometimes I fear it listens to what we say." He stood tall, paced along the monitors, checking each one. "The coin was made as a safeguard. Maybe he knew, that man I used to be, maybe he understood that one day the mirror would destroy us all. The coin is a matrix, an unform. But it will only work if the two halves are joined, and they are so powerful I had to hide them far apart, dimensions apart." He paused, listening. "And now one half is in this house. That scares me. Sarah's idea was ingenious, but without running water over it, the coin is exposed and vulnerable. I have to get it, Becky, and I should try now, before They come back." He turned. "Will you help me?"

What could she do but say: "Of course. What do we have to do?"

Wharton lay on his back under the moon, staring up. The pale disc shone down on him. Was there a face in it? A man in the moon? A lost man, marooned?

If so, he was that man. He was in deep trouble.

As soon as Summer had walked back into the Wood, things had changed. For a start she'd looked at him almost with disgust, muttered, "Get this creature out of my sight," and stalked off under the trees, her red dress shriveling to a cobweb of gray.

A tall and disdainful Shee had brought him to this bare clearing and left him here. No food. No chair. Nothing.

And when he'd finally said "Hello? Anyone?" nothing had happened. The moth-Shee and the others were nowhere to be seen.

At first he had been glad just to lie wearily on the grass and try to understand what had happened back there. *What the hell did Jake think he was doing?* And Venn—if the revolutionaries had him prisoner, the man was likely to end up on the guillotine. What a mess! And he, Wharton, the only one with any common sense, was stuck in here in this crazy forest and there was no one to— He stopped.

Sat up.

This was his chance. Before he could talk himself out of it, he was on his feet.

The Wood was still. The faintest of warm breezes touched his cheek. Through gaps in the heavy foliage the midsummer stars glinted; the clearing was lit with the magical silvery sheen of moonlight.

A small thread of path led away between two trees.

He took a step toward it; no Shee appeared.

He reached the trees and peered around them. The path led downhill, the tree roots almost forming steps.

He started down.

His breathing was loud; his heart thumped in his chest. *Calm down, George!* he ordered himself, but halfway down the twisty steps he knew he felt only fear.

Every tree was a wizened being, every bole and hole a dark eye. Brambles scratched him. The soil was baked hard and thudded with his footsteps.

He reached the bottom panting for breath and found

himself in a dank cleft under a darkness of clotted branches. Far off, one moonbeam gleamed.

Which way to the Abbey?

An owl hoot came from close by; he jumped, jerked about.

It came again, a soft savage message of intent, and he remembered how he had once seen Summer transform into that bird, break out in beak and claw under the great storm she had called down.

He started to run.

Maybe that was his mistake.

The thud of his feet became a thud in his head, and then a thud in the earth; it became a drum that someone was beating, an urgent rhythm.

When he stopped, it went on.

The Wood woke. Branches gusted and crackled. Leaves drifted down. A cloud masked the moon.

He ought to go back, play safe, but he wouldn't. Stubbornness burst out in him; he set his shoulders, lifted his chin. No one scared George Wharton, he thought.

Even as he thought it, a vibration gathered in the air, a swarm of something came out of the trees like a buzz of dusty bees and was all over him, their stings ferocious and real, and he was squirming, yelling, beating them off, until gasping, he whirled around.

And there was nothing there.

A branch snapped; a hare pelted out past him. He backed after it down the path.

The piping began then, haunting music, sweet and cheerful, but it filled him with dread. He knew this story. He knew what was coming.

He stood still. And looked up.

Through all the dark branches, their party clothes crackling to carapace and wing, their eyes unblinking, their silvery hair crisping to feathers, their fingers hooking to claw and talon, the Shee were gathering in their host, some as hounds, some as hawks, some as half-human runners, some riding silver horses with skeletal heads, galloping on cloud and branch and grass, swift as vengeance under the trees.

Wharton panicked. Even as he turned and fled he knew it was the worse thing he could do. The bray of a silvery horn rang out joyfully behind him. He leaped a fallen trunk and plunged into the Wood, running heedless, falling and picking himself up, thrashing through thicket and briar and sudden empty space. He gasped hard and breathless up a slope where thin young trees grew so close he had to duck and weave and squeeze between them, the ground all humped and hollowed with banks of decayed leaves, the hounds yelping so he could feel their teeth snapping at his ankles, at his heels, at his—

A hand shot up and grabbed him, yanked him down

into a burrow of brown earth, clamped itself over his mouth.

A hand with dirty fingers as small as a rat's.

"Will you shut your noise!" a testy voice growled in his ear.

Wharton's eyes went wide. He rolled over.

"Piers?" he whispered.

17

Many went to the scaffold with great bravery.
Others wept and screamed. The crowd in the square
became a many-headed beast that roared and
slavered, an insatiable monster of vengeance, and in
its voice I heard the centuries of disease and poverty
and want.

So I too cried out.

Maxim Chevelin,
A History of the Late Revolution in France

VENN OPENED HIS eyes, but that didn't help.

He was in a dark place and it was rocking under
him. A great jolt shuddered through him. He tried to
sit up, but felt at once that his hands were tied behind
his back; he was lying, facedown, in a layer of mud in
the bottom of some lurching vehicle.

The word *tumbril* came into his mind. He struggled
harder.

Someone whispered, "Stay still, monsieur. Best to
play dead."

Venn's ribs ached. He had been beaten and kicked
with some relish. He eased his head aside. "Where are
they taking us?"

"We think to the Conciergerie." The answer came from a young woman sitting above him. Her silk dress was bedraggled; her whisper showed her raw terror.

"And then, no doubt, an appointment with Madame Guillotine." This speaker was a tall man, his powdered wig still on, his once beautiful coat torn, but he sat in the cart with great hauteur. "An appointment, *mes amis,* that I do not intend to keep."

Venn realized that the cart was crowded with prisoners. The girl whispered, "Monsieur . . . how do you intend to escape?"

"Like this, mademoiselle. Boldly and openly, as befits a true son of France." He stood up. *"Vive le roi!"* he cried. Then he leaped over the side of the open cart.

The girl gasped. Venn struggled up. They were crossing a high bridge over the Seine; he saw the moonlit rooftops of Paris, the rearing towers of Notre Dame. The prisoner had leaped up onto the palisade of the bridge, kicking away men that grabbed at his ankles.

One shot rang out, a musket crack. The air stank of cordite.

When the smoke cleared, the man was gone.

"Mon Dieu," the girl whispered in horror. "Such a noble hero! And they killed him."

Venn wasn't so sure. He thought maybe the man had jumped before the shot. But even so, his chances in the dark undertow of the river wouldn't be good.

He closed his eyes and, through the sickening pain in his head, thought of the despair that must have lain under that pride.

Not a solution he intended to try.

They rattled on, the prisoners silent. Venn worked at his bonds, managing to loosen them slightly. Dried blood was in his hair.

After a while he gave up and sank back

Anger was hot in him, anger at Jake and at Summer. And at himself. Because now Janus had the purple flower, had taken it before their eyes, and with it who knows how much power over Summer. The thought of Janus and Summer in some vengeful league turned him cold with fear.

Abrupt darkness closed over him.

The cart rumbled under an arch, bumped over cobbles, then stopped. "Out," someone snarled. "All of you!"

Venn was last. He closed his eyes and deliberately hung limp, so they had to drag him and half carry him between two of them. If he had the least chance he would crack their heads together and run for it.

But the doors that slammed behind him were vast oaken barriers, and the men were armed, and his own sword was gone.

Then panic flashed through him.

The bracelet.

So far he had been lucky; it was jammed well up under his sleeve and his captors must not have noticed it. But as soon as they did they'd take it, and then he'd have to fight for his life and the whole future of the mirror.

He heard them unlock a heavy door. It grated on its hinges; a foul stench gusted out of the darkness inside.

They flung him in, facedown.

He made no sound, lay bruised on the stones, his face in musty straw that leaped with fleas.

Only when he was sure they were gone did he lift his head and sit up.

The gloom implied a small space, a high ceiling.

He said softly, "Is anyone here?"

No answer.

First he worked on the bonds. They had been hastily tied, and he finally managed to wrench them loose enough to slip them off. Rubbing his scorched skin, he tugged the bracelet down and examined it, holding it close to his eyes in the dark.

It seemed unharmed, though there was a slight dent in the silver head of the serpent. He flipped open the amber eye and touched the dark space where the tiny fossil had been, now lodged in the mirror frame. Twice before the mirror had shown them *journeymen*. Could Maskelyne see him now?

"Do you hear me?" he said quietly. "Anyone? It's me. Venn."

Nothing.

He had no way of knowing if they heard him or not. Outside, in the corridor, heavy boots approached.

He shoved the silvery ring inside his shirt.

The footsteps passed.

Venn sat still, breathing out, making himself relax. And suddenly, quite out of nowhere, he thought of Leah.

Her face emerged from some locked and clotted place in his memory, as if at that moment a darkness had been stripped from it, some terrible clinging growths torn from it.

He sat amazed at his own folly.

How could he have forgotten her? How had he let Summer beguile him? The time he had lost! He saw Leah's face, and she was smiling at him, but it was the painted face of the portrait in his room, and for a moment he had to struggle to remember the real, infuriating, careless woman, the woman who lay late in bed and read novels, who was always late, who knew how to mock him softly. The one he loved. The one he wanted back.

The thought of her made him curl his hands into knots. And yet even now, he knew there was a thin, cruel sliver of jealousy in him, sharp as a shard of glass, when he thought of Summer smiling, not at Wharton, who was no one, but at Janus.

He shook the thought away. *Leah*. Leah was all that mattered.

And escape.

→·←

"So where is it, this house of the Black Cat?"

Sarah said, "Somewhere near the Seine. Built out over the water." She sat hugging her knees, with Gideon's silvery jacket draped over her maid's dress. Even in the steamy heat of the hothouse, she felt chilled and dispirited and unutterably weary.

They had hidden here as the château burned. It had been chaos back there—even now dark figures were running and piling up looted goods on the dark lawns. The destruction sickened her, because she recognized it. She had seen it in the End time.

Gideon said calmly, "Try not to get involved. We're only passing through."

"That's a real Shee attitude."

He tipped his head. "Mortal history seems to be full of terrible times."

"And we walk straight into them."

"At least we can walk out again."

She looked up. "I really hope so. Because my fight is for the most terrible time of all."

Gideon nodded, but her fierceness hurt him. He had thought she would be grateful to him for coming to find her, but she seemed to have forgotten that already.

She was such a mystery to him!

He stood up and rubbed another patch in the steamy glass and stared out. "When it gets light—which should be soon, because this is the shortest night—we should head for the city and find the mirror."

Sarah rubbed her dark skirt. "Jake said Moll knew where his father was. Do you think that's true?"

Gideon considered, hands in pockets. "She seems a tricky creature."

"Fond of Jake."

"Maybe." He turned. "But Jake promised to go back for her and never did. She must have waited years for him. What if this is some sort of revenge, Sarah? Paying him back for her lost hope with some of his own?"

She didn't like that idea at all. "She's just some little urchin. I really can't believe she'd do that."

"You don't know her. None of us do. And believe me, waiting for rescue that never comes destroys anything human in you."

He was talking about himself, she knew. She ran her hands through her hair, exasperated. One thing she didn't need was something else to worry about. She came and joined him at the window. "We have to believe Jake is in no danger. But Venn is."

"Venn! Venn can look after himself."

Sarah snorted. "Not from what I've seen. Summer almost owns him."

Gideon slid her a green, sideways glance. Lowering his voice, he said, "You must be worried about the coin."

That touched a nerve. She said, "The coin is safe. It's guarded." Then her whole body stiffened. She leaned forward, stared out into the tumult on the lawns, then said, "Come on. Quickly!"

"What . . . ? Wait!"

But she was already gone, running across the grass, her shadow huge in the leaping flame light. "Sarah!" Gideon drew his sword and raced after her.

The night was an inferno. Sparks and scraps of burning cloth flew past him. The château was unbelievably brilliant, the flames reaching high, the stench almost too much for him.

He found Sarah at a pile of tumbled goods, among ragged men picking over the spoils. One of them glared at her; Gideon lifted the blade, wary.

"Here! Look!" She was kneeling by some contraption on its side, scorched but otherwise undamaged. It seemed to him like the statue of a masked figure holding a pen in one hand, some mortal mechanism.

"What is that?"

"One of the automata." She pushed it upright with an effort. "It belonged to Moll."

"What do we want with that?"

Sarah looked at him, direct, hard—what he thought of as her *metallic* look.

"It's given me an idea," she said.

→·←

The carriage rattled swiftly over the bridge. The moon lay low on the Seine, a track of light leading to it.

Ahead, Jake saw the prison of the Conciergerie rising, a silhouette against the sky, its towers crowned with coned roofs, its barred windows dull with torchlight.

Panic and fierce excitement gripped him at the sight of it. "We must be mad."

Moll patted his arm. "Trust me, Jake. We'll have your dad out of there as fast as an oyster from the shell." As the carriage rolled to a stop at the gates she glared at the aristocrat. "Out please, monsieur. Come on, Jake."

The small man breathed a prayer. Jake didn't move.

"Come on, cully!"

"I can't, Moll."

"Can't?"

"I can't take this man into some dungeon and hand him over to people who'll cut his head off."

She stared. "They'd have done that anyway, Jake."

"Would they? How do we even know?"

"But . . . Lord, Jake, he's nothing to you. Some rich toff. And your dad—"

"My father wouldn't want me to do it." His voice was low, fierce. He knew that now, knew it as if some voice had whispered it in his ear. "He'd be appalled, Moll, and he'd be furious. We don't need this man. We can do this on our own."

She looked at him, her small heart-shaped face framed with its tangle of hair. Her look was unreadable, and for a moment he was afraid that she despised him now, but instead she shook her head and said slowly, "Lord luv you, Jake, I think you're barmy! I really do. Chucking out our best card. But it's your party."

She leaned over, turned the handle, and threw open the carriage door.

"Get out, mate. Your lucky day."

The vicomte stared. His handkerchief was a twisted rag in his hands. "You mean . . ."

Moll jerked her head. "Leg it. Before my friend changes his mind."

He understood the gesture, if not the words. Awkwardly he grasped the carriage framework, lowered himself down. For a moment he looked back at the two of them, and his eyes were dark with fear in the warm Parisian night. "What do I do? Where do I go?"

"Can't help you there, luv," Moll said sadly. "Bribe your way to England would be my advice."

He stared at her. Made a deep bow. Then, like a bright moth from the window, he was gone.

Moll rubbed her nose. The carriage lurched and creaked as Long Tom clambered in. "What's going on, Moll? What's the idea? I thought the toff was our ticket in."

"Change of plan," she said, glancing at Jake. "If you've got one, that is."

Jake's old confidence had come back. The decision to take control had made him feel sure, invulnerable. He put his arm round her and hugged her, feeling the thin bones. "No problem, Moll. You and me, we can do anything. Time travelers and thieves and pirate-princesses, us."

She giggled.

But Tom muttered, "We can't blag our way in without a prisoner."

"You've got a prisoner." Jake took off his sword and handed it to him with elaborate politeness, hilt first. "You've got me."

18

And as the Abbot returned, slow and broken-
hearted through the Wood, he looked up and saw
that every dark tree had silver eyes. And he cross'd
himself and hastened, because it came to him that
he was in a place beyond the knowledge of man. And
that if he remained there one more hour he would be
lost for all eternity in its mazes and dreams . . .

The Chronicle of Wintercombe

"HOW ARE YOU still here?"

"Because I'm either brave or stupid." Piers lay curled
in the hollow, and it was all Wharton could do to make
him out. The white lab coat had become a suit of complete camouflage, so carefully formed of overlapping
brown and sepia leaves and patches of bark that he
blended perfectly with the background.

"Keep still now," he muttered.

Above them the Shee host passed. It rippled like a
gale driving a scatter of leaves, so light, delicate. Or
like a flock of birds, the wind of its wings raising dust
and flickering in the moonlight. There must be so
many of them! Wharton kept his head down and felt
the soil trickle down his neck.

Would they sense him here? He lay curled in the hollow of his own breathing.

Finally, the silence of the Wood was all that was out there.

Piers murmured in his ear, "Okay. We need to move. As soon as they realize you've vanished, they'll come back."

"Move where?" The hollow was a cramped scrape under the bracken, leading nowhere.

He felt Piers's soft laugh.

"Out of this Wood."

"How can we cross it with all of Them—"

"Not across, idiot. Nobody catches Piers. We go *under*."

Something peculiar happened.

Wharton felt giddy and oddly hot. He had the strangest feeling that the hollow grew around them. The tree roots next to his hand became enormous. A nibbled acorn lying next to him was as big as his chest.

He said, "Piers . . ."

Piers grinned. "Don't worry, big man. Trust me. Come on."

Because there was a tunnel now, and they were racing down it, and Wharton realized he was running, or he thought he was running, but did you run with your hands and feet and with your face so close to the earth? Had his nose always this been long and lean? And as he shot after Piers, he marveled that he could flee so fast, and without getting breathless at all.

And then, the smells!

He ran in an overwhelming stench of soil, leaves, the stink of sucked worms, the pungent sweetness of rotting fungi. He lifted his nose and sniffed, and there were unknown parts of him that were thin and wiry and quivered, that translated scent into a new language, into the colors of this place that were nameless, dimmed and dull, all drabs and grays and palenesses.

There was an itch on his skin and he licked it.

It was a peculiar thing to do, but it seemed normal.

Under roots, over swarming anthills, through a network of dark tunnels where the earth roof dropped worms onto his neck, he ran with loping strides and small swift feet. He heard all the chatter of the underground world, all its fumbles and scrapes; the muffled thuds of rabbits, the soft rasp of a badger's tongue. He knew that all around him, spreading like the invisible filaments of mycelium, lay the labyrinthine roads and ways of the underworld, a place without human or Shee, without light or any direction but the invisible magnetism of the deep rocks.

Piers was a sleek shadow ahead, and when he stopped and sniffed and began to scrabble upward, Wharton pushed in beside him and dug too, scraping the soil expertly with his hands that were long and hard and narrow.

Cold hit him.

⇾·⇽

A black patch of sky, brilliant with stars.

He poked his head out, slithered up, found himself on a bleak and featureless surface that stretched as far as he could see in every direction.

Piers slithered out beside him.

They sat, staring around. They were breathless and grimy with soil and their nails were broken and black.

Finally Wharton managed to say, "What the hell was I, down there? And where's Wintercombe Abbey?"

Piers ignored the first question. He looked around at the strange rocky landscape, irritated. "We should be there. The Shee are always moving everything about. There's never any sense or order to them."

Wharton was already shivering in the bitter cold. "Piers. Don't tell me."

The small man shrugged and stood. His lab coat was back, and under it his most scarlet waistcoat. He scratched his small wisp of beard.

"Yep."

"No!"

"Afraid so." He looked up at the impossible stars. "Has to be the bloody Summerland. Doesn't it."

⇾·⇽

The sky in the east was a paleness; Rebecca could see a point of fire that was the planet Venus, shining brilliant and low over the Wood. Worried, she said, "Wait just half an hour. Just for more light."

Maskelyne shook his head, tying the rope tight. "It's already too dangerous. It's Midsummer Eve and anything might happen."

The wooden bird that had come with them, and was now perched on the bare curtain-rail of the attic room, made a cheep, and said, "Well yes, but then I think you're crazy to go after it at all."

"He wouldn't have to, if you went," Rebecca snapped.

The bird looked aggrieved. "I told you, last time I saw Summer she had me in her talons and I was about to get my head torn off. No way am I going out there."

The room was the highest attic they had been able to find in the vast dim house. Maskelyne had wanted to go alone but Rebecca had insisted on coming, locking the cats and the wailing baby and the marmoset in the lab with the silent, black mirror. All the way up through the building they had found corridors and stairs and landings wreathed with ivy and sprouting flowers, until, on the highest corner of the gallery, Maskelyne had lifted a tendril of honeysuckle from the floor and said, "Look at this."

Sweet scent crisped from it.

He had stared at the branch for a hopeless moment. "How can we ever win this house back from her, Becky?"

The door to the roof, when they had found it, had been warped and wrapped tight with weed, impossible to open. Here, though, the ivy had broken the window and was thick on the attic floorboards. Maskelyne tested the rope and fixed it securely to the window frame.

"The wood looks rotten," she murmured.

"Probably is."

"Then let me go. I'm lighter."

"Than a ghost?" He smiled. "I doubt it."

Before she could answer he had climbed up onto the sill, wriggled through, and swung himself out. In the pale predawn glimmer, the Wood was dark below, its branches close, its leaves a mass of shadow against the very walls of the house.

"Be careful." She leaned out, twisting to look up.

A silhouette of darkness, he was edging along the narrow strip of roof toward the nearest chimney stack. As she watched, the wooden bird came and perched on her shoulder, its claws digging painfully in.

"Did Sarah really get out there?" she whispered.

"Oh, by the door it was easier." The bird tipped its head. "She really knows this house, you know. She's got all sorts of hiding places round it."

Rebecca nodded, not listening. Maskelyne had reached the chimney. He was lost in its shadow. Then his voice came softly back to them. "I've found the rope she tied here."

"Follow it," the bird said. "Somewhere at the end you'll find the gutter."

"Go back down, Becky."

"No. I'm staying." She frowned. "Just hurry up."

And then he was gone, and only a few scrapes over the tiles betrayed where he went.

Maskelyne moved cautiously along the rope. The rooftops of the building were an uneven landscape of slopes and gulleys, gutters and gables, the tiles great slabs of tawny limestone, clotted with moss and lichen, warm even at night to the touch. He climbed over ridges and slid down a steep slope, one hand tight on the rope, to find a level and wide walkway leading between a maze of chimneys. He followed it carefully, glancing nervously at the eastern sky.

Venus was fading, a pale speck. The sun would rise in the next hour.

Already, in the Wood, he could sense the stir of birds, their heads coming from under their wings, their dark, intent eyes opening.

At the end of the walkway the rope had been looped through a rusty stanchion next to an ancient metal ladder leading to a lower section of roof. He swung around and climbed swiftly down it.

Sarah certainly knew the house. He wondered how often she had climbed and explored it as a child, learning the complicated ruin it would become at the end of time.

At the bottom of the ladder was a gutter. He crouched quickly.

The gutter was deep and would carry all the water from the steep roof behind him. Normally it would have been wet, but with the long days of summer heat, even the small cushions of lichen near the drainpipe were desiccated and dry as dust.

In the bottom of the gutter, taped securely at the deepest point, was a plastic-wrapped package.

He tugged it away, the tape making a sharp ripping noise.

At that moment, as if his action had caused it, the molten tip of the midsummer moon pierced the corner of the chimney. Its horizontal rays lit his face; Maskelyne whipped the package into his pocket, and turned.

On the topmost rung of the ladder a white owl was perched.

Its feathers lifted in the dawn wind.

Its great dark eyes, circled with yellow, were fixed on him.

"*Is that you, Lady Summer,*" he whispered.

→·←

Venn explored the damp cell wall with both hands.

It was solid stone. But there were niches and jutting slabs, and from somewhere above him, a tiny sliver of pale light was entering. It slid down, thin as a wand, and he stood in it and looked up and imagined the narrow crack somewhere in the darkness of the high ceiling. The moon was setting over Paris.

Behind him, the door unlocked.

He turned, fast, but it was a stranger who entered, a thin, officious-looking man in a brown coat and tricorn hat with a sheaf of papers in his hand. He peered at Venn, then at the papers, and put his hat carefully under his arm before speaking.

"You are English, I think."

Venn drew himself up. "Absolutely. I'm not a citizen of Paris. My name is Venn and I insist you release me now."

"Do you? But there is a problem." The official raised a bland face. "We know very well who you are, monsieur. You are a criminal."

"*What!*"

"We are fully aware that this night you entered the house of the Vicomte de Sauvigne and stole the priceless jewel known as the Sauvigne emeralds."

Venn stared, his eyes glacial. "You're mistaken."

"I think not. We have the coachman whose place and livery you took to enter. We have witnesses who place you at the scene. You have been denounced, and are guilty."

"Even you can't believe . . ." He stopped, suddenly seeing where this would lead. "Wait a minute. What do revolutionaries care about theft from a nobleman?"

"Nothing." The man fixed Venn with a calm gray eye. "Those parasites have lived on the blood of the workers of France; now their fate is their own. All you have to do is to tell me where these jewels are, and you will be released at once."

Venn folded his arms. "So greed is still greed, even for principled men like you. But I have to tell you, monsieur, that I don't know where these jewels are. I'm not your thief." He almost felt amused at the thought that he was only too likely to be executed for Moll's daring crime. And then he thought, Will they search me for them?

The official made a note on his paper. "A grave mistake."

"You can't just execute me without a trial."

"You are denounced. The trial is unnecessary. Sentence will be carried out at dawn."

"The guillotine?"

The shrug was silken. "Your time has ended, monsieur."

Venn's laugh was harsh. "Time is the only thing I do have plenty of."

The man stared at him as if he was mad. "You have an hour in which to change your mind. You can be on your way back to your own country before sunrise."

Venn watched the man bow out, then sat, grim.

He knew enough about this period to know that any trial would have been a farce anyway and the result the same. At dawn they would come and take him out, with others, to the Place de la Révolution to be screamed at and jeered by the crowd. The blade would fall; his head would be off. All very simple. And quick.

He pushed his hair back, gazed around the dim cell, and nodded.

He had one hour.

Before they came for him.

⇢⇠

A cart was easy enough to find, but a horse was tricky. The stables were empty—either the horses had already been stolen or had fled the scorch of the flames, and many of the carriages were overturned and burned.

Finally Gideon slipped away into the dark formal gardens, where he stood beside the fountains, listening with his Shee-sharp senses.

The moon was low, a glimmer in the west. He could feel the approach of the sun, could sense it climbing, second by second, up the long ascent to the horizon. Very soon it would be peering over at him with its flaming gaze.

He could also smell the horse. It was close, nickering with fear. He could smell the salt of its sweat.

Carefully, he moved toward it, down the gravel paths strewn with looted clothes, bronzes, food, precious paintings, torn curtains. Scorched paper gusted past him.

Fugitive men and shadowy women flitted by, their arms full.

He found the beast deep in the shrubbery, its trailing harness broken and snagged on a branch. When he spoke to it with the words of the Shee, it stood still, trembling, and allowed him to come close, to touch its damp skin, rub his hand over its long, inquisitive nose.

Gideon smiled.

Animals delighted him.

He gathered up the reins, climbed on a log, and slipped lithely up onto the creature's back, turned its head toward the darkened summerhouse. "Steady now," he whispered. "We need your help. And you'll be away from all this flame and smoke, I promise you."

The horse whickered and shook its mane. He walked it to the summerhouse, where the cart was waiting, the dark figure of the automaton already loaded and covered with a charred cloth. As he jumped down, Sarah came so suddenly out of the air he knew she had been invisible.

"You shouldn't do that!"

"Don't tell me what to do," she snapped. And then, with that swift reversal that was so like Summer, she gave her mirthless laugh. "Even though I know you're right."

Quickly they tethered the horse to the cart and jumped up. Gideon took the reins, though he had no idea what to do with them. Instead he spoke to the horse.

"Take us back to Paris," he said. "Quickly."

Sarah grinned.

But the horse flicked its ears, turned its head, and began to run toward the glow in the eastern sky.

19

The elementals and goblins, the firesnakes that dwell in deep meres, the fish-headed men and the hounds that ride across the moon, these haunt my dremes. These speak in my ear. But I know the words to dismay them.

From The Scrutiny of Secrets by Mortimer Dee

WITH MOLL GRINNING at him through her tangle of hair and Long Tom's blade nudged into his back Jake didn't find it too difficult to look scared and cowed.

The Conciergerie was an ancient, dismal fortress, and it was crammed with prisoners. Through every door and grille faces peered out, hands reached for them, desperate pleas and promises echoed. There must be hundreds. How would he find his father among all these?

Moll had thought of that. She nodded at Tom, who shoved Jake up to the nearest guard and snarled, "Orders. This one goes out in the morning with the doctor's lot."

"Doctor?"

"The citizen whose protests are so loud."

"Ah, him." The jailer shrugged, taking a bite from a chicken leg. "Too late."

Jake's heart gave a leap of terror. It was all he could do not to gasp out the question, but Moll did it for him. "How, too late?"

The man winked at her. "He's been moved, sweetheart."

Jake gave her a mute look. She said, "Moved where?"

"To the cell in the Place de la Révolution, right beside Madame Guillotine herself. To spend the rest of the night hearing the citizens of Paris bay for his blood." He chewed and laughed, shaking his head. "And then at dawn, an appointment with Death himself." The jailer stood, gestured them ahead of him. They turned and walked down a dark and dripping corridor, and he stopped before a low door and took a great ring of keys from his pocket. "We'll put this one in here for now, citizens, and I'll—"

He turned, straight into the hilt of Tom's sword. The blow was swift and brutal; the man went down like a sack of coals.

Jake grabbed the keys from the dust. "Let's go!" He ran backward along the corridor. "We'll let them go! All of them. Create as much chaos as we can."

"Are you crazy?" Moll gasped. She snatched the keys from him. "Get a grip, Jake. Yer dad's not—"

"No, but Venn's here somewhere!"

That stopped her. She swore softly. "Oh hellfire, so he is! Jake, you are such trouble. Next time I *journey,* I'm just going to leave you tucked up in your warm little bed."

But she was grinning, her eyes were bright, and he knew she was loving every second of this, of the exhilaration and the danger.

Quickly she unlocked the nearest door and flung it open. "Out!" she screeched. "Everyone! Run, you dull beggars!"

The crowd of disheveled prisoners, many of them from the masked ball, stared at her in disbelief. Jake saw frizzled hair, wide eyes, painted beauty spots, torn silk dresses. But no Venn.

Then he was racing after Moll, with Tom walking backward, musket steady, keeping guard behind. All down the corridor they unlocked every door; the cells were packed with the vicomte's guests, but Venn was not among them.

As the crowd grew bold, surging out, Moll yelled, "Go with them."

"What?"

"Go with them. Get to this holding cell and get in. Let them capture you if you have to. We'll find Venn."

For a moment, in all that tumult, doubt struck him. He looked at her through the shoving crowd in the dingy corridor. Then Moll reached out and took his arm in her dirty fingers. She shook it softly. "Don't you trust me, Jake?"

"Moll—"

"I'd never let you get hurt, Jake. We're mates. Right?"

He nodded. But something made him say, "I should have come back for you. I'm sorry, Moll."

"That's okay, cully." She smiled, tight. "I forgive you."

He was no longer sure he could forgive himself, not for this flash of doubt. But there was only one way to show her that he trusted her entirely, so he turned and walked, pushing through the crowd of fleeing prisoners, straight toward the outer doors, already crammed with guards and weapons.

Once there, he took one look back.

But Moll and Tom had vanished.

Maskelyne had only one thought and that was to keep the coin from Summer's claws.

He took a step backward.

The owl eyed him. He waited for her to speak, to ripple into another shape, but she did nothing but watch, and for a moment he doubted himself, and wondered if this was really only a normal bird.

Her feathers lifted in the dawn wind.

But all his centuries-old senses tingled with the danger of her, the prickle of the sweet scent of the Shee, and just beyond hearing, their unbearable music.

Behind his back, clutched tight, was the plastic bubble wrap.

The owl opened her wings and flew.

He gasped, ducking. She soared over him, and she was greater than any owl should be, and through her wings the moonlight was fractured; it dazzled his eyes. He stepped back. His footing slipped. And then he was on hands and face, sliding, sliding down, grabbing at tiles, at lichen, at anything, until his feet jarred into the gutter and he hung there, splayed in the pale night.

But the package was still in his hand.

He looked up. With a shriek that made him jerk aside, she dived, and only his speed saved him; he felt the savage beak tear his hand, the warm blood between his fingers. He fought against her, desperate to summon some defense, but in seconds she was back, screaming straight at his eyes.

He yelled, and the gutter gave way; he fell over the edge of the roof and landed with a breathless crack on a lower section.

The wrapped coin bounced out of his hand. He grabbed for it but it was gone, slithering down and rattling over the thick tiles, coming to a stop wedged in the top of an ancient downpipe.

Breathless and sore, Maskelyne lay and stared at it.

She would plummet down in seconds and snatch it.

He stretched after it, his arm reaching to its uttermost limit, straining, his fingers touching the plastic, squirming after it, finally, with huge relief, gripping it.

"Have you got it?" Rebecca was half out of the window, anxious.

"Yes. Get back inside!"

She turned, but it was too late; the shadow over the moon was a ghostly blur. He closed his eyes, searched deep in the broken places of his memory. The words were fragments, he spoke them as if they caused him pain, spat them out as if his lips bled from them.

> Let all the seeds attend me.
> Let all the sepals open.
> Let all the weeds speak.
>
> In swarm and cloud.
> In bright currents of air.
> In the shafts of the sun.
>
> To hide, to cover, make secret,
> To mask, to intervene.
> Let them attend me now.

Turning, he saw the owl against the stars. But also there came out of the air, sudden and drifting in vast airy clouds, the billion, million seeds of summer, white clouds of dandelion fluff and rose bay willow herb, the flung spores of puffball, the crackle of pollen.

The sky was clogged with them; they came down

like unseasonal snow, warm and whirling. He felt them in his hair, against his face, and the sky was blanked out by them, even the ridge of the roof below him was lost.

From somewhere he heard the owl's high-pitched rage, knew she would land, change shape, so, heedless of danger, he let go and slipped down, crashing up against the solid mass of a chimney.

"Maskelyne!"

Rebecca had climbed right out of the window and was balanced on the frail ledge that led to the roof. She was crazy, but he realized he loved her for that. He hesitated barely a moment. Then he yelled, "Catch!"

The package circled through the air. It went high, and for a moment he knew she'd miss it, that Summer would swoop and snatch it away, and fly to the Wood with it in her beak.

Then Rebecca's hand shot out; she caught the package deftly and was already turning, diving down, wriggling in under the sash.

He laughed.

Among the softly falling snow of seed he lay there and laughed and listened to the owl as she rose and circled high above the Wood.

"I'm in!" Rebecca hissed. "Now you."

He caterpillared down the steep roof. Reaching the narrow ledge, he grasped the window and clambered in, slamming it tight. They both slid to the floor of the dusty attic, and sat side by side.

"That was so scary!" she muttered, at last.

He looked at the parcel. "Open it."

Feverishly she tore the bubble wrapping open and the cellophane off. Then she tipped a small gold thing into her palm and held it up.

From the windowsill the wooden bird gave a chirrup of delight. "That's it! Fantastic! You would not believe the trouble I went to over that thing! She kept it in this red box, and there were whole galaxies in there . . ."

They hardly heard.

The gold coin had been cut in half; its edge was jagged and uneven. The profile of the Greek god was sliced away, the surface worn by centuries of long-dead fingers. Rebecca stared at it in awe. Could such a little thing mean so much?

But she had no doubt when she saw the way Maskelyne looked at it. He reached out and she put the piece of gold into his hand, and saw how he held it up and how the moon caught its chipped edge.

"So long ago," he murmured. "So far away."

A great clang silenced him. It came from deep in the house, far below them.

"What was that?" Rebecca said.

They listened for a moment. Then she caught the smallest, slightest whistle of piping. It made her spine shiver.

Maskelyne stood; he crossed instantly to close the door. "Don't listen. We dare not listen to it."

The bird sat in an odd unhappy silence.

And, with a chill of dread, she knew the Shee were inside the house.

➤⋅⋅⧏

"Slow down," Wharton muttered. "I'm getting out of breath."

Piers stopped and looked back. "You're not, actually. It's just that you're not breathing at all."

"Rubbish."

Piers sighed. "Mortal. There is no air on the moon!"

Wharton stood stock-still under the jet-black sky and looked around him. The bare rocky landscape stretched to the horizon—but now that he came to think about it, that horizon was oddly close. There wasn't a single living thing on the plain but himself and Piers. Not far ahead a low wall of rock reared against the stars.

"Why is it night? Surely—"

"It's not night. There's just no atmosphere."

"But if we were on the moon, wouldn't we be bounding around all over the place? Not to mention dead?"

"The Shee invent whole worlds. They don't feel the need to be accurate." Piers turned and plodded on.

As they gained the crest of higher ground Wharton stopped and gasped.

Before him, so huge it filled the sky, the Earth was rising.

"Oh my *God*!" he said.

Of course he had seen all the photos, the images from space probes, the Apollo missions. But this huge, weightless, beautiful bauble of blues and greens and swirls of white—this rare vision—he could barely believe it existed, or that he saw it.

But then . . . this was all the Summerland. So it probably didn't exist at all. And yet, what if down there was a whole other Earth than the one he knew, an alternative Earth imagined by immortal creatures. What unbelievable continents, what crazy cities might be down there!

For a moment the whole concept fascinated him.

Piers said, "They really annoy me. I mean, that's why I went off on my own. They have no idea about *order*." He looked around.

The crater wall was craggy and abrupt; its shadow was ink black.

Wharton giggled, still staring up.

"I suppose this means I'm really the Man in the Moon now. Where's my lantern and my dog . . . was it a dog? And a bush . . . there was a bush . . ."

Piers frowned. He had seen mortals go quite insane when faced with the illogic of the Summerland. All he needed was the big teacher to crack up now.

"Come on," he muttered.

He knew it would be here somewhere.

Wharton dragged himself reluctantly from the glory of the rising planet. "What are we looking for?"

"A hole. A small chink."

Wharton giggled again, but ignoring him, Piers bent and scrabbled in the dust and rock at the crater wall's base. "There's got to be something here."

But it was Wharton who said, "Look at that!"

A point of light, pure and golden and warm. It pierced the pure black of shadow like a keyhole in a door.

"That's it." With considerable satisfaction, Piers rubbed his small fingers together.

"It's a hole. Through to what?"

Piers felt beside it, grasped a knob of rock, and pulled.

With a crack like the opening of an air-lock, a whole rectangle of stone was dragged open, debris dropping from the lintel, a cloud of dust rising to make Wharton cough.

A butterfly gusted through.

Beyond was a green lawn and a pale sky between trees. And deep in the combe, dark as a silhouette, the roofs and turrets of Wintercombe Abbey.

"Brilliant, Piers!" Wharton said, hoarse.

Piers tried to look modest. But it was a complete failure.

20

And sometimes, sewing in the heat by the open windows, I smell the gorse on the moor, and the far-off salt of the tide. And I think what a house of mystery it is, and how in distant rooms there are small footsteps, and comings and goings, and doors left open when no one is there.

Tonight, as every night, I will be sure my bedroom door is locked.

Letter of Lady Mary Venn to her sister

BY THE TIME Jake was marched into the Place de la Révolution between two armed and eager citizens, his coat was torn and he was hot and hungry, and bitterly angry. But all that vanished from his mind as soon as he saw the crowd.

Heat and fury rose from it; a terrible stench of sweat and ordure. The noise it made was totally unlike the voices of people. It was a howling, pounding, raw blood-lust that was more ferocious than anything he had been steeling himself to expect.

It cowed him.

Petrified him.

The men shoved their way through and pushed him

into a small wooden shack, heavily guarded, that had been built up against the walls of a nearby building.

He ducked under the doorway and it was slammed behind him. He stared around.

One flickering lamp guttered in a corner. About twenty prisoners, men, women, and even some children, huddled in misery on rickety benches. Their faces turned to him as one, but their eyes were blank, as if they didn't see him, as if seeing him would be too much of a concession to hope.

Outside, the cries and shouts erupted again, shaking the frail timbers.

"Dad?" Jake whispered.

He moved forward.

The prisoners edged away from him, withdrawing their bedraggled skirts and shoes. He took another step, saw the darkest corner, those that lay there, weeping, sobbing, too terrified even to raise their heads.

And he saw a man, bending over them, talking softly, holding a girl's hand. A man who had somehow gotten water from somewhere, and a clean handkerchief, and was trying to make some hopeless, stupid bandage.

A thin man whose wig was lost and whose hair was dark and whose face was the face Jake dreamed of.

His father.

Jake walked over and crouched in the mud and took the bandage and held it steady.

David looked up.

It wasn't like the other time, in Florence. They didn't hug or cry; his father wasn't half crazy with heat and fever. Instead David grinned with pure relief, and nodded, and slid one arm around Jake's shoulders and squeezed really hard. "You know, I've been hoping you'd drop in, Jake."

Jake's eyes were bright. He said, "This time we're all here. It's okay now."

"Good. Because I have to say I was getting just a touch panicky. Venn always cuts things fine. But before we go, you could just hold her wrist for me."

With a choked laugh Jake held the girl's hand while his father bound the handkerchief around a deep cut. He adjusted the knot delicately and bowed. *"Merci,"* she whispered. And then, "Your son?"

David nodded. "My son."

"I am so sorry, Doctor. So very sorry."

Her distress pierced their aura of safety. Jake scrambled up. "Where's the bracelet?"

"Safe." David drew him discreetly to the corner. "On a chain round my neck."

"Why didn't you use it, before?"

"Too scared. Too worried about going back, and back. And I've never been able to find the mirror. It must be close. But last time I saw you . . . when that man with the scar . . ."

"Maskelyne."

"After he told me about the amber stone, I opened it and found a small coiled fossil . . ."

Jake nodded.

"But I had no mirror. I've searched Paris for it. My guess is it's at Versailles. Louis XVI loved mirrors."

Jake looked around. "And where's Alicia? What happened to her?"

In the darkness a smile of purest delight crossed his father's worn face. "Oh Jake, that old lady! What a character! When we *journeyed* out of the rubble of her house we ended up here, together, about a year ago in this time. She adored it. She set up a salon and had all the noblemen of the city at her séances. Next thing, I heard she'd persuaded one of them—some elderly suitor dripping with money—to marry her and whisk her off to Venice."

"Venice!" Jake loved the thought. Alicia in a lace gown in a gondola on the Grand Canal! He felt again her frail hand among the rubble of a blitzed house. "That's fantastic."

"I've had a letter—she's very happy. Of course she knew what would happen here—we both did. We discussed it—she wanted me to go with them. But I said no. Said I'd wait for you."

He put his arms around Jake. "Because I knew you'd come."

Behind Jake, the door opened. Daylight slanted in. "One more head to roll," a voice snapped.

Another prisoner, tall against the dawn, was shoved inside.

Over Jake's shoulder, David saw Venn.

>+<

Sarah said, "Be very careful with it."

They unloaded the automaton next to a stall selling pies. The stench of grease and meat turned her stomach.

The crowd was wild. Gideon slid down beside her, and they gazed in horror at the bedlam.

A mass of people, eating, drinking, laughing, gambling; a celebration of death, and in the center of it all, dark against the red slash of dawn, the guillotine.

"They think they've won," she whispered.

Gideon's sharp green eyes flicked across the faces in fascination. "And have they?"

Her knowledge was poor. She shrugged. "You'd need to ask Rebecca. But every revolution ends badly, doesn't it? Freedom doesn't last. Freedom is too dangerous. There are always more tyrants. Napoleon. Janus."

A small girl in a ragged dress came and sat crosslegged on the floor at her feet and nodded sagely. "Too bloody right." She glanced up. "Time to strike a blow for common sense, then. You got here fast, Sarah."

Sarah stared. The gloriously dressed creature from the ball was gone—this was an urchin, thin, her face sharp and clever, her eyes lit with a wild enjoyment.

"So did you, Moll," she said quietly. "Where's Jake?"

"Gone to find David." Moll stood. On her wrist was a silver bracelet; they watched as she made the slightest adjustment. "Going to find him now. I'll need him to make a very small *journey* back with me," she said. "Just half an hour. To make a few adjustments. To give Venn a hand."

→→-←←

The scramble through the entangled house was a nightmare.

Maskelyne led the way, the half coin clutched deep in his pocket. Rebecca followed, the tiny bird's talons digging anxiously in her shoulder. They hurried along the attic corridor and forced their way down the twisting servants' stair, but now all the rails were wreathed in honeysuckle and the floorboards had sprouted with flaring red poppies, as if the seed-fall Maskelyne had conjured had infiltrated every cranny and magically grown.

Below them, the house was haunted. The very walls and floors of it seemed to be warping out of alignment, the ceilings sloping, the windows choked up with greenery, slashed with shafts of moonlight. The Long

Gallery was a warm green gloom; roots sprawled across the floorboards.

All around, soft laughter, shifts of movement, the creak of a shutter, the flutter of a butterfly in the corner of her eye, told Rebecca that Wintercombe was part of the Wood now, that already Summer inhabited it completely. Despite the heat, she shivered. Seeds hung in the air; spores were breathed in. Soft rustles drifted through the sprouting leaves. She felt eyes watching her, then heard, closer, the mysterious, enchanting snatch of music she feared, so breathtakingly sweet all she wanted to do was stop and listen to it.

When Maskelyne touched her arm, she had to refocus to see him.

Had she been standing still?

He tugged her on, faster. "Concentrate hard, Becky. Think of the mirror, and the baby. We have to get to them before the Shee do!"

He pulled her down onto hands and knees. "Down there."

The wide room had become a hollow way, a tunnel of brambles. She crawled into it, felt it tug at her hair, snag on her T-shirt. Behind her, Maskelyne breathed harshly. Deep below the floorboards the fairy music mocked.

Soon her palms were sore; splinters cut her. She was sweating, strangely breathless, as if the very air was changing to some primeval, unbreathable steam, and she was scared to breathe it, because the spores would sprout inside her, she would become a woman of flowers.

The boards had softened. She could feel with every touch of her hand that they were bending, rotting, that white threads of tiny mildew threaded them. Fungus clustered in the cracks.

She was terrified to put her weight down.

Maskelyne breathed, "Becky . . ."

"They'll give way."

"No. That's what they want you to think. Get on, Becky, quickly."

"I can't."

He said, his voice husky and dry, "Trust me. We're nearly at the door."

She couldn't see it. She didn't believe in the house anymore. She was an animal in some green tunnel in the Wood and it led nowhere, and she would be crawling through it forever.

Then a thorn stabbed her. She gasped with the pain and saw, just on her left, a crack of darkness.

A cool, misty draft gusted from it.

A cat meowed urgently behind it.

She struggled a hand up toward the lock. As if in retaliation, greenery wreathed her, entwined around her, squeezed the breath from her. It had tendrils tight as hands, pale as lightless fungus. It broke up into bees and wasps. It whipped around her wrists and ankles.

She screamed.

"Hurry, Becky!"

The key was in; she ground it around.

Then she threw her whole weight against the warped wood. It groaned.

And crashed open.

→→←←

Jake turned his head.

David stood silent.

It was Venn who spoke. His voice was cool with his usual careless, icy composure; his eyes blue in the gloom. He said, "I'm sorry I've been so long, David. We've had a few problems. Summer tried to stop me. She very nearly succeeded."

David raised his eyebrows, then said, "You look different, O. Thinner. Paler. But I'm very glad you're here."

Behind him, the guards lined up. "Time to go, milords and ladies," one mocked. "Time to bow your heads to Madame Guillotine."

David said, "*Time*. We have all there is and yet it never seems to be enough." He walked up to Venn. They clasped hands, a brief, warm grip, and Jake saw his father's eyes were damp. Then David stepped back and cleared his throat, and said with elaborate unconcern, "Well, what's the plan? I suppose the mirror is near?"

Jake and Venn shared a glance.

"I mean, there *is* a plan. Right?"

"That depends," Venn said.

"On?"

"A girl," Jake muttered. "Aged fifteen, going on fifty."

"Great! I don't suppose you checked if our names are on some roll of the dead here?"

Venn snorted. "Not if I can help it, they're not." He looked at Jake. "Where *is* Moll?"

"Looking for you. Or so I thought."

Venn breathed out in frustration. But there was no more time to talk. The guards grabbed them and hauled them out; the roar and fury of the crowd exploded around them.

Jake was jostled and shoved. Ragged men and angry women jeered and spat and raged at him; it was a maelstrom of foreign words and raw hatred. He grabbed his father's arm and clung on tight because whatever happened, they wouldn't be separated now. Venn, already ahead, drew much of the crowd's fury because of his height and bearing and because he walked alert, oblivious of their noise, his keen eyes raking the ranks of faces.

Jake searched too. Where was Moll? Sarah? Surely they must be—

Then from up ahead came the sound that had haunted him since he first heard it. The sudden, terrifying *slice* of the descending blade.

He gripped David tight.

His father stumbled.

And as Jake turned to help him, he saw it.

Bizarrely, astonishingly familiar. A stillness in the frenzied crowd. A calm-faced man in Oriental costume, turbaned, sitting in a multicolored booth, a white-plumed pen in its hand.

The Scribe automaton.

He stared around, instantly, for Moll.

Instead he saw Gideon.

The changeling's silvery coat was ragged; he wore a tricolor sash draped over it at a rakish angle and was calling out. "Fortunes! Your fortunes told here! Find what your future holds!"

It wasn't French, but people seemed to understand; a small section of the crowd had gathered there, as if bored with the executions. The stall stood among others, a huddle of pie-sellers, women selling wine, sweetmeats, sausages, chairs, parasols.

Jake glanced around. He couldn't see Sarah. But at least he knew they were not alone.

The group halted. At that moment Gideon saw him,

and yelled, "You! Young monsieur! A last request? Let my masterpiece tell us all your crimes!"

Jake managed one step toward him. The guard's pike flashed sideways.

The Scribe's face was calm, its eyes blue and sharp, fixed on him.

He looked down.

The Scribe's hand moved. It was white and delicate and he knew it was Sarah's. It wrote five careful words on the blank paper.

WHEN THE BELL RINGS BE READY.

Men were already dragging him away, but he had seen. He looked around. Venn had reached the foot of the scaffold. The terrible slice of the blade rang out again. He struggled close to his father.

"It's okay. Something's going to happen."

"Then it had better be quick." David was white with worry.

Even as he spoke, a sonorous clang rang out, urgent even over the tumult of the crowd. It rang again, and Jake knew it was a great bell and behind it was a smell of acrid scorching, a screech of alarm.

Thick and gray, from somewhere unseen, smoke was billowing.

He moved. He shoved the guard aside, punched him hard in the stomach. The man doubled with a gasp, his pike clattering to the floor. Jake dived for it, but a sword was shoved in his hand; Gideon was beside him with a pistol. "Let's go! Hurry!"

"Dad." He wasn't leaving without him. But Moll was tugging his other arm; she had come from nowhere.

"I'll get him, Jake. No worries."

Before he could answer, she had darted into the panicking crowd. Gideon slashed the sword; the crowd scattered and he dragged Jake through, but Jake dug his heels in and turned.

"No!"

"She's got him! Look."

It was true. Suddenly his father was there, breathless, Moll pointing a pistol in the face of anyone who even looked at her.

"What about Venn?" Sarah had squirmed out. Now she stared around. "Where is he?"

"We need to sort that," Moll said. Venn was already at the scaffold.

"No!" Sarah shoved past Jake, into the crowd.

"Sarah!"

"Get to safety! Get to the mirror!"

He wanted to grab her. But in seconds, she was lost to sight.

Moll adjusted the bracelet and grabbed his hand. "No time now, Jake. We need to go and find some time. Come on."

Venn sensed the commotion, heard the clang of the bell. He turned at once with lithe speed, but two guards already had him; they hauled him up the steps and threw him onto his knees. The wooden platform was a bloody mess in front of him, red with the stench of horror.

He wanted to twist around and look up, but they held him down and he knew that only seconds of time were left to him.

He wanted to smile, but his mouth could only twist in bitter anger.

He wanted to say something memorable, but *"Leah"* was all he could whisper.

$$\rightarrow\!\!\leftarrow$$

Moll and Jake materialized in a dark space still loud with the muffled yell of the crowd, as if they hadn't *journeyed* at all, and he gasped, "Moll!"

"Only ten minutes back, Jake. That's all. We're under the guillotine. Look there."

He glanced up. Over his head was a bolted trapdoor.

"Give us a bunk," she hissed. Before he could move she was on his back, reaching up, working the rusted bolt with vigor, trying to force it back.

"Hurry!"

"I am! But it's stiff."

Suddenly a man ducked under the timbers and saw them. He opened his mouth to yell but Jake moved first.

Dropping Moll, he had his sword out with one swift slash. The guard raised his own weapon. The steel met.

Dimly aware of Moll climbing hurriedly back up, Jake circled with the wary instinct of a fencer. But when the attack came it was ferocious and fierce; he fought calmly, coldly, every nerve tense, but this was a real fight, not some practice in the gym, and a stray whip of his opponent's blade stroked blood from his wrist with terrifying speed.

Sweat stung his eyes. He thrust, parried quarte, thrust again, ducked. The man crashed against him, grabbed at the hilt; Jake shoved him away, and they both toppled, awkward and locked together, back against the wooden frame, hitting it with a thud so hard that the whole structure shuddered.

Jake felt pain shoot down his back; then he was on his feet, looking down at the man's body.

The guard didn't move.

Moll leaped down. "Killed him, Jake?" She bent quickly. "Nope. He's just a bit stunned." She grinned up at him. "Nice one, cully. And the bolt's loose. Let's go."

She caught his arm and touched the bracelet in that odd way and they were back in the shouting crowd and his father's arm was on his as if that sudden and bewildering interlude of fear had never happened.

But there was a stinging cut on his wrist. And a

puzzling, odd question ringing in his mind, that he couldn't quite grasp. He looked up.

No time to think about that now.

Venn was under the guillotine.

→··←

Trapped by the press of bodies, Sarah yelled, fought, kicked her way to the foot of the scaffold.

"Venn!" she screamed. Behind her Jake's voice rang somewhere in the din. The dripping blade was hauled up.

She stood still. The crowd went quiet.

She forgot to breathe, forgot to pray as the blade jerked, rattled.

And dropped.

My love . . .
melted as the snow, seems to me now
as the remembrance of an idle gaud
which in my childhood I did dote upon . . .

21

And behold this is a mechanism to deprive death
of its guilt. No man's hand is blooded. The killing is
perform'd by earth's own power, and time's workings,
relentless and implacable. We are not to blame. We
cannot stop them even if we would.

Maxim Chevalin,
A History of the Late Revolution in France

VENN'S DREAM WAS the last of all the dreams, and
what else could it be but a dream?

Because above him the blade of the guillotine stopped.

Not with a shudder, or a jerk, or as if something had
jammed in it, but impossibly. In mid-slice.

He twisted around, stared up at the red, honed edge;
then, with his body's visceral terror tingling to a new
alertness, he leaped back, pulled his head and shoulders out, and stood up.

Time had paused. That was his first thought. Time
had somehow stopped, and the blade of the guillotine
was held still, and all the crowd with it. In an eerie
silence he looked down at them, and they were frozen
in an instant of blood-lust and fury. It was a terrible

sight. Their faces were contorted, their fists clenched. A woman's mouth was wide in mid-scream, a man was leaping up, both feet off the ground.

Venn stared around. He was the only thing here that moved. Birds hung in flight. A cloud half blurring the sun did not even make the slightest drift of shadow.

He rubbed a weary hand over his face. Then he walked to the edge of the filthy platform. There was Sarah, her face caught in terror, her arm flung out toward him.

Beyond, half lost in the still people, he could see David, twisting aside. Gideon was there with them, and a whole host of fairground sideshows and food stalls, stopped in mid-sizzle, the sausage flipped from the pan, the playing cards half rippled.

There was total silence.

It was the silence that scared him most.

Wanting to fill it with anything, he raged, "Summer! Is this your doing?"

No one answered. But somewhere out there, in that mass of bodies that hung and balanced at impossible angles, something glinted.

Tiny. Brief.

The flicker of sunlight on a shiny surface.

He held his breath, stared out. Every eye was on him, but none of them could see him anymore; as he scrambled away from the bloody blade, no gaze followed him. They were living, but lifeless, and for a moment he thought of them as a great mass of waxworks, as if the time-stop had changed them from humans to a tangle of beings neither dead nor alive.

Again. *A tiny sparkle.*

Venn took a step to the rail. "Who are you? Who's out there?"

His voice was harsh with fear. He made himself stand firm, surveying the crowd one by one, face by hideous face.

Was he trapped in some timeless world forever, alone? Was there really anyone else here but him?

Then, unmistakably, he saw the light move. It reflected from a pair of round blue spectacles, covering the eyes of a man in the crowd. A man not frozen in some off-guard pose. A man standing casually, calm and interested, his arms folded, gazing up at Venn.

A man who was breathing.

Almost with relief, Venn's voice went steely. "So it's you."

For a moment Janus did not answer. Then he nodded, and that movement was a shock in this timeless place. "Who else?"

Venn was suddenly furious. "How can you stop time! How the hell can you do that?"

Janus shrugged. He began to move carefully through the crowd, edging between the rigid bodies, ducking under the stiff punched fists. "I doubt that's what annoys you, Venn," he said softly.

"What?"

"What annoys you is that by stopping time I have saved your life." Janus reached the steps to the platform and climbed the first of them. He stood there, a small man in a gray uniform, leaning on the rail and gazing up. Venn caught the flash of the sun on the lenses that hid the man's eyes.

"And that must be so difficult for you." Janus nodded, as if to himself. "Oberon Venn would probably have found it more heroic to go fearlessly to the guillotine than be saved by his enemy."

Venn folded his arms. "If you think that, you don't know me."

Janus smiled. And in his lapel, tucked in safely, Venn saw the purple flower.

He tried not to show by the least tightening of a muscle what it meant, but Janus smiled as if he had noticed. "Actually," he said, "I just wanted to talk. I did try to come through to your Abbey, but . . ."

"I kept you out."

"With such unnecessary dramatics. Besides, it was Maskelyne who barred my way." He tapped a finger thoughtfully on the wooden rail. "What do you know about our friend with the scar, Venn? Very little, I expect."

Venn frowned. That was true enough.

"For instance, did you know that he is a being who has lived many lifetimes? Beware of him. He worked with me, or will work with me, far in the future. Beware of the scarred man, Venn. He's there now, in your house, with the mirror, which is all he cares about. Can you trust him?"

"More than you," Venn growled. "What do you want?"

This time Janus laughed. "We want the same thing, you and I. The safety of the mirror."

Venn's eyes narrowed. "There's no way we're the same."

"I think so." Janus glanced over at Sarah, frozen in her fear. "And that girl . . . look, that escaped invisible girl of mine, she's the one who is our enemy."

"No."

"Yes." The tyrant's voice was soft. "I need what she has, Venn."

"Which is?"

"The coin."

"The half coin? *Sarah's got it?*"

"She stole it from Summer. Didn't you know? The right side of the broken face of Zeus. Stole it and has been hiding it in your very house. What a treachery that is. Don't you think so? How it must upset you, to know that."

They looked at each other for a moment, a moment open with strange possibilities.

Then Janus said, "We'll make an agreement here and now. I allow you to escape death. I allow you to complete your work, to rescue your beloved Leah. In return, when you have finished, you give me the broken coin."

Venn stood still. His voice was flint hard. He said, "You really want it, don't you. *Anyone would think you know where the other half is.*"

A flicker of alarm passed over Janus's face like a ripple over the mirror, but Venn saw it, and it was more than alarm. It was fear. As if he had guessed right.

Fierce joy filled him, revenge warmed him. He snapped, "I don't make agreements with tyrants."

Janus said nothing, but took the flower from his buttonhole. He twirled it in his fingers, the purple petals held in their undying beauty. "I was afraid you might say that. But you must remember that I still have this. Just imagine, Venn, if after your unfortunate death under the guillotine Summer and I should become allies. Imagine that!"

He didn't want to. "Summer is no one's ally."

Janus shrugged, turned, began to descend. "Well, we'll see about that, shall we?"

Venn leaped after him, but even as he touched the ground a peculiar shiver moved among the still bodies as if a flame had run along a trail of gunpowder. Behind the crowd a creature like a wolf rose up, its pelt flame-red. It growled, alert, its eyes watching him, dark as coals.

Janus said, "Get the broken coin for me. In return I give your life. Agreed?"

Venn was silent.

He could say yes and then break his word. If he had Leah, what would he care anymore about the mirror? But he had promised Sarah she could do what she wanted with it. And besides, he loathed this small, sly man who seemed to hold all of the future in his hands. Centuries of Venn arrogance rose up inside him. He raised his head and stared Janus down. *"I told you. I don't make agreements with tyrants."*

Janus stepped onto the blood-soaked ground and sighed.

"I have to say I expected it. You are a very tiresome, and if I may say, ungrateful man. Good-bye, Venn."

He lifted his hand.

→⦁←

Time jumped back.

The crowd exploded into screaming bedlam.

Before Venn had time to know he was back under the blade, it slammed down.

→⦁←

"Okay. So what's the plan? Do we storm the house?"

"You tell me. You're the sergeant major, mortal."

Wharton frowned. It was true he had done ten years as an NCO, but in all that time he had never had to face an enemy as wispy and unpredictable as the Shee.

"Anyway," Piers muttered, "just crashing in is too dangerous. It looks like the whole crazy Host is flitting around in there."

They lay flat in the long grass of the overgrown lawn, watching the building.

Wintercombe Abbey was a riot of music and dance. Every window blazed light. Every door was wide. Inside, the Shee-songs echoed, far and sad and strange. Lights shimmered, purple and blue and green, glimpsed in tantalizing fragments through the smothered windows.

To Wharton the whole shape of the building had been lost; it was part of the Wood now, a green branching structure of leaves and moonlight.

"Maskelyne and Rebecca will be holding out," he said

"Oh, let's hope so." Piers sounded worried. "Because that lot must have crawled and flitted everywhere. Kitchens, corridors, cellars. The whole place is infested."

Wharton let his eyes range across the dark ridges of roof and chimney, turret and towers. For a moment he thought he saw movement up there on the east wing, but then a cloud of bats rose in a silent swirl and he pulled a face and said, "Okay. Points of entry. Cloister door?"

"You must be joking!"

"Up the ivy into the attic."

"No chance."

"West wing coal chute."

"If you want them to shovel you onto the fire." Piers's voice was gloomy in the dimness.

Wharton twisted to look at him, irritated. "Look, you know this place. You're the goblin in the bloody cottage. Give me some help here!"

Piers sighed. He twisted over and lay flat on his back, staring up at the stars. Finally he said, "There's only one way you can get in and that's down the river."

"The Wintercombe?"

"Where else? It's running water. They hate running water. Get in it and swim down the ravine, and you'll end up in the gorge below the Monk's Walk. Then it's a question of climbing up the cliff, and squeezing in through the old windows—only a few have any glass left in them."

Wharton blew out his cheeks in dismay.

Piers grinned up at him. "Too much for a clapped-out old squaddy?"

Wharton thought maybe it was. But there was no way he'd say that to this little mocking creature. He shrugged. "Walk in the park, Piers. Walk in the bloody park."

Moll's diary.

Of course I knew the old sod was never up to it.

I'd got him the bracelet and there was the mirror, but Lord what a palaver and a mess he made of it. Everything so careful, so scaredy-cat. And me with this plan growing in me like the beanstalk in the story; because he couldn't see what you could do.

"Get rich JHS!" I told him. "You could be lord of the whole universe with this!"

But he never had the guts.

So, finally, yes, okay Jake, I nicked the bracelet and went off with it. Betrayed him. I felt a bit bad about that, so after the first job we pulled, I sent a wad of dosh.

Never thought he'd do anything so stupid, though.

When I heard about the explosion I went straight round there. Great scorch marks down the walls.

Sad really.

House was all locked up, but easy as pie to get into, and there it was. The obsidian mirror. Leaning all cool and arrogant against the burnt wallpaper, among all that black charred mess.

I knew then the old fool had journeyed without the bracelet.

Idiot.

So, anyway, that was the start of it, Jake. We borrowed the mirror. Couldn't leave it there, could we? Took it out at night in a hansom cab. And so I commenced my life of crime, and what a mad bit of fun it's been, and all them jewels I've had away and the times I've seen, Lord, Jake, you wouldn't believe.

But I was always really looking out.

For you, Jake.

And when I saw David, I knew it was time to come and get you.

22

I have had some experience of life. I believe myself fully capable of offering an excellent example to the boys of a sound moral outlook and the importance of hard work.

George Wharton, letter of application to Compton's School

SARAH STARED.

In the blink of an eye, Venn disappeared.

Then, before she could move he was back, the blade already falling, the crowd screaming with joy.

She screamed too.

But a trapdoor burst open under Venn's feet; he crashed down and the blade sliced only air.

The scaffold shuddered. The crowd surged back.

Sarah stood stunned, unable to believe what she'd seen, but the next moment Venn had picked himself up, scrambled out, and was right there next to her, grabbing her arm. "Run! Let's go!"

They hurtled through the packed people. She yelled "Jake!" and saw him ahead, waving her on. With a great rattle of wheels, a dark carriage drove around the corner of a building and thundered toward them, the horses whipped to fury.

Women scattered with screams of panic.

Long Tom hauled on the reins; the doors flew open.

Moll was already leaping up onto the box beside him. "In!" she screamed. "Everyone!"

Jake pushed David on; his father flung out a hand and held the door and hauled himself up. Jake scrambled after, but before Gideon could follow, the crowd had grabbed him and torn him down; they fell on him. For a sickening moment all Jake saw was his pale face lost in a sea of hands.

Suddenly, Venn and Sarah were there. Venn snatched a sword and swung it at the flinching men. "Get back!"

Jake jumped down; Gideon scrambled up. They turned to face the mob.

The three of them stood at bay, all in a line, while behind, Sarah clung in the doorway.

"God," Venn muttered, seething with fury. "I'd like to take the whole lot of them on right now."

For a wild moment Jake was totally with him.

Gideon said, "It would be so much like . . . being alive—"

But Moll's voice cut like acid through their ardour. "Nice heroics, cullies, but no time. Get in or we go without you!"

The horses reared. Jake turned, and Venn and Gideon crashed on top of him. Then the carriage was galloping at speed, and someone was picking Jake up and he realized he was on the worn leather bench with someone's arm thrown casually around his shoulders, and it was his father's arm. And all he wanted to do was shout and scream and stamp for joy.

Instead he leaned back while Venn picked himself up and Sarah smiled and Gideon dusted down his silver coat and watched with green envious eyes.

"Well," David said calmly. "If that's a plan, I'd like to see what chaos is."

→⤝←

"Will you take it easy!" Wharton slid down the remaining mud of the bank and fetched up against a dark granite boulder. "I'm nearly there."

Piers was braced above, a white face against the moonlight. "Okay. Letting go now."

"No! Wait! I'm not— *Piers!*" But Wharton was already slithering, the moon-pale rope dissolving around his waist back into the cobwebs Piers had made it from, and feet-first, he cascaded over the steep bank and plunged deep into the roaring black water.

God, it was icy!

Hitting the bottom with his feet, he crumpled, pushed, rose in a cloud of silt, and burst back to the surface as a frozen man, white and gasping.

A boulder rose up; he slammed against it.

"Piers!"

Water took his words, swallowed them, spat them out. He fought to keep his head above the surging current, but the river was incredibly fast; it crashed him against rocks, ducked him, battered him, sucked him down. In the deepest dark he was so cold he was warm, and for a moment was back in the summery wood lying on the green grass in the sun.

Then he was drowning deep in the green leaves of a van Gogh painting, which seemed, oddly enough, to be growing on an elder bush in the ravine. He spat and coughed until Piers said in his ear, "Time to climb up now."

He opened his eyes. He was clinging desperately to a barren cliff, and beside him on the rock a warty green toad was watching with emerald eyes.

He looked up. "My God!" he breathed.

Wintercombe Abbey soared above like a gothic nightmare. Bats showered from it; the moon balanced on its topmost turret. It was black and smooth as the mirror. He could never climb up there.

He gave orders, but his body refused to obey. Instead it clung obstinate and shivering to the bank.

He took a breath; it was a knife in his throat.

"Scared, mortal?" The words were a sly croak in his ear. "I'm not surprised. The Shee always say the big men are the ones who crack first."

Wharton growled. He reached out, grabbed a rock. Hauled himself up onto it.

The toad hopped onto his shoulder. "See you up top. I'll have the kettle on."

A wet flop of tiny hands on his head. He roared with fury and pulled himself out of the river.

Immediately the warmth of the summer night enfolded him. He sighed with relief, water running from his clothes, trickling and dripping. Then he was climbing, hands and feet splayed against the rock face, and the surface was dry and crumbly in places, and in others clotted with great cushions of plump emerald moss.

He was halfway up when he felt something.

A dread in his nerves and muscles. A gathering of darkness.

He risked a quick look at the sky.

Were they birds or bats? Hard to tell. They were rising in a great spiral from the towers of Wintercombe, and whatever their shape, he knew they were Shee.

"Piers!" he whispered. "Piers, look."

No reply. He cursed silently, intently.

Then he climbed faster.

But the row of windows of the Monk's Walk was far above when the cloud dissolved, and came down around him like black rain. Not birds but things shaped like the grotesque gargoyles of the house; crazy patchwork creatures of bat-wing and gryphon-beak and mermaid-tail and human eyes. They perched on the rocks and slithered onto the slanted slabs of the cliff-face, and in the roar of the waters they sat and looked at him, and all their eyes were hollows of silver, and all their claws as sharp as the pain in his bruised fingers.

He scowled, grabbed for the next rock. Instead his fingers closed around a small, white bare foot.

The owner of it giggled. "Oh, George. You're so bold."

Summer was sitting on the narrowest ledge that slanted down the rock. Her short dark hair glinted; she wore earrings of pearl and a moon pale dress with lacy craters.

He snatched his hand back and hung there, fingers aching, splayed feet jammed in footholds.

She said, "I just thought I'd come and have a chat—"

"*Chat!* For God's sake, Summer I'm clinging for my life here."

"About my proposal, George! About giving you another chance at life. Remember that? All the things you thought you might do?"

He did remember and for a moment it was all he wanted, to be anywhere away from this crumbling cliff whose fragments were plopping into the river far below.

She smoothed the dress over her bare knees. "If you

want I can get my people to lift you, George. Take your clothes in their beaks and lift you up and fly with you to the roof, where you'd be safe. Then I'd wait while you popped in and got me the coin."

"Coin?"

"Don't pretend you don't know. That girl Sarah has it."

He stared. And then laughed.

It surprised even himself—it was a laugh of finality, exasperation, of real amusement.

Summer frowned. "Don't do that."

His foot slid; he scraped it back up quickly. Then he said, "Okay, Summer. Here it is. *I am never going into partnership with you.* I don't want the mirror destroyed but I'd rather trust Sarah than you. I'd never betray Jake. Ever. And certainly I've made plenty of mistakes in my worthless life, but they were *my* mistakes and if I had another existence I would almost certainly make them all over again. So any fantasy you have that you can win me over ends here. Sorry."

He knew she would cast him down. But that was all right.

He had said what he needed to say.

She was so silent he raised fearful eyes to look at her.

But all that looked back at him were the cold yellow eyes of a hawk, and they were embedded in her human face, and she shrieked, a sound so harsh and dark that all the stars seemed to tingle with terror of it.

And then she pointed one red-painted nail at him, and he let go.

And fell.

And fell.

And fell.

→·←

The carriage rattled through the dark alleys of Paris toward the Seine.

The five passengers had been silent a long time. It was as if the turmoil they had gone through had cleaned them out, used up all their energies, drained them of speech. Except for Moll, who could be heard boasting to Long Tom outside on the box about her *journey* back to save Venn. "A few tools, a few minutes. Bolt off the trapdoor, Bob's your uncle."

They heard Tom laugh. "Neat as a pin, Moll. They don't call you Contessa for nothing."

Finally Sarah raised her head and fixed Venn with a hard stare.

"What else happened back there?" she demanded.

The others watched as Venn rubbed a hand down his face. He looked gaunt and worn, and that peculiar glint of the Shee that had entered him over the last few months was suddenly more apparent than before.

"Happened?"

"The blade fell. I saw it. The blade fell and you were under it." She closed her eyes, remembering the great horror that had swamped her. "And then . . . *You were gone*. For a second. Then you were back there."

Venn looked at her, his stare arctic. "You imagined it. You blinked."

"*I felt it*. A shudder in time."

Jake listened, intent.

Sarah leaned forward. "And that means one of two things to me, and both of them bad. Either Summer intervened. Or Janus did."

The coach rattled, slower now; it turned a corner, and the stench of the river grew strong.

Jake said, "Summer wouldn't—"

"Neither would Janus." Venn's eyes were steady on Sarah's. "And if . . . *if* . . . they did. If they offered me all the world in return for the safety of the mirror, do you think I'd take it, Sarah?"

For a long time she did not answer. When she did her voice was a whisper, "No."

He smiled a wintry smile. "Correct."

David leaned forward. "Of course you wouldn't. All you want is Leah."

Gideon raised an eyebrow, looked at Jake.

"What?" David said. "What have I missed?"

Venn looked down. "Like I told you, Summer distracted me, David. She . . . enticed me away. You don't know what it's been like. But I swear"—he looked up, sharp—"that that's over. Forever."

David looked dismayed. He said, "It has to be, O, it has to be now."

Jake looked at Sarah, and Gideon. Neither of them seemed happy, or sure they believed Venn's vow.

In an uneasy silence, the carriage wheels bumped over cobbles and finally stopped, and the door opened and there was Moll, grinning at them all.

"Back home safe and sound! And not a hair chopped off anyone's head! I told you I could do it, Jake, didn't I? Aren't you pleased, Jake?"

He was so pleased he jumped out and caught her up and swung her around as if she was still that tiny urchin he had known, and she screeched and grinned with delight.

Dawn was a red slash of light over the housetops. Below the piles of the wharf, the dark river glimmered with reflected fires. Paris slept an exhausted sleep.

When they had all climbed down, Tom muttered "See you, Moll," and drove the carriage quietly away into the dark.

"Where's he going?"

"To collect the gang. We have to get everyone back." Suddenly her grin was gone; she turned and led the way inside. "Come on, quick now."

The long room above the river was dim; the fire had died during the night and only a few dull ashes lay in the hearth. Without another word Moll crossed the dusty floor and twitched the cover from the mirror. And as soon as he saw his own dim face in it, Jake knew what was puzzling him.

"At last!" David almost ran to it. "I've searched for this so hard! Where . . . how did you find it?"

Moll shrugged. "Research. Saw a drawing in one of the books on Versailles. Room full of mirrors, hundreds of them. And this one among them, bold as brass. As if it was staring out at me saying *Here I am. Come and find me.* So we came. Brought it here before the palace got trashed. Those crazy citizens out there can make a hell of a mess."

David put his hand out and touched the mirror.

The obsidian glass gave a small ripple, barely seen.

"It recognizes you," Jake breathed.

"Not him. The bracelet," Gideon muttered.

David nodded. He reached into his dirty lace coat and pulled out the bracelet he had carried for so long on a silver chain, then slipped in onto his wrist and clicked it shut.

Venn lifted his own arm and the two snakes stared at each other. "First time together since we messed up the experiment," David muttered. "So long ago." Then, as if it took all his summoned courage to ask the question, he looked at Venn. "Exactly how long since I've been gone, O?"

It was Jake who answered. "One year, ten months, nine days."

"My God. Is that all?"

"All? It was forever!"

Fear was back in his father's eyes. "Yes, but don't you see, Jake? For me . . . here and in Florence . . . it's been longer. Maybe three, four years. I'm years older than I should be. When I go back . . . will I have lost time, or gained it?"

For a moment they all shared the puzzling impossibility of it.

It was Gideon who broke the spell. "It doesn't matter now. We need to hurry," he said uneasily. "Who knows what the Shee are doing back there."

"Right." Venn turned, purposeful. "Sarah, take my hand. You too, Gideon. We *journey* together. Jake and David, all of us, linked in one line. With the two bracelets it should be possible. And we go directly into the mirror."

He adjusted the controls carefully on each of the bracelets, synchronizing them, and showed David the small ammonite in the top of the silver frame.

"Amazing," David muttered.

Venn nodded, and turned to the mirror. "Can you hear us, Piers? Maskelyne? Can anyone hear?"

Next to him, Sarah watched.

The darkness of the mirror altered. Something drifted in its depths, like a dark leaf falling from a branch. For some reason it sent a dread through her. She stepped closer, staring hard, but only her own face, pale and tired and strangely thin, stared back at her. And then Jake said, "What the hell is that?" and she realized that the mirror was no longer black.

It was green.

A deep gloom, as if it reflected the very depths of the Wood.

Venn swore a bitter oath. "The Shee are in the Abbey."

She saw that there were tendrils of ivy over the surface of the glass; that a great tree root had splintered the floor beside it.

"Where's Maskelyne? And Rebecca?"

Venn's face was dark, and she wondered if he had feared this all along. "That's a good question." He turned. "We go. Now!"

Without waiting for an answer he grabbed Sarah's hand, and she quickly caught up Gideon's. Jake held on tight to his father. Then he turned and held out a hand to Moll.

"Coming?" he said.

She shrugged, tugging the red cap from her curly hair and tossing it down. "Might as well. Already missed the last omnibus, Jake."

He gripped her small dirty fingers.

"Here goes," David muttered, nervous. Jake held him tight.

They walked forward.

And all around them, the mirror exploded into vacuum.

23

When the Wood shall enfold the World, then there shall be wonders told.

There shall be dreams and diamonds.

There shall be a kiss through the smallest chink of time.

From The Scrutiny of Secrets *by Mortimer Dee*

REBECCA RAISED HER head wearily and said, "Light. At last."

Outside, beyond the green gloom of the Wood, they saw the light of dawn.

Everywhere on turrets and branches and boughs, the birds of Wintercombe burst into song.

The shortest night was ending, the sun was rising. She longed for it, and yet in a way she was dreading it too, because this would be Midsummer Day, and the scorching heat of summer would crisp the leaves of the gorse and the bracken, and it would be the day of her greatest power.

"Can't you do anything at all?"

"I've tried." Maskelyne dragged leaves from his dark hair. He looked angry, bitter with defeat. "Believe me.

But even I can't challenge the power of the Shee on this day."

They had crawled and wormed their way along the Monk's Walk until they could get no farther. Now, sitting exhausted against the cool wall under the windows Rebecca peered ahead into dimness. The lab where the mirror leaned was inaccessible; a sheer mass of bramble had sprouted into a dark portcullis completely blocking the passageway.

They had no way of knowing how things were beyond, and she was worried about Lorenzo, but certainly the cats were still there. Even as Rebecca looked now she saw a black paw emerge from the brambles, and then, flattened almost to the floor, a small head with green eyes looking at them.

The cat mewed urgently.

"What does it say?" she hissed.

Maskelyne looked at it gloomily. "I have no idea."

"Piers would know."

"I'm not Piers." But he was listening, intently. Then he said, "I think I can hear the baby crying."

She shook her head in despair, imagining the cradle wreathed in leaves, the Shee with their long fingers bending over Lorenzo in fascination. *"What if they take him!* We need to get through!"

Remembering, she snatched the small wooden bird from her pocket. "You! You might get through."

"No way!" The creature opened its eyes wide. "Are you crazy? This place is infested. If even one of them lays eyes on me . . ."

Even as it spoke it gave a cheep of terror and fled back in.

Maskelyne knelt, alert.

Something had jumped in the dimness of the stone corridor. Then it was on the sill; a small wet toad with pimpled skin.

It flicked a long tongue out, caught a fly and ate it. And quite suddenly became a small man in a rapidly changing series of clothes—doublet, dark suit with top hat, red waistcoat, and finally lab coat, as if he had rippled through an imaginary wardrobe and selected the right outfit. His gold earring glinted in the coming light.

"Piers, for God's sake!" Rebecca leaped up. "Where have you *been* so long! Where's George?"

"Down below." Piers scratched his skin, which still had too many warts, irritably. "Take a look."

She leaned out of the pointed window, and saw the rocks clustered with watching Shee, Summer in a dress as white as a swan, a man hanging desperately on the most precarious of handholds.

She put her hand to her mouth.

And screamed as he fell.

Wharton heard her. He thought it was his own terror, the scream that was torn from him, or the screech of the faery queen's laughter. Then all the breath went out of him as he hit the rock face and slid and grabbed and slid.

Blood oozed on his fingers; winded, he blinked grit from his eyes.

He yelled and swore and slipped again.

He couldn't see, daren't look up or down because the Shee would cluster on him now like flies on a carcass.

He was finished.

"George!" The cry was Rebecca's; it rang oddly in the crannies of the cavern. He rubbed his stinging eyes on his sleeve. Was he even the right way up? Was his neck broken? He had no idea.

Something hit him with a smack on the shoulder. He grabbed it like a lifeline, hauled himself around, and then he was climbing, faster than he had thought he could ever climb again, knees tight, ankles locked, hands gripping the rope, and it was a strange spell-rope too, all made of bines and bramble, but he had no time to think of that, because around him the Shee hung and laughed and watched, butterfly-bright.

Where was Summer?

He reached the window. Hands grabbed him; he was hauled roughly in and at once crashed to the stone floor with a moan of relief.

"Where is she?" Maskelyne hissed.

Rebecca was leaning out, looking up. "There."

On the topmost gable of the house a white bird perched. A swan? Long-necked, elegant, it watched them with dark, careless eyes, and then, as the red glimmer of dawn touched it, it rose up and opened its wings wide.

The feathers were tipped with crimson, like blood.

Wharton pulled his head back in and looked at the clogged corridor. "What do we do now?"

Rebecca considered the tangle of brambles, and turned to Piers. "We need to be small, Piers. Really, really small. Can you do that?"

Piers flexed his fingers. "Here we go again. Ready?"

And then something happened that she had no words for, and when it was over had no idea if it had really happened. Because how could the brambles have become so enormous, and the gaps between them suddenly so wide? How could she have been running like that, flat and fleet, and how could her heart have pounded and her eyesight been so sharp and the colors all lost? How could fear become a creature so huge, with green eyes and whiskers, a thing that picked her up with a velvet mouth, and carried her, shaking her, dumping her, flattened, under one paw?

". . . hear what I said, Primo! Let her go right now!"

The cat leaped back, mewing with sulky venom.

Breathless, she was sprawled face-down on the lab floor, and Wharton was helping her up. "Are you okay? Bloody cat! That could have been so . . . nasty."

She caught her breath. "Did we just . . . ? I mean, was that really—"

"Best not to ask." He turned, quickly. "At least we're in."

Indeed, they were in the lab, and it was untouched by the spell of the Wood. In fact, the tendrils of ivy and branches turned back sharply at the door as if at some solid invisible barrier, and she saw one or two cool-eyed and silver-haired Shee beyond, staring in with calm curiosity, as if Maskelyne had guarded the mirror with every spell he knew.

Pushing past Piers, she hurried to the cradle.

Lorenzo was awake, eyes wide and dark, but lying quietly. Hugging him with loving abandon was the marmoset, Horatio, his tail wrapped cozily around the baby's feet.

"Look at that!" she breathed.

Maskelyne said, "Becky. Come quick."

The mirror shivered. The malachite webbing tensed. The air hummed with a rising frequency.

"They're coming back!" Wharton was already there, eager. "Jake's coming back. Thank God!"

The mirror opened.

So dark, so far and deep was its vacuum, they felt all the world would be sucked into it.

And then, without another movement, there they were—Venn and Sarah and Gideon, standing in the room, and with them came a strange smell, a flicker of alien light, and it made Rebecca think of the one time she had *journeyed,* and the terrible heat and stench of Florence, and the wonder of that past world.

Venn took one look at the green gloom in the corridor and said, "I knew it."

Gideon whistled. "They've been busy. The place is overrun!"

But the others were silent. It was Sarah who turned and stared and turned again. And then said, "Where's Jake? And David?"

→·←

In fact Jake was standing in a street.

For a moment he felt no emotion but surprise, and then a dreadful fear crawled through him, until he knew his father's hand was tight on his and nothing else mattered.

David swore. "Oh no. Surely not again . . ."

Jake saw that Moll was there, but not the others. And he knew this street. He had seen it in Victorian times, when John Harcourt Symmes had lived here, and he had seen it bombed into oblivion when

Symmes's daughter, Alicia, had gripped his hand from under its rubble.

But today it was just a quiet, moonlit London square, its trees shadowy, its chimneys silver, its cobbles wet from a recent shower of rain.

David breathed out. "Moll," he said. "What have you done?"

"It's not another kidnap, cullies. Just a little detour," she said breezily. "Just want to show you the old gaffe, Jake. Won't take a sec."

She ran across the road.

"What's she up to?" David whispered.

"You really never know." Jake went to follow, then saw her suddenly step back into the shadow of a lamppost and wave them into stillness. A sturdy policeman was plodding down the pavement, rattling the area gates and closing any that were open, humming tunelessly under his breath.

What year was this? Jake guessed, by the clop of distant carriages and the dim advertisements, that it was possibly only a few months before Alicia would come to claim her inheritance.

When the man had turned the corner, they flitted noiselessly across and up the three steps to Symmes's front door.

Moll took out a key and slid it into the lock, turning it quickly.

Inside, the hall was dark; she lit the gaslamp and turned up the flame until it was steady and they saw the dim tiled hall and the stairs.

"Good Lord." David looked around fondly. "Never thought I'd get to see this house again. I was here with Symmes, Jake, for at least a year, working on the mirror."

"Yes. I know." Nagged by a growing unease, Jake was watching Moll. She grinned, and slipped her cold hand in his. "Come on."

The rooms downstairs were dim, the furniture shrouded with ghostly coverings.

She led them to the familiar door of Symmes's study, and opened it. On the threshold she stood back with a proud smile. "There you go, Jake. Cop a load of that."

"Hell *fire*!" David whispered.

The room was ablaze with light. It shone from the lamp on the desk, and it was reflected in the jewels. They lay carelessly on the desk and chairs and carpet, spilling from boxes and caskets—a diamond necklace, a set of emeralds, a purse of gold coins arranged in elaborate stacks as if a child had played with them like bricks or counters.

"For heaven's sake, Moll." David walked over and took up a ruby tiara. The precious stones shook in his hand. "These alone must be worth millions! Did you . . . ? Is this all . . . ?"

She shrugged, modest. "All my own work, David

luv. Well, the gang too, of course. Not that we bother much with it. Tough to fence, some pieces. Just stacks up here, a bit." She took out the Sauvigne emeralds and tossed them among the rest.

Jake shook his head. He was dazed with the thought of what she had done. "Moll, look. None of this is here when Alicia comes. The house is bare. We need to pack it all up and . . ." And what? He thought about taking it with them, but that appalled him. Crazy ideas about putting it all back slid through his head. "Maybe in our own time we can . . ."

He stopped.

Moll was sitting on a small stool, watching him with her steady, measuring gaze.

He said, "Once I promised I'd come back for you. I never did. That was wrong. So now . . . now I am asking you, Moll, to come. Back with us."

"To the twenty-first century?"

"Yes."

"Where there's all those machines and not much disease?"

"Still disease. But better than here."

"Where girls get educated?"

"Yes."

His father was watching, sitting silent at the table.

"And you really want me to come. That so, Jake?" Moll tucked her hands under her knees.

Something was wrong. He blundered on. "You can't carry on doing this. It's far too dangerous. Jumping about in time, doing what you want. It's mad. Anything could happen. "

"That's what I like about it," she said softly.

"Moll . . ."

"No, Jake. It's time for you to listen." She sat back, legs stretched out, ankles crossed. "See, I'm not the little urchin now, cully. It's Moll the pirate-princess now. And I like it. We can't go back Jake, not with all the time machines in the world, we just can't. That's something I've learned."

She came over and took one of the necklaces and held it up. Tiny rainbows shimmered in the diamond drops. "I never took all this stuff for what it's worth, Jake. I told you. Adventure, danger, the sheer fun of it—that's what I want. I want to be someone unique in all the world, a rip-roaring girl, a wild, free, fierce lady with no one saying Moll do this and Moll do that." She put the jewels down and suddenly she had his hands, both of them, and was grinning up at him. "I've heard all about your machines and your wars and your laws and it ain't for me, cully. *Far* too prim and proper. Far too scary."

"Moll . . ."

She spun him around, and he had to gasp out a laugh. "Moll, see sense! I want—"

"No you don't." She stopped suddenly. "You don't, Jake. Or you would have come before. And I don't blame you anymore either, because you're right. We can be big friends, you and me. For always. Just like this."

She let him go and stepped back, her face suddenly a little red. "Don't want you to see me get old, Jake. All crabbed up and rusty. Not that I'm planning to get like that! Going to do things my way, you know?"

He nodded. Watching her, he thought that he had known it would be like this. From a small friendless child she had become someone who could be anything, do anything. That was a freedom no one would give up, least of all this small, feisty, cheerful girl he loved.

He said, "I get it, Moll."

"Knew you would, cully. Knew you would."

"But, you have to promise me to be so careful. And . . . maybe . . . in the future—"

She said, "No promises, Jake. That was where we went all wrong last time. But you'll take a few presents. I like presents, David, don't you?"

"You've already given me my son back," David muttered. "Nothing else is that precious."

Moll grinned. Taking a handful of the jewels, she selected the finest—diamonds, sapphires blue as the sea, emerald drops fit for a queen's ears. "Maybe. But I want you to take these. You can use them for money, or give them to your lady-loves." She thrust them into David's hands.

"Moll . . ."

"And something else, Jake. Just for you."

She opened a drawer in Symmes's desk and took out a small diary, in black leather, its pages held with a tiny lock, the key taped to it. She looked at it a moment, then held it out.

He took it.

MOLL'S DIARY was scrawled on the front.

He said, "I'm not sure I should read this."

"Up to you, cully. Only don't get all puffed up when you do, because I was just a kid, Jake. Don't let it all go to your head."

He said, "Does it tell me how to *journey* without the mirror. Because you did that, going back to save Venn."

She shrugged. "It's all in there. And one big thing in there you'll need. Or Venn will. The back pages are the work Symmes and I did about *journeying* to the future. After he met you and Venn it was all he thought about, and he learned loads. It's possible. It's how I came and snatched you."

He stared. "The future? But . . ."

She eyed him. "You'll need it. When you go after Janus."

For a long time there was only silence in the room.

Then Jake came over and carefully kissed her on the forehead. "Love you, Moll."

A little red, she stepped back. "Love you too, Jake. If you want a bit of thieving, any time, mind, you just ask. And I'll come."

She lifted her wrist and touched the bracelet, and looked back at him.

David stood, the jewels in his hands, as time rippled.

"Okay?" she whispered.

"Okay," Jake said.

24

If any man can make a promise and keep it, Venn
is that man. His willpower is all that has brought him
through many encounters with danger. He is said to
have despaired for a while, following his wife's death,
and for me that will have contributed to what later
happened to him, the bizarre event of the lost days.
He would have bitterly resented the waste of time.

Jean Lamartine, The Strange Life of Oberon Venn

"DON'T WORRY. They left with us. They'll get here." Venn flung a furious look around. "But what's happened to my house? You, Piers! What the hell sort of protection do you call this!"

Piers got no further than opening his mouth.

Wharton snapped, "It's not his fault the Shee are all over us. If anyone's, it's yours."

Venn swiveled a frosty glare at him, but Gideon's cool voice broke in. "Mortals waste a lot of time arguing. The Shee never argue. Maybe that's why they live so free and easy."

Wharton glanced at him sidelong. Venn turned quickly on Sarah, and Maskelyne. "We have another problem. Janus has an . . . artifact. A purple flower. It's a spell that will give him some . . . well, not control but"—he flicked a glance at Wharton—"some sort of hold over Summer. We have to get it back. If he joins forces with her, we're finished. Ideas?"

Rebecca stared at him in dismay. "How did he get that?"

Both Gideon and Wharton looked uncomfortable. Maskelyne stood quickly. "That was mine." He spun on Gideon. "You took it from my book."

Gideon shrugged an easy shrug. "Sorry. I thought it might help us against Summer." But he didn't seem sorry at all, Rebecca thought.

"Only if you want her besotted with you," Maskelyne snapped. "It has to be recovered! At once." He was standing by the mirror, and she saw again how he had no reflection in it, but was tall and dark as it was. And she felt it was some copy of him, some dark double.

Sarah paced the floor in agitation. "I can't believe this! Janus and Summer! Together! That's unthinkable!" She spun on Maskelyne. "We have to get him here. Call him. He'll come."

"Then what?" Rebecca said.

"Can we hold him in some way?"

"No. He has complete power over the mirror." Maskelyne's voice was husky and sour; he reached up and touched the scar on his face with light fingers, a thing he rarely did.

"But . . ." He paced, thoughtful. "It may be possible for me to destroy the purple artifact. I'd need at least five minutes. To invite him here is dangerous, and possibly deadly. It's you, Sarah, he wants. You'll have to keep him talking."

She nodded, thinking anxiously of the coin, safely hidden in its hiding place on the roof. If Janus found out where that was, it was over for them all. She would die rather than tell him. But the coin had to be the bait.

She looked up. "Okay. Let's do it."

They cleared a space. Horatio swung shrieking into the vaults and sat on a gargoyle's head, watching. The cats crawled away and hid themselves under tables and benches. Gideon carried the cradle as far from the mirror as possible, and placed it safely against the wall, looking down on the sleepy baby. The creature fascinated him, its wild wails, its constant hunger, its strangely attractive shape and smell.

The Shee had nothing like it.

Maybe that was why they stole such small, soft humans.

Why they had stolen him.

"Ready?" Venn was asking.

He dragged his thoughts back. "Yes. Ready."

He took out the glass weapon and held it behind his back.

They gathered in a silent, nervous semicircle around the dark glass. Venn cast a quick glance around. The tangled brambles in the corridor outside glimmered with the curious peeping eyes of the Shee. He turned away from them. "Right. Sarah. It's up to you."

She took a breath and approached the mirror.

In it she saw a girl wearing a dark dress, her fair hair tousled and windblown, her face still smudged with the dirt of Paris. She looked into her own eyes, at her own complexity and her own fear. As she called out, she saw her own mouth making the words. "You, Janus! You, lurking there at the end of the world. I want to talk to you!"

Nothing.

Not even a ripple of the surface.

At the controls Maskelyne muttered, "He hears. Try again."

With both hands Sarah gripped the unreadable silver letters of the frame. She felt between her fingers the power of the mirror, the plummeting depths within it, the eternity it contained.

She said, "I have what you want. I have the half coin, the coin with the head of Zeus. *The coin that will destroy the mirror.*"

Wharton stared. Gideon's green eyes widened. But Venn, she saw, was not surprised. And neither was Maskelyne.

Doubt stabbed her.

Then, just before the mirror shimmered with eagerness, in its dark reflection of the lab, she saw something that made her catch her breath. Peeping from the pocket of Rebecca's light summer cardigan, was the tiny curious eye and wooden beak of the talking bird.

She turned her head, fast as a cat.

Maskelyne looked up.

Their eyes met. *She knew he had the coin.*

But Janus was already in the room.

Wharton saw how the man came quickly, striding eagerly again down that long corridor that seemed to open in the glass. Grasping Gideon's elbow, he muttered, "It will be a Replicant, so if there's any sign of it taking Sarah, you blast it to bloody bits. I'm not having her sacrificed to solve Venn's problems. Got that?"

The changeling nodded. His face was pale as ivory. But his hand was steady.

Venn moved up quickly and stood beside Sarah.

Janus came out, his footsteps the only sound. The moment of his stepping through the glass was silent; there was only the faintest spiteful spit from one of the hidden cats, and a rustle in the roof overhead. Then there he was, small and self-contained, his arms at his sides, boldly standing among his enemies.

Wharton had to admire the man's guts, until he remembered it was only a Replicant.

Janus watched Sarah, his eyes secret behind the blue lenses. "You have the coin?"

She shrugged.

"You, and not Summer?"

"Not Summer." She held him with her fierce defiance, willed herself not to be daunted by him, to remember that she hated him.

He smiled. "And, I suppose, you'll just give it to me? I'm not a stupid man, Sarah. I hardly believe that."

"We'll trade it," Venn snapped.

"What could be as precious to you?"

Venn was silent.

The room hummed. From the corner of his eye Wharton glanced at Gideon's hand. It held the weapon tight.

The Replicant lifted its fingers to the flower in its lapel. It touched the purple petals. "Is this what you want, Venn?"

Then it happened, and it happened too fast.

Perhaps Maskelyne wasn't ready, perhaps whatever energies he had managed to gather were not enough, because the bolt of light that flashed through the mirror was barely a shimmer. Even so the room rocked, a glass fell and smashed. Wharton grabbed the edge of the table.

Pure energy, the flare surged up and crackled around Janus. He looked startled, but then gave a small laugh and stood still; when it snapped away and left both him and the flower unharmed, he met their dismay with a nod of the head.

"Well. I didn't think you were this desperate. Of course I can see you wouldn't want me to be with Summer. But such jealousy, Venn! It shocks me. And your wife still so lost, still so dead! I'm beginning to think you can't love her at all. *You who don't make agreements with tyrants.*"

Venn stood silent, his skin Shee-pale.

"I'm afraid I don't believe they would ever let you give me the coin, Sarah. But come back with me now, into the mirror." Taunting, Janus held up the flower. "They can have this in return for you."

She was still.

Alarmed, Wharton watched her, his whole body poised to grab her if she even moved a finger, because he *knew* she was considering it, her cropped head to one side, knew she was thinking of some desperate, despairing final *journey.*

But it was Maskelyne who moved. He stood up and Janus twisted, alert at once. "Ah! My friend the scarred man. You tried to destroy me once before and failed. I should have dealt with you then."

The Replicant seemed to do nothing, but Maskelyne froze, seemingly caught for a second in a strange moment of memory.

"Let him go!" Rebecca snapped.

Janus shrugged. At once, as if the movement had released him, Horatio swung down from the dark. Hanging from his tail he snatched the purple flower from the Replicant's fingers, leaped onto the top of the mirror, and clung there, chattering with joy.

Janus immediately grabbed Sarah.

Gideon whipped the weapon up, but before he could fire, Maskelyne snapped one icy command.

The Replicant's eyes widened. It shattered like glass; became a stinging hail of fragments. Wharton dodged; Sarah flung herself back, one hand over her eyes. The pieces tinkled and fell on the table and workbench and floor, and they were pieces of a vitrified man, fingers and slivers of his face, sharp shards of his hair and eyes, a creature of smashed glass.

With a clash and clatter the last sliver rocked. They watched in appalled silence. Venn helped Sarah pick herself up. She shook glassy fragments, in horror, from her hair.

Then they all looked at Maskelyne.

The scarred man stood rigid, his eyes dark as the mirror. He said nothing as the marmoset, shaking in terror, dropped into Sarah's arms, and clung to her, its tiny splayed fingers grasping tight to the dark rough sleeves of her housemaid's dress.

When he spoke, his voice was choked and hard. "The mirror belongs to me. No one else."

→⊷←

Even as he said it, a small white object came drifting down from the darkness of the vaulted roof. It fell with an easy, gentle, swaying motion, landing at Venn's feet.

A swan's feather.

Summer was sitting on one of the rafters, as if it were some high trapeze. Her bare feet dangled, one of them still becoming unwebbed. She wore a dress of soft white down, and as she slid down to land lightly, the fabric stirred feather-light about her.

A small silver tiara glinted in her hair.

"That was so impressive!"

Maskelyne said sourly, "I'm pleased you think so, lady." He turned and walked away to the farthest corner of the room and sat in a chair, head down. Rebecca hurried after him.

Summer watched them, then smiled. "How sweet. Let's patch up our quarrel too, Oberon."

"Gladly. When you let my house go. Get your people out."

"Ah, but you owe me." She was eyeing the purple flower curiously. "Just what is that thing? It makes me shiver. Makes me feel . . . strange. Give it to me, Venn."

He took it from the monkey's paw. But instead of handing it to her he held it up and deliberately shredded it, pulling the petals off rapidly one by one, snapping the stem and tossing the broken ruin on the floor, where it blackened and curled, as if it burned in an invisible fire.

Wharton could only feel relief.

Summer pouted. "Oh really! It was so pretty. You're always so *harsh,* Venn."

"Believe me, I was doing you a favor. I was wrong ever to use it. It would have made you love a monster."

She smiled up, amused. "Love!" Her laugh was a tinkle of scorn. "I don't love. Not even you. So I'm to have nothing I want, not that, and not a bracelet and not my sweet changeling?" She flicked a glance at Wharton, and then past him at Gideon.

Gideon looked away.

"What ransom do I get then, Oberon, to entice me to leave?" She was close to him now, and her hand reached out toward his, a delicate white hand that Sarah longed to slap away.

"You can have these," a voice said behind her.

She turned.

Jake was there. Jake with his father, David, standing close behind him. And in David's hands, dripping from his fingers, such jewels! Diamonds, rubies, sapphires.

A queen's ransom.

Wharton muttered, "My God, Jake, have you robbed a bank?"

Jake laughed. He nodded to his father, who held out his hands to Summer, and as she snatched the brilliant strings of stones from him and giggled with them against her neck, he looked at Venn and Venn looked at him.

Summer decked herself with the jewels. Gazing at herself in the mirror, she put them all on, and Sarah wondered at the intensity of her delight, because in a few minutes, surely, those same trinkets would bore her. She said quickly, "Will you release the house?"

Summer turned on bare toes. "From what?"

"The Wood."

The faery queen gave a careless glance at the bramble-tangled corridor.

"What Wood?" she laughed.

Branches shrank. Leaves dropped into dust. Sarah turned and pushed through the arch into the Monk's Walk, seeing how the tendrils of ivy shriveled, how the green webbed bines of the Wood slithered back like snakes.

Small puffballs of fungus exploded into clouds of spore. Butterflies fled. The rich, rotten dampness of loam and soil faded.

Piers hurried past her. "Oh at last. My poor kitchens!"

She followed him, down the stone passage, out into the Long Gallery.

Midsummer Day had dawned. The sky was the palest blue. Through open casements golden sunlight slanted, and in the long wide room she saw the trees crumble, shiver, and break before her eyes to a strange green dust that sparkled and drifted in the early light.

She looked back.

Summer gave Venn the lightest of kisses. Then she went to Gideon, stood on tiptoe, and whispered something in his ear.

His pale skin flushed.

So softly only Sarah heard, he said, "This is your day, Summer."

Outside, over the Wood, the sun burned. And all the birds cried out.

25

Take a brush and take a broom
Take a silver dishclout
Sweep the winter from the room,
Throw the withered weeds out.

Now the summer rules the Wood
sorrow fades away.
Open the door that leads to the moon,
and dance on the longest day.

Ballad of Lord Winter and Lady Summer

IT WAS MIDSUMMER and Wharton had never known one so hot.

He came down at noon after a long delicious sleep, wearing light trousers and an old loose shirt with paint stains on it. In the kitchen, Piers was humming cheerfully over the range, where a whole raft of pans and pots were bubbling.

Wharton stood and inhaled the glorious smells. "Good Lord, Piers. You must be cooking up some feast."

"A banquet of celebration and delight." The small

man grinned, balancing a row of plates down one arm.

"Just as well. Jake's dad looks half-starved and we've all had a very busy night."

How could it all have happened in one night? For a moment, standing there in his socks and sandals, Wharton had the strangest feeling the whole thing had just been some crazy dream, and he scratched his head absently, wondering why the length of his ears should worry him.

"Where is everyone?"

"Not sure. Maybe outside?"

Picking up some toast and a mug of tea, Wharton wandered down the corridors.

The Abbey was cool and peaceful. All the windows were wide, a delicate breeze stirred the dust. And, good grief, there was certainly plenty of that. Over busts and shelves and books and paintings, a soft carpet on the wooden boards and rugs, it lay like a fine ash, as if the magic tangle of the wild Wood had shriveled away to this green powder, this whisper of seed and sepal.

He peered into the study and the dining room but they were empty, and in the Great Hall only Horatio was there, performing solitary acrobatics across the Elizabethan rafters.

The black-and-white tiles of the front hall were scattered with dead leaves, but the door was wide, and he crossed to it and went out, and the sweetness of the summer noon hit him like a perfumed wave, like a symphony of pollen and heat.

Sarah was sitting on the steps, in shorts and T-shirt.

He creaked down beside her.

"Look at them, George," she said. "Just look at them."

Jake and David lounged in striped deckchairs on the lawn. David was lying back, feet up, showered, dressed in fresh cream slacks, talking at length, waving an arm, explaining as if he could never stop. Jake perched on the end of the chair, in expensive sunglasses, listening. Or maybe not even listening, just looking.

Looking at his father.

Wharton said, "He looks content."

That was an understatement, Sarah thought. Happiness was coming from Jake like a glow; it was there in the skin of his face, the angle of the dark lenses.

She said, "He's got just what he wants."

"Indeed." Wharton mused. In all the time he had known Jake, he had never seen the boy's restless energies so satisfied.

"And I'm glad. Don't get me wrong, George."

He looked at her. "But?"

"But nothing's over."

"Jake knows that."

"I hope so." She turned to him, anxious. "His father's

home and safe, but mine, and my mother, is still in some filthy prison far in the future." For a moment, that knowledge was a sickness inside her. "Janus rules there. Leah is still dead. The mirror is not destroyed."

She stretched out her legs in the sun, her voice acid. "And I don't even have the Zeus coin anymore."

"So Maskelyne really has it? "

"Oh yes. I climbed up and checked this morning. It's gone."

"Then . . ."

"Do you think Maskelyne wants the mirror destroyed? Of course he doesn't. He's obsessed with the thing." She shook her head. She saw again her father's arm trailing as they dragged him away. "I'm no nearer what I came for than I was in the winter. I've failed, George! Totally failed."

"Don't you be so sure." Wharton sipped thoughtfully from the mug. "A lot has changed. Venn has changed."

"Enough to abandon his wife to save a future world he's never seen?" She shook her head. "I don't think so."

Wharton was silent. Then he said, "Well then, maybe he should see it."

She turned slowly. "What?"

"Maybe he should see it. The future. Your end time, Sarah. If you want to convince him."

"That's not possible. Unless . . ."

"Jake says Moll has given him the way to journey into the future." He drank the last dregs of the tea and put the mug down on the hot stone of the step. "So . . . It's just a thought."

She looked at him.

"Cheers, George," she said quietly.

➤·❖·◄

"I think it's about time you trusted me," Rebecca said.

Maskelyne had his back to her, in the old greenhouse with its broken panes. Piers's crop of tomato plants were tangled in wires on each side, their fruits small yet and still green.

"I do trust you."

"Then tell me about your work with Janus."

Maskelyne shrugged. "There isn't much to say, Becky. Except once I had no scar. Once I was a different man. But if you touch evil, if you think you can work with evil, it scars you. It's deadly. It explodes in your face. And believe me, Janus is a man without mercy. I've seen what he will do."

"Will you give Sarah the broken coin?"

"No." He came over then and took her hands and held them between his. "I will keep it safe. Neither she nor Janus will find it. I'll keep it safe until the time comes to use it."

"And who decides that?"

For a moment she didn't want to hear his answer.

"I do," he said.

"Like as if you're God or something."

"Or something. But I won't hurt them, Becky. I promise you. I will make up for whatever I once did. The Zeus coin is more powerful than Sarah can even imagine. It could destroy us all, and I won't let that happen."

Who are you? she wanted to ask him. Who are you really?

But she was afraid of what the answer might be.

She pulled away, turned and walked out, and he came after her. Crossing the lawn, she looked up at the brilliance of the blue sky. "Venn won't be happy."

Maskelyne gave his rare smile. "Venn never is."

⇢⇠

Venn carried the stepladder into the bedroom and propped it against the wall; quickly he climbed up and grasped the painting.

Between his hands, in his embrace, Leah laughed calmly out at him. He said to her, "I'm sorry. I've been stupid."

She would really have laughed at that. She had a careless, shrugging way that he had loved. *"Whatever happens, Venn, the sun will rise tomorrow,"* she had always said about any problem. And yet for her, one day, it hadn't.

He lifted the portrait down; it was heavy, and the

green scum of the Wood lay on it; he brushed that off, angry.

As he carried it out of the room, the corridor stretched before him; it became a road, and the road was not straight but veered on a sharp bend, and he was laughing and talking and driving too fast and the speed of the car exhilarated them both.

The wheel was warm and leathery under his hands. He jerked it aside.

And stopped and closed his eyes as the memory splintered, as the lorry loomed and the winshield shattered.

As the sky was below him.

As she screamed.

➵⊶

"Venn?"

Gideon's whisper was quiet.

Venn opened his eyes.

The changeling sat in the window seat, knees up. The silver suit was dissolving back to forest green, the boy's skin so pale he seemed like some wraith trapped in a haunted house.

Venn paused. He propped the painting against a bookcase.

"What are you doing?" Gideon said.

"Taking this downstairs. I'm going to place it right next to the mirror. So I can see it there, while we're working. Because now that David is back, we are going to work. Night and day, every hour, every minute, until we know how to get her back."

Gideon smiled, his eyes glints of green. "Summer got to you, didn't she."

"This time. But never again."

"You and I both know that's an empty boast. That's why you're moving the painting. Because you're afraid you'll forget about Leah again." Gideon knelt up on the sill. He unlatched the window and let it open.

Venn stared. "I thought you wanted to stay safe?"

The warm breeze blew Gideon's pale hair. He lifted his face to it, breathed it in deeply. Then he said, "I do. But I have to go back."

Venn was silent.

"Summer will never leave you alone if I don't. She needs a mortal to torment, any mortal, but most of all, me. And in truth I'm sick of being trapped here. At least the Summerland is a bigger prison." He turned. "But later . . . when you've done what you need to, promise me you'll let me try and go home."

Venn gave a wintry smile. "You can try. But it will be hopeless."

For a moment they were both still in the sun-dappled corridor. Dust motes slanted down the dark paneling. A bee buzzed in and bumped the glass.

Then Gideon murmured, "You hear them too, don't you."

Venn did. Together they listened to the eerie, tormenting, distant music. Far and sweet and clear it drifted down the aisles of the Wood, a heartbreaking beauty, an enticing promise that would never be kept and always be broken. It infiltrated their hearts like a sickness.

Finally Gideon whispered "They don't get it, about the Shee, do they? Jake and the rest."

"No." Venn's gaze was distant and absorbed. "No. They don't get it."

His fingers, against the gilded wood of the portrait frame, tapped the delicate rhythm.

Lunch was set out on the lawn, on a long table that Piers had dragged outside. Everyone came, even Gideon, though Sarah noticed how his eyes kept straying to watch the edges of the Wood, and how the butterflies that skittered over danced more playfully around him.

There was cold meat and salad and fruit and platefuls of delicious little creamy desserts, bowls of strawberries and ice cream that seemed to stay cold despite the heat, because the day was scorching, the blueness of the sky almost oppressive as it reached even to the crisped barrier of the moor.

"I think," David said, pouring a huge mug of tea,

"that this afternoon I am going to take the car and go down to the cove and sit on the beach. Anyone who wants to can come. I haven't seen the sea for . . ." He shrugged. "Centuries."

Jake laughed.

"But first I need to phone your mother in the States. She might be vaguely interested to know I've turned up again."

He got up and wandered in. Jake's eyes followed him. Sarah moved to the empty seat.

"Happy?"

He smiled. "What do you think?"

She nodded, watching a ladybug crawl between them on the white tablecloth.

Something in her silence made him look at her.

She said, "Janus won't give up. Nor will I. If Venn succeeds, the whole thing starts up, the rising power and fame of the mirror, the way it was traded and fought over, the people that were killed for it, the wars that were fought over it. You don't know any of that. And then, at the end, it becomes a black hole eating my world, my family, my friends. We can stop that, Jake, right at the source."

He was watching her. "Now that I've got what I want, you mean."

"Yes."

"You want me to help you stop Venn. But don't you see, if we do that, if he never gets Leah back, Summer will take him."

She shrugged, looking out at the Wood. "Better that than the alternative."

It chilled him. Because he knew she was right.

※→※←

David put the phone down with relief because it had only been the answering machine, and saw Venn looking at him through the open doorway.

"Coming to the beach, O? Brisk walk?"

"No."

"Listen. I always knew you'd come for me."

Venn looked uneasy. "It's Jake you should thank, David. If he hadn't broken out of school and come storming in here to sort things out, I might still be sunk in darkness and despair. He's a bright kid."

"Takes after me." David laughed, awkward. Then he stepped closer. "What I mean to say is, now I'm back, we'll work like stink. We'll get Leah."

Venn moved aside to let Piers push an old-fashioned pram past him. "We will. And this time, nothing will stop me. Nothing, David. I swear that."

※→※←

The long afternoon walking the beach ended in a sunset that seared the west. As they drove back to the Abbey and up the drive, Jake sat with his elbow out of the window, feeling calmer than he had for months. The worst was over. His father was here. For a moment, a fleeting memory of Moll creased his mind, but that was fine, he would see her again.

After all, they had a time machine, and were close to knowing exactly how to use it.

"Look at that," his father muttered.

Between the darkening branches of the Wood, the Abbey rose like a dark shadow. But it was lit with a light that made Jake frown, a strange, green, shimmering glow.

"Put your foot down," he muttered, worried. "That's not right."

David drove hurriedly down the overgrown drive.

As they came out onto the lawns he gave a gasp, and Jake flung the door open and leaped out, his heart thudding, all calm gone, because surely that glimmer was made by the Shee and that must mean they were back and—

He hurtled around a tree and stopped, staring.

The lawns were hung with soft blue lights, like lanterns. In the house were hundreds of tiny movements and glints and glimmers, flitting shapes, a face with silver hair appearing briefly at a window, a flock of starlings on a chimney.

Venn and Sarah were standing outside, watching. Jake raced across to them. "What's happening?"

Venn smiled, sour. "They're tidying up."

Piers came down the steps with a rug, shook it, grinned, and went back in.

"Piers? Or the Shee?"

"Summer seems to have given orders." As he said it a window opened by itself above, and a great cloud of the green dust was hurled out, billowing into the air.

Sarah giggled. "Brushes and brooms and all sorts of things. But they seem to be making more mess than ever."

As she said it a door opened and a thin figure came out, walking quickly toward them. Gideon wore his green frock-coat. There was dust in his hair, and his skin was pale under the moon. He came and stood in front of them, hands in pockets, and his eyes were green and distracted.

"Don't forget me," he said

Sarah said, "You don't have to do this."

"Call it my sacrifice. It's been good being a mortal. It's made me remember myself. But . . . maybe I've been with them too long to stop now."

"They don't have time," Jake said "So how . . ."

Gideon shrugged. "I know what I mean." He turned and walked through the long grass of the lawn toward the Wood. "If you call, I'll come. If she lets me."

He raised a hand. Sarah shook her head; Jake frowned.

"You're not Shee," he said with sudden fury. "You're one of us. Don't forget that."

Gideon nodded. "Maybe."

Then he was only a shadow among shadows.

And then nothing at all.

KEEP READING FOR A SAMPLE OF
THE FIRST BOOK IN THE TRILOGY,

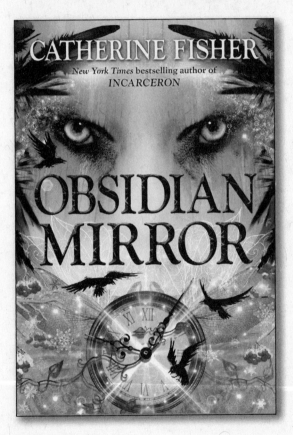

1

I have discovered something totally impossible.
I will be rich. Celebrated. A hero of science.

And yet in truth I am so bewildered that I can
only sit for hours in this room and gaze out at the
rain.

What can I do with such terrifying knowledge?
How can I ever dare use it?

Journal of John Harcourt Symmes, December 1846

THE BOY PUT on the mask outside the door. It was
a heavy black fencing mask and inside its mesh he felt
different.

It made him dark, supple, dangerous.

An actor.

An assassin.

He was wearing the costume for *Hamlet,* Act 5,
the duel with Laertes, and he had the fencing sword
ready in his hand. He had to be very careful. This
could all go badly wrong, and not just in the way
he wanted. He took a deep breath and peered in
through the glass panel. The rehearsal seemed to
have paused; people were sitting around and Mr.
Wharton was explaining something, waving an

arm expressively to Mark Patten, who was playing Laertes.

He opened the door and went in. At once, as if someone had switched it on, he burst into a world of chattering voices and music and loud hammering behind the scenery. Mr. Wharton turned around and glared at him. "Seb! Where have you been?" Without waiting for an answer he swung back. "Well, maybe now we can get on. Are you sure you've got the blunt sword? And you remember the jump over the table?"

The boy nodded and climbed up on the stage. It was shadowy there; the lights weren't set up properly, and the cardboard scenery leaned at awkward angles. A mirror reflected him, slanting. He saw he was too tall, that the costume was a little tight. His eyes were dark and steely.

"Ready?"

He just nodded.

"Please yourself," Wharton muttered. The Head of Humanities—a big man, ex-army—looked hot and harassed, his collar undone, hair sticking up where he'd run a sweaty hand through it. "Right, boys. All set to run through the duel?"

Run through. That was apt. The boy put the foil tip to the floor and carefully flexed the supple steel blade. He watched Laertes come up onstage. Patten, the one with the big-shot father. The one with the mouth.

"Okay." Wharton glanced at the script. "So. Let's go from *'I'll be your foil . . .'* And let's have it sad, Seb, really sad and noble. You're confused, you're angry—your father has been killed and all you want is revenge, but instead of the real killer, you have to fight this guy you hardly know. You're sick to the soul. Got it?"

He nodded, silent. They had no idea how much he got it.

The others took their places. He waited, inside the mesh of his hatred, his heart thumping like a machine out of control, the leather grip of the foil already sweaty in his hand.

Wharton scrambled down and sat in the front row. The lights flickered, a shudder of scarlet in the shadowy hall. His hand on the sword-hilt was suddenly bloodred.

"Sorry," someone shouted from the back.

"Okay. Laertes and Hamlet duel. Do the moves exactly as we practiced yesterday." Mr. Wharton tipped his glasses to the end of his nose. "In your own time."

Patten faced his opponent. "Get it right this time, prat," he whispered.

"Oh, I will." The answer was a bare breath, intent.

Patten stared. *"What . . . ?"*

But the boy dressed as Hamlet had already lifted his sword and was speaking, his voice hoarse with the built-up tension of weeks. *"I'll be your foil, Laertes; in mine ignorance, your skill shall, like a star in the darkest night, stick fiery off indeed.*"

"*You mock me, sir,*" Laertes snarled.

"*No. By this hand.*"

He moved forward. They gripped fists, but he squeezed too hard, crushing Patten's fingers.

"What the hell." Patten stepped back. "You're not Seb!"

The boy smiled. And instantly he attacked, slashing with the foil. Patten's sword came up in alarmed defense. "Hey! Idiot! Wait!"

He didn't wait. He shoved against Patten's chest, sending him flailing back into crashing scenery.

Wharton jumped to his feet. "That's all wrong. Boys! *Seb!*"

Thrust. Parry. Attack and keep on attacking. Fight the anger. Fight the pain and the loss. And then his head seemed suddenly to clear, and he was free and laughing, breathing easier, knocking away Patten's wild blade, ignoring the shouts, the people jumping up onto the stage, Wharton's roar of "Stop this at once!" He chose his moment and aimed coldly above the guard, at the bare white flesh between sleeve and glove. Then, as if it weren't even him doing this, he struck.

Patten howled. A great howl of pain and fury. He leaped back, flung down his foil and grabbed his wrist.

Blood was already dripping through his fingers. "He's sodding mad! It's a sharp sword! *I've been stabbed!*"

Clatter. Shouts. The cardboard balcony rippling backward into a dusty, oddly muffled collapse. Hands grabbing him, tight around his neck, hauling him back, snatching the weapon from his fingers. He let them. He stood calm, breathing hard, in a circle of staring boys. He'd done it. They couldn't ignore him anymore.

Abruptly, as if a spotlight had come on, brilliant glare blinded him. He realized Wharton had snatched the mask off him and was standing there, staring in astonishment and fury at his white face.

"Jake. *Jake Wilde!* What the *hell* do you think you're doing?"

He tried not to smile. "I think you know the answer to that. *Sir.*"

"Where's Seb? What have you . . ."

"Locked in his room. I haven't hurt him." He made himself sound cold. Icy. That's what they should see, these staring, brainless kids, even though he wanted to scream and shout in their faces.

Behind the teacher, Mark Patten had crumpled onto the stage; someone had a first-aid kit and was wrapping his wrist in a tight white bandage that immediately went red. Patten looked up, his eyes panicky and furious. "You're finished in this school, Wilde, finished.

You've really flipped this time. My father's one of the governors, and if they don't expel you there'll be hell to pay. What are you, some sort of sodding nutcase?"

"That's enough." Wharton turned. "Get him down to the med room. The rest of you, out of here. Now! Rehearsals are canceled."

It took a while for everyone to go, an explosion of gossip and rumor roaring out into the corridors of the school, the last boys lingering curiously. Wharton kept a resolute silence until there was no one left but Jake and himself in the hall, and the echoes from outside fading away. Then he took his glasses off, put them in his jacket pocket, and said, "Well. You've really made your point this time."

"I hope so."

"They'll expel you."

"That's what I want."

Eye to eye, they faced each other. Mr. Wharton said, "You can trust me, Jake. I've told you that before. Whatever it is, whatever's wrong, tell me and—"

"Nothing's wrong. I hate the school. I'm out of here. That's all."

It wasn't all. Both of them knew it. But standing in the ruins of his stage, Wharton realized that was all he was going to get. Coldly he said, "Get out of that costume and be at the Head's office in five minutes."

Jake turned. He went without a word.

For a moment Wharton stared at the wreckage. Then he snatched up the foil and marched. He slammed through the fire doors of the corridors, raced up the stairs and flung open the office with HEADMASTER printed in the frosted glass.

"Is he in?" he said, breathless.

The secretary looked up. "Yes, but . . ."

He stalked past her desk and into the inner room.

The Head was eating pastries. A tray of them lay on the desk, next to a china mug of coffee that was releasing such a rich aroma that it made Wharton instantly nostalgic for his favorite coffee shop back home in Shepton Mallet, where he'd liked to read the papers every morning. Before he'd come to this hell-hole of a school.

"George!" The Head had his elbows on the desk. "I was expecting you."

"You've heard?"

"I've heard." Behind him, outside the huge window, the Swiss Alps rose in their glorious beauty against a pure blue sky. "Patten's gone to the hospital. God knows what his father will do."

Wharton sat heavily. They were silent a moment. Then he said, "You realize what this means? Wilde's got us now, exactly where he wants us. That was criminal assault and there were plenty of witnesses. It's a police matter. He knows if we don't get him out of the country, the publicity for the school will be dire."

The Head sighed. "And Patten, of all boys! Are they enemies?"

"No love lost. But the choice was deliberate. And clever. Wilde knows Patten will make more fuss than anyone else."

There was deep snow on the alpine valleys, gleaming and brilliant in the sunlight. For a moment Wharton longed to be skiing down it. Far from here.

"Well, we expel him. End of problem. For us, at any rate." The Head was a thin streak of a man, his hair always shinily greased. He poured some coffee. "Have a pastry."

"Thanks. But I'm dieting." How did the man stay so skinny? Wharton dumped sugar in the coffee gloomily. Then he said, "Clever is one word for him. Sadistic is another. He's wrecked my play."

The Head watched the spoon make angry circles in the mug. "Calm down, George, or you'll have a heart attack. What you need is a holiday, back in dear old Britain."

"Can't afford it. Not on what you pay."

"Ha!" The Head stood up and strolled to the window. "Jake Wilde. Bit of a problem."

Wharton sipped his coffee. The Head was a master of understatement. Wilde was the absolute rebel of the school and the torment of everyone's life, especially his.

The boy was intelligent, a good athlete, a fine musician. But he was also an arrogant schemer who made no secret of his loathing of Compton's School and everyone in it.

"Remind me," the Head said grimly.

Wharton shrugged. "Where to start. There was the monkey. He's still got that stashed somewhere, I think. The fire alarms. The school concert. The mayor's car. And who could forget the Halloween party fiasco . . ."

The Head groaned.

"Not to mention writing his entire exam paper on *Hamlet* in mirror-writing."

"Hardly in the same league."

"Bloody annoying, though." Wharton was silent, thinking of Jake's hard, brittle stare. *You did say you wanted something totally original, sir.* "If it was me, I'd expel him just for the way he says *sir*."

"I've bent over backward to ignore all of it," the Head said. "Because his guardian pays top whack to keep him here, and we need the money."

"I don't blame the man. But we can't ignore this." Wharton touched the foil; it rolled a little on the table and the Head picked it up and examined the sharp point.

"Unbelievable! He could have killed someone. I suppose he thinks as he's the school's fencing champion he could handle it. Well, if he wants to be expelled, I'm happy to oblige." Dropping the sword, the Head came back and touched the intercom button. "Madame. Would you please send for—"

"He's here, Headmaster."

"I'm sorry?"

"Jake Wilde. He's waiting."

The Head made a face as if he'd eaten a wasp. "Send him in."

Jake came in and stood stiffly by the desk. The room smelled of coffee, and he could see by the gloom of the two men that he'd defeated them at last.

"Mr. Wilde." The Head pushed the pastries aside. "You understand that your actions today have finally finished you at Compton's School?"

"Yes. Sir." Now he could afford to sound polite.

"Never in my career have I come across anyone so totally irresponsible. So utterly dangerous. Have you any idea of what the consequences could have been?"

Jake stared stonily in front of him. The Head's tirade went on for at least five minutes, but all of them knew it was just an act that had to be played. He managed to tune out most of it, thinking about Horatio, and how tricky it would be to get him on the plane. A few phrases came to him distantly. "Incredible folly . . . honor of the school . . . returning home in disgrace . . ."

Then the room was quiet. Jake looked up. The Head was looking at him with a calm curiosity, and when he spoke again his voice was different, as if he meant it now.

"Have we failed you so badly, Jake? Is it so absolutely terrible to be here?"

Jake preferred the riot act. He shrugged. "It's nothing personal. Any school—it would have been the same."

"I suppose that should make me happier. It doesn't. And what will your guardian have to say?"

Jake's face hardened. "No idea. I've never spoken to him."

The men were silent. Wharton said, "Surely in the holidays you go home. . . ."

"Mr. Venn is very generous." Jake's contempt was icy. "He pays for a very nice hotel in Cannes, where I spend the holidays. Every holiday. Alone."

Wharton frowned. Surely the boy's mother was alive? This seemed an odd situation. Was it behind this bizarre behavior? He caught Jake's eye. Jake stared icily back. The old *Don't ask me any more questions* stare.

"Well, it's about time we informed Mr. Venn all that's about to change." The Head turned to his computer.

"Headmaster?" Wharton edged in his chair. "Maybe . . . even now, if Jake . . ."

Jake's gaze didn't waver. "No. I want to go. If you make me stay I'll end up killing someone."

Wharton shut his mouth. The boy was mad.

"Let's hope he's online." The Head typed a rapid e-mail. "Though I suppose your guardian has a big staff to run his estate while he's off exploring the Antarctic or whatever?"

"He doesn't do expeditions anymore. He's a recluse."

The Head was busy, so Wharton said, "Recluse?"

"He doesn't leave home. Wintercombe Abbey."

"I know what recluse means." Wharton felt hot. The boy was such an annoying little . . . But he kept his temper. "Since when?"

"Since his wife died." The words were hard and cold, and Wharton was chilled by Jake's lack of the least sympathy. Something was very wrong here. He'd read about the famous Oberon Venn—polar explorer, mountaineer, archaeologist, the only man to have come back alive from the terrible ascent of the west face of Katra Simba. A heroic figure. Someone young men should look up to. But maybe not the best person to be suddenly landed with someone else's child.

"Your father knew him?"

Jake was silent, as if he resented the question. "My father was his best friend."

Far off, a bell rang. Footsteps clattered down the corridor outside. The Head said, "He seems a man of few words. Here's his answer."

He turned the screen so that Wharton and Jake could read it. It said:

SEND HIM HERE. I'LL DEAL WITH THIS.

Wharton felt as if an arctic wind had blown out of the screen. He almost stepped back.

Jake didn't flinch. "I'll leave tomorrow. Thank you for all—"

"You'll leave when I say." The Head clicked off the screen and looked at him over it. "Can't you tell us what this is all about, Jake? You're a promising student . . . maybe even the brightest boy in the place. Do you really want to rot in some English comp?"

Jake set his face with the icy glitter Wharton loathed. "I told you. It's not about the school. It's about me." He glared at the screen. "Me and him."

The Head leaned back in his chair. As if he could see it was hopeless, he shrugged slightly. "Have it your way. I'll arrange a flight. Go and pack your things."

"They've been packed for days."

The Head glanced at Wharton. "And you can pack yours, George."

"Me? But . . ."

"Someone has to take him home. Have a few days off for Christmas while you're there."

"I can take myself," Jake snapped.

"And I have a ton of work to do, Headmaster. The play . . ."

"Can wait. In loco parentis, I'm afraid."

They both stared at him, and the Head grinned his dark grin. "I don't know which of you looks the most horrified. Bon voyage, gentlemen. And good luck, Mr. Wilde."

Outside in the corridor, Wharton blew out his cheeks and gazed desperately up toward the staff room. Then he looked at Jake and Jake looked at him.

"Better do as he says," he said, gruff.

"I'm sorry." The boy's voice was still arrogant, but there was something new in it. "Sorry you're dragged into this. But I have to go and get the truth out of Venn. To confront him with what I know."

"And what *do* you know?" Wharton was baffled now.

The lunch bell rang. Jake Wilde turned and was jostled down the corridor as the boys poured along to the dining room in a noisy, hungry wave. In all the uproar Wharton almost missed his reply. The words were so quiet. So venomous. But for a moment, he was sure Jake had said, *"I know he murdered my father."*

New York Times bestselling author
and queen of fantasy Catherine Fisher's
OBSIDIAN MIRROR series!

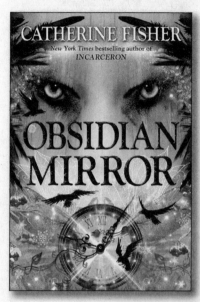

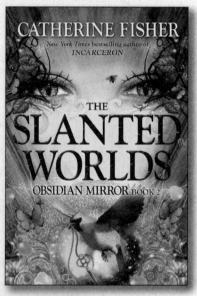

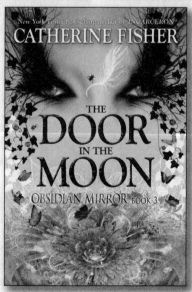

Read more from bestselling author
Catherine Fisher!